MAGE FARM

LUNARA STATION BOOK TWO

CLARA WOODS

Copyright © 2019 Clara Woods

All rights reserved.

ISBN-13: 978-1-6934-3955-1

For my parents. You always knew that his would happen one day.

PROLOGUE

IT COULD FEEL BILLIONS, possibly countless presences existing all around. In front of its inner eye, every single one was visible and—there—it could see one area that was the most corrupt. A faraway place, but distance did not matter.

There was more. A second infection, one it had seen before. It took it all in, planning the next steps.

Shifting its focus, it could see its own army, grown since the last time. They always grew. Incalculable mindless souls. This enemy had even more souls, but that was not a problem. It had never been a problem. Cassandral's will would always prevail.

It leapt down, off the pedestal where it had passed the eons of slumber, stretching its wings in the large stone chamber. Small swirls of a breeze from outside tingled all over its body. It wanted to go there, take off into the sky, its true home. But the low rumble and scratching of stone against stone from inside the building reminded the Cava Dara of its purpose.

Its own section of Cassandral's army was right here, and it had to attend to it. To lead the minions into the most corrupted area.

It turned and walked through the tunnel toward where the army was awakening.

1 UPL STATION

GIVING A LOUD CLICK, the clamps engaged on the *Star Rambler*, the fifty-year-old Galaxy Gate which Lenah Callo and her crew had been calling home for the past month. With that, the ship was tightly held in place on UPL station.

Too late to turn around now, Lenah thought with a burst of worry. She wasn't sure what exactly was causing that feeling. The United Planetary Legion were the good guys, the only entity with the power to command all corporate armies. Given the Cava Dara threat, they would do just that. However, Lenah couldn't shake the queasiness in her stomach. Shouldn't she be happy to get rid of the Mapstone and its terrible responsibility? Not to mention their hostage. Determined, Lenah got out of the pilot's seat and made her way to the common room, where the rest of her crew was assembled around the dining table.

Only, it wasn't a dining table at all anymore. With the screens, computers, and screws lying around, it resembled more a mad scientist's lab.

The mad scientists themselves, Uz and Doctor Lund, crouched over a small drone, while Persia and Cassius each sat in an adjacent chair. Cassius was frowning at what they were doing, but Persia seemed to be hiding a smirk.

"What's going on?" Lenah asked as she entered. No one even acknowledged they had just landed.

"They've gotten it to work," Persia said, finally looking in Lenah's direction.

"That's incredible," she started. "But why don't you look more excited?"

Uz looked up. "Something is wrong with this thing."

"Wrong?"

"Must be the translation. Some miscalibration maybe."

Lenah looked at the drone they had taken from the temple of the Syrr, an extinct race of small humanoids, only two weeks earlier.

Her crew had unlocked the message of the Mapstone and learned that ancient beings called Cava Dara were about to attack humanity, triggered by the archaic belief that no race should ever augment themselves using magic. To the Cava Dara, the mage farm, a facility producing storage drives for magic, unnaturally enhanced humanity. The powerful UPL were their best bet to stop them. And the drone, a Syrr construction, was going to be full of useful information, or so Lenah hoped. It was made of stone, and, instead of cables, its inner workings were carved out of various gemstones. It was a show of miraculous craftmanship and it was equally astonishing, that Uz had been able to interface it with modern technology.

Not only that, but Uz had used the language file they had found in Lunara Station's Knowledge Center to translate the Syrr language into today's G-Standard. Without that, the native Syrr tongue sounded just like a random series of hisses, which made communication impossible.

Besides, the drone, after being very chatty when it had first approached them in the temple, had been very quiet during their journey ever since. If that was due to some technical malfunction or because they had taken it from its home against its will, they didn't know.

"Does it speak G-Standard at all?" Lenah asked Uz.

"Sure, it does…" Persia softly spoke beside her.

"We'll show you," Doctor Lund added, connecting the hard drive with the language overwrite to the drone and pressing a button with a grand gesture.

The toddler-sized machine immediately opened its eyes, moving them around slowly and taking them all in. Gradually, it flapped its intricate wings and hovered up, stopping close to the ceiling, so high that everyone, even Uz, had to crane their necks upward.

Its features looked distinctly male, albeit in a significantly reduced scale. A big nose and thin lips sat on an angular face that was carved into the dark gray material. The forehead was furrowed with tiny wrinkles, giving it the appearance of an old man.

Lenah couldn't help but think that it looked very serious. Did these old Syrr, a culture that had been obliterated six thousand years ago, have the capability to develop personalities for their drones? Maybe it was just the fact that its face was carved in such detail from stone.

Uz reached out to where it was buzzing in the air on its small wings, beautifully crafted from hundreds of delicate stone joints. It evaded her and came to hover closer to Lenah.

"Um, hello," Lenah said.

It didn't answer.

"Can you understand me?"

The drone still didn't speak, but its face got a sour expression as if deeply disapproving of what Lenah had said.

She tried engaging again. "I'm Lenah. What's your name?"

"You are not that young as to not know your limitations toward the Elder," a gnarled and at the same time high-pitched voice spoke back to her.

"I —. Excuse me?" Lenah asked, dumbfounded.

"If you are anything like Syrr, like most races, your younglings are born small. While you are smaller than most of your species I have seen, you still look old enough to understand the difference between elder wisdom and youthful indiscretion. If I excused you, it would mean to accept your misbehaviors. I shall not."

Lenah stared. Had she just been called tiny by an even tinier piece of stone?

"Is this a joke?" Lenah looked at Uz and Doctor Lund to confirm if they were pranking her. Judging by their frustrated faces, that was not the case.

"Are you angry that we took you?" Lenah said, turning back to the drone, who cocked its head but didn't otherwise acknowledge. She watched as it stayed silent, noticing how it didn't seem to breathe. Despite the detailed craftsmanship, this was only a machine.

Lenah continued. "Now that we speak the same language, we can explain why we took you. I hope you'll understand once you see how important a role you can play in saving my species—humanity—from the same destiny as yours. Am I right that the Cava Dara destroyed your kind?"

"At least you know of the superiority of age, even if your manners suggest otherwise," the drone spoke back as if talking to a small child it was scolding. Lenah looked at Uz, who clenched her jaw, then pressed a button on the hard drive that still connected to the little machine. It closed its eyes and would have fallen, had Doctor Lund not been prepared and carefully caught it.

"And that's why it seems miscalibrated," Uz said to Lenah. "It just won't tell us anything but speak of Elders and respect." She rolled her eyes in a very un-Cassidian expression. Uz might be the only Cassidian who didn't like to speak of Elders or follow the traditional Cassidian Way. She preferred to tinker with computers or spaceships.

Lenah hid her grin. Uz seemed genuinely frustrated, which was understandable, given how much time she'd spent getting the drone to speak their language. "Are you sure that it's an issue with the translation software? Maybe it's just a stupid drone."

"I get the distinct feeling that the drone would take offense to you calling it stupid," Persia said with a smirk. "It could just be this stuffy."

"No one is *this* stuffy. Not even Lenah is, and she's from the families." Cassius offered his opinion for the first time. He had taken to making comments like that over the past two weeks. Lenah couldn't say she minded. It was a big improvement over being addressed as 'rich girl' in a tone of disdain—like he had over the first couple of weeks of knowing her. She had decided to take it as a good sign, even though being reminded of where she came from, didn't fill her with any pride these days.

"We've landed. I'm surprised you're here and not looking all cyborgy and standing armed at the hatch," Lenah said instead, remembering the original reason she had come to talk to them.

"Wow, that's good flying. I didn't even realize." Persia patted Lenah on the arm. "I remember my first landing with you, and even though I was slightly intoxicated, I couldn't miss the fact that we were violently banging all around other spaceships."

"It was trees. And you were wasted," Lenah objected but grinned. Her flying *had* improved a great deal since her first time over a month ago.

Doctor Lund took the lead getting up from the table. "Finally, we can get rid of *her*," he murmured, clearly relieved to be handing their hostage, Corinna Cheung, over to UPL responsibility. Lenah wouldn't disagree. Having another mind mage on board, one that was stronger than herself, hadn't been fun.

2 CONSTRAINTS

BEING ON UPL STATION, humanity's center of power, made Lenah feel small and insignificant. She might be bringing the Mapstone and news of a threat to humanity, but she fully expected to stick out as a nobody from a backwater planet. As a last-minute thought, she made a quick stop to her cabin and adjusted her hair into a tight, low bun. It made her feel slightly better. Pulling her wavy, brown hair into buns had been a constant of her previous life as a family executive.

When she joined the others in the cargo hold, Persia, Uz, and Doctor Lund were already in front of the closed hatch, having apparently decided to leave the drone be for now. Persia stepped from one foot to the other and was peering out the view window. She had a pistol barely hidden inside her sweater.

"Expecting trouble so soon?" Lenah asked, but she couldn't blame them. In fact, she had brought her own pistol.

Just in case. "At least try not to clutch the handle of your weapon too tight when you greet the ambassadors."

The diplomacy part of this mission would be Lenah's job, as she had spent years aiding her father and his corporation, Starwide Research, in acquiring the necessary funding to grow a prospering business of mage farms. She had sat across from self-important politicians many times and expected this meeting to be just like that.

UPL space station was a giant, white sphere in low orbit of Arcadia, the planet where most corporations, at least the ones with enough power, kept embassies. The proximity served the many corporate representatives, who came up to UPL station all the time. If anyone could be singled out as humanity's most powerful institution, it was the United Planetary Legion, and their station was certainly built to impress.

Silver windowpanes were interlaced into the smooth, white paneling in intricate patterns, giving the station the look of an oversized piece of jewelry. The only indication that this was a working space station, and not an adornment, were the vents and knobs protruding from the underside of the otherwise smooth white-and-silver surface. Lenah, who had been to Arcadia many times and was used to fancy environments, still couldn't help but be impressed. Her ragged crew was indeed out of place here. And, she reminded herself, that included her now.

She wasn't here as a member of the Callo family. Not that the Callos were ever invited to come here. Starwide Research was not a corporation recognized officially by UPL and, therefore, wasn't allowed to have a corporate army, though Lenah's father was pushing hard for it.

Lenah smoothed the surface of her black jacket. The shoulder was torn open where a laser had grazed her a few weeks earlier, and the smuggler ship hadn't come with any sewing equipment. All she had been able to do, was wash out most of the bloodstains. She had even cleaned her shoes. Nothing like a first impression.

"You cleaned up nicely. Haven't seen you look like this since the cyborg whisked us away on this adventure," Persia remarked, turning away from the view window. Her own boyishly short haircut had been growing out, and her attempts to brush it back failed more and more every day. At least, the ex-gladiator hadn't brought her hammer this time. It tended to call attention in public places, a fact that Persia seemed utterly oblivious to. Though Lenah had to admit that it had come in handy several times already.

Lenah smoothed her hair and was about to answer when Cassius walked in. He had Corinna, their hostage of almost two weeks, thrown over his shoulder and easily held on to her with his cyborg arm. Only three weeks ago, it had been Lenah and Persia being his hostages, and now Lenah counted herself lucky that she'd never been carried upside down over his shoulder like a sack of rice. Corinna's head hung limply next to his hip, bobbing sideways with each of his steps and coming perilously close to the wall of the *Star Rambler*'s corridor. She was still unconscious and should stay like that for a while longer; a necessary precaution. No one wanted an enemy mind mage influencing people on their ship. Without the drugs, Corinna could have influenced them to do her bidding, and Lenah wasn't strong enough to counteract Corinna's power easily. She'd only won with some luck back on Masis III.

A man in a white politician's caftan walked toward the ship, visible through the one small window in the hatch. Taking a deep breath, Lenah thumbed the hatch's button, and the *Star Rambler* opened to UPL station's landing bay. She stepped out first, followed by Doctor Lund.

"Greetings, Lenah Callo," the white-robed man said with a smile. "Welcome to UPL station. I hope you had a pleasant flight."

"Very good, thank you." At least for the past ten days, that was true. "We come here to fulfill Run 118," Lenah continued, referring to the codeword that had been specified in the posting for the Mapstone. Lenah felt its weight in her pocket and couldn't wait to exchange it for the hefty sum of one million CGC.

"Understood." The man nodded. "We have been waiting for you."

That took Lenah aback. She hadn't announced that she would be coming with the stone. Forcefully, the queasy feeling in her stomach was back. Wherever they went, it seemed that someone was already expecting them.

The man's focus suddenly shifted to somewhere behind Lenah, and she turned to see Cassius walk out with Corinna still draped over his shoulder. His c-nano arm glittered in the bright light of the landing bay, and, combined with his tall build, he was the walking image of cyborg strength in his prime.

Let's hope that intimidates them at least a little bit, Lenah thought, glad he was there with them. She doubted they could quickly exchange the stone for one million CGC and leave again. There would be questions. But maybe there would be fewer questions with a cyborg looming by their side.

Lenah also had her mind magic, an advantage she wouldn't hesitate to use if it got them out of some difficult questioning.

"We also bring you this woman." She pointed toward Corinna. "She was in charge of an illegal plundering mission on Masis III. She wanted to keep the Mapstone for herself. Corinna Cheung of Cheung Corp."

Lenah had expected that to cause a reaction from the man. Unlike Starwide Research, Cheung Corp was a corporation recognized by UPL, and Corinna was a corporate leader known all over the galaxy. But the man's face stayed expressionless.

Cassius's eyes met Lenah's, and she could see her own worry reflected in his gaze.

"Very well, let's get you settled. Ambassador Dreistein wants to meet you." The UPL man snapped his hand and turned around, quickly vanishing out of the hangar's hatch. Lenah looked at Doctor Lund, who shrugged at her. She followed the man, grasping the stone in her pocket as the *Star Rambler* vanished out of sight.

They walked through large, white hallways for several silent minutes. In the beginning, they met other groups of people who were either walking or driving on small hovering stands to their destinations, but after a while, they were alone.

"Where are you taking us?" Lenah asked the man, suspicion once more rising within her. "You said we are going to meet the ambassador?"

"Yes," he said, sounding bored and not even turning around. "We're almost there."

They continued like this for another thirty seconds, until the man finally stopped in the middle of the corridor. "Here we are." He turned around, an expression of pity on his face. A second later, his image became blurry as dozens of laser beams stood between him and Lenah.

"Back, it's a trap," Lenah yelled, whirling around. She bolted back the way they had come, but an identical grid of laser beams was blocking their way. Lenah turned to the UPL man again. "You will explain. Are you taking us as prisoners?" She reached out with her senses to touch his mind. *Why hadn't she done so before?* This was no place for high moral ground; this was a place to make use of any advantage you could.

Now she had to convince him to shut down the lasers. Or, if it wasn't him accessing the control, to relay the order to do so. But she couldn't see anything. Usually, if she concentrated on it, minds started to become visible to her as a cloudy aura wrapped around a person. There was nothing there. Only the laser beams.

Lenah spun, scanning her group and looking for the familiar minds of Persia or Cassius. She felt nothing. *What the stars had just happened to her mind magic?*

"That's not in my power to share," the man answered Lenah's earlier question. "Please excuse me, I'm only following instructions: to keep you and your group contained under high security." He nodded as if that was an apology. "I wasn't lying about your meeting with the ambassador. When he's ready, he'll come to speak to you." With that, he turned and walked away, quickly vanishing behind a hatch that lead out of the corridor.

"Shit!" Lenah couldn't keep back her frustration—about UPL, for being such crooks when they were going to have to save humanity, or about herself, for having walked so easily into the trap.

"Shit," Persia echoed her. "Now what?"

Lenah stepped carefully up to the laser barrier with the intention of inspecting it further, when the section of the floor they were standing on suddenly moved downward like an elevator cart.

The light from the corridor above quickly diminished until they were cast in darkness. The white square above them became smaller the further down they went.

"What's happening?" Doctor Lund yelled into Lenah's ear, clutching on to her arm for balance. She took a wide stance, afraid that a sudden movement would send her spinning into the laser bars. No one answered, and the only sound was Doctor Lund's mutterings of "not again, no please, not again". Lenah imagined what he was referring to. He must be reliving his recent experience as a prisoner on the *Star Rambler*.

They went further down for several more minutes. Finally, the movement stopped, and a bright light hummed on around them. It reflected intensely—blindingly—off four white walls. A low mechanical sound caught her attention from above, and she saw a white panel closing over the open ceiling. A moment later, the laser grids went out, leaving them in what could only be called a prison cell. No door, no windows.

"Just great. Who would have thought UPL are even worse than their fame? They didn't even take *her*," Cassius muttered, finally putting down Corinna whom he'd been carrying all this time.

"She's going to be so mad when she wakes up. Did anyone bring more of those sleep medications?" Uz said, looking at Doctor Lund with wide open eyes.

He shook his head.

"If she's like me, then at least she won't be able to use her abilities," Lenah answered, feeling her shoulders slump. She got out her pistol and aimed it at the wall. Not that she expected it to do anything. After all, why would they be allowed to keep their weapons? But maybe this Ambassador Dreistein would show up quicker if she started vandalizing their spotless white space station.

What Lenah didn't expect, was for the laser to bounce back and almost burn her. She only managed to dodge sideways at the last moment. "Shit!" she repeated.

"Smart cells," Cassius commented from behind.

"Smart cells? You've been in these before? Why didn't you say something?"

He grimaced. "It didn't seem important until you started shooting the walls."

Lenah let go of a tense breath, surprised about herself. She usually had a better handle on her impulses. Being without her powers made her twitchy. She distracted herself by wondering what Cassius could have done to get himself into a smart cell. She knew, of course, that he was a criminal and the son of a smuggler, and a few days ago, the fact that he knew all about the insides of a prison cell would have been obvious to her. But she thought of him as Cassius now; the cyborg on her crew and a good person despite a troubled past. A tickle stirred deep in her stomach as his eyes met hers, and Lenah looked away quickly. "How do we get out of here?" she asked.

"We don't. Right now, there's nothing we can do but wait." Cassius looked at her sharply. "What did you mean before; you're unable to use your abilities?"

Lenah nodded, sinking to the floor. All energy had left her. "I can't see any of your minds nor could I touch the one of the UPL man."

"That's really weird, isn't it?" Persia asked, and Lenah nodded.

"Either a strange reaction with something around here or not a coincidence at all," Uz mused, looking about as if the answer was written on the white walls.

"How could it *not* be a coincidence? Mind magic is secret, right? Even Lenah didn't know what it was called until two weeks ago," Persia said.

Lenah didn't answer. She wasn't so sure about that. If Corinna had known about it, then it was entirely possible that UPL did as well. Maybe being unable to use her powers wasn't so strange after all. Lenah couldn't influence her father, for instance. And if there were two mind mages, there were likely more. What she didn't understand yet was the reasons to keep it a secret.

3 CORINNA

"CORINNA'S WAKING UP." Cassius's voice roused Lenah from her uncomfortable sleep on the floor. She had tried not to doze off, but, apparently, sleep had found her. They had been in the cell for over twelve hours, and, according to her wristpiece, it was now the morning of the next day.

As fast as she could, Lenah scrambled up and instinctively pulled up her mental shields. Over the past couple of weeks, the group had learned that Corinna would try to attack as fast as possible after waking from her drug-induced sleep. This time, when Lenah attempted to lift the mental wall in front of her and Cassius, nothing happened.

"My abilities still don't work," she told Cassius grimly.

At her words, he silently shoved her to the side to take the position next to Corinna. "Should I?" He waved his hand over Corinna's neck to indicate if he should touch a nerve there, keeping the woman unconscious.

Lenah was tempted but also curious. Was something wrong with her own abilities or was it just here, on UPL station?

"Wait to see what she does. I want to know if she's able to use her abilities or not," she whispered, so low she could barely hear herself.

Cassius, picking it up perfectly thanks to his hearing implants, rubbed his temple. "Seems risky. What if she influences me?"

He had a point. If Corinna's mind magic still worked and she willed Cassius to attack them all, they wouldn't stand a chance against his cyborg strength.

"Then move back," Lenah whispered. "Knock *me* out if I start doing something stupid."

Cassius's lips lifted to form a smile, and he started to speak, but Corinna's eyes fluttered, and he moved backward instead.

Good. Lenah wasn't sure she wanted to hear his opinion about her doing something stupid. She already felt like it had been foolish to come here.

Lenah looked down at the woman on the floor. Corinna Cheung had been her idol for many years; a woman who led a vastly successful company and didn't feel too fancy to fly a spaceship despite her high position. But that had been before Lenah discovered how Corinna had tried to single-handedly claim knowledge of the Cava Dara threat and hide the involvement of her company, declaring to be able to handle it all by herself. *Too fucking heroic.*

Dark-brown eyes looked up at Lenah, but the expected attack didn't follow. Instead, Corinna blinked several times, then furled her brows together for one moment before the expressionless mask returned.

"How's your ability doing?" Lenah asked her.

Corinna glowered back.

For a woman with a messy bun on her head and clothes stained from two weeks of constant wear, she sure managed to look intimidating.

"What did you do to me? I no longer feel drugged." That was all Lenah wanted to hear. Making Corinna think she was the only one who had issues with her mind magic was good. After all, they were trapped with her in the same cell for stars knew how much longer. Let Corinna think Lenah could still access her magic.

"Where are we?" Corinna started to sit up, and Lenah didn't hold her back.

"UPL station."

"Ah," Corinna nodded, as if that explained everything.

She wouldn't know something about mind magic not working here, would she?

"Doesn't look like they were fond of seeing you. Why are we in a smart cell?"

Of course, the businesswoman famously called The Queen in the smuggler world would know all about smart cells.

"This is their lobby. We're waiting to meet the ambassador."

Corinna shot Lenah an exasperated look. "Please don't tell me you gave these people the stone?"

"Sure thing, I won't tell you." Lenah smirked as Corinna glared at her.

"I didn't take you to be so immature, Lenah Callo."

Corinna actually managed to make Lenah feel childish about the comment. But she decided that those jokes belonged to the Lenah she had become: the free-spirited pilot of a ship, no longer bound to the empty life of corporate formalities.

Before she could think of a good answer, their cell suddenly jolted, and they were moving sideways and then up. By the time the cell halted inside another white, empty room, everyone was standing. Once more, they were trapped inside a square of laser beams functioning as very effective bars. Persia had pulled her weapon, and Cassius looked around, so tense that all his muscles were straining and visible.

"Miss Cheung and Miss Callo, please step forward onto the blue line. Everyone else, stay behind," the cheerful but metallic voice of an A.I. system said through an invisible speaker. Who put a happy voice into a prison cell speaker? *Totally beside the situation*. Moments later, a blue line appeared at one end of the cell.

"They want to separate us," Cassius growled from behind Lenah.

"Can we do anything about it?" Lenah whispered back. "Why are Corinna and I being singled out?" She specifically meant why wasn't Persia, the one who had actually stolen the stone, being called out but didn't want to be so direct.

"Let's see," Cassius said and took a resolute step forward, pulling Lenah by the arm until they were both standing on the blue line. Corinna was still half sitting, half lying on the floor.

"Only Lenah Callo and Corinna Cheung on the blue line," came the A.I.'s voice again. "Everyone else step back, or we will engage less friendly methods."

"Less friendly methods? It's not like you've been very welcoming so far. We haven't even gotten a single sip of water or access to a sanitary facility," Lenah replied.

"I apologize. You will get access to both soon. That is the case for all of you, if you follow the instructions."

"The hell I will," Cassius said. "We all go, or no one does." He motioned for Persia, Uz, and Doctor Lund to step forward.

"Cassius, I don't think this is a good id—" Lenah managed while the voice from the speaker said:

"Negative."

Then, without further warning, they were all pushed backward by some kind of stunner beam. Only, it was invisible and very targeted. They landed a couple of meters back, on the floor. Cassius was the only one who instantly leaped up, but it was only to get targeted by yet another beam and get knocked back down. This time, he struggled to get up, but didn't try to jump forward again. Instead, he growled toward the ceiling where the voice was coming from, then looked at Lenah, giving her a look that she interpreted as an apology.

Lenah nodded and smiled. She'd have to go alone. Maybe once she was out, she could escape and help free them. Or pressure someone into telling her why they had been arrested. It seemed a foul move by UPL first to offer to pay one million credits for the stone, then arrest the party bringing it.

Lenah bent down to help Corinna up, who glowered at her but accepted the assistance. Once standing, Corinna bobbled on shaky legs and continued to lean heavily on Lenah, who pulled her over toward the blue line.

"Thank you." The A.I.'s voice was as cheerful as ever.

Lenah stumbled forward as laser lines suddenly blinked to life, separating her and Corinna from the others. They were left standing in a small space of barely an arm's length in between the walls of lasers. The fear of tripping and falling was hard to suppress. Lenah grabbed better hold of Corinna. It wouldn't do that they had made all the effort to get her to UPL only for Lenah to drop her into a laser.

After a long and silent minute, footsteps sounded in the distance. They grew louder, and, finally, a tall figure walked around the corner. It wasn't the same man that had trapped them, but he looked almost identical: white robe, similar features. It reminded Lenah of the information broker in Port Dumas. So much so that she wondered if these men too were using some weak warp magic to conceal their real features. The man stopped a few meters away, and the wall separating them vanished.

"Follow me."

Then he turned around and left Lenah to deal with Corinna's weight alone.

Deciding to postpone confrontation for the time being, Lenah tried to catch up to him as she dragged Corinna, but he always stayed a couple of meters in front of her.

After a few minutes of walking and sweating—Corinna was by no means able to support herself—they reached a wall with four white doors. Lenah concluded that she hated the color. Everything here was made of it, and it was blinding and confusing. Likely it was done on purpose. Even before they had been taken captive, she would have had a hard time finding the way back to the ship. Now, with the absence of any windows and the monotony of the corridors, she was completely lost. Lenah suspected that they might be in the lower part of the sphere with the cell movement having felt mostly downward, but it wasn't more than just a gut feeling. How did this man even find his way around?

"In here, please, Miss Cheung. You, in there, Miss Callo." The man spoke for the first time in minutes, pointing to two of the doors. Lenah noticed how he used please with Corinna but not with her.

"I really don't see the point of this," Corinna wheezed. The walk had visibly exhausted her, and Lenah agreed with her point.

"Me neither. I came here to make a transaction and deliver a criminal. Being locked in a cell *with* the criminal was not the treatment I was expecting."

Corinna scowled at Lenah but didn't say anything to her. Instead, she turned to the man, who was still standing two meters away.

"I wish to speak with High Ambassador Pantha. And, please, get this person off me."

"You will speak to *an* Ambassador, Miss Cheung. But, unfortunately, the High Ambassador is not currently on the station. If you will step into your designated room, please."

Lenah didn't like how the man was so friendly with Corinna. Or was she imagining that he was a lot nicer to her?

So be it, she finally decided and let go of Corinna to step toward the room. She didn't turn at the sound of Corinna going down to the floor. Let her deal with her own problems; after all, she'd asked for Lenah to let her go. Maybe Lenah was petty, but it gave her some strength, and she figured she'd soon need all the strength she could muster.

4 FAVORITES

THEY MADE LENAH WAIT. She had been in the interrogation room—there was no other way to call a room with a table split in half by another wall of laser grids—for a full hour, though it felt more like three. Before that, two robed men had come in and searched her, then left with the stone. Pleas for a bathroom break and some water had gone unanswered.

She hadn't used the past hour for any good. Lenah had paced, tapped her foot, and barely kept herself from hitting her palm into the table in front of her. She hadn't done it, thinking of the cameras that were most likely filming her every motion.

Despite knowing that she needed to be at her very best for the conversation—interrogation—that was coming, she hadn't managed to keep her cool. The worst part of her power was being without it. Was such a lack of control how normal people felt all the time? How did they prepare?

If they'd let Lenah, she'd be open and bring up all the facts as soon as possible. Everyone listened to facts. That's what Lenah sent out when using her powers. Images of how proud the investors were when they made triple gains for putting CGCs into Starwide Research's mage farm. Wrapped around her mind magic were always facts. Today, she had come to UPL with strong facts. Video proof. She touched her wristpiece that carried the recording of the ancient computer on Masis III.

Lenah had also brought the stone to them. Any reasonable person would see the need to react to this threat. They would send out corporate armies under UPL command. They would have the mage farm shut down. Why was it taking so long?

Finally, when Lenah was about to pass out from thirst and boredom, another white-robed man with the same features as the others before him appeared in the room.

"Come this way." Reluctantly, Lenah stood up. Now, with a strategy forming in her head, she wanted to start the interrogation. But if UPL wanted to torture her without actually doing *anything*, they sure were doing a pretty decent job.

The man led her to a large sanitary unit down the corridor and locked the door. There, Lenah was allowed a few minutes to freshen up. She sighed, drying her hands against the wall dryer and already feeling better. Why hadn't they allowed this before? She gasped and realized it most likely wasn't a coincidence. They had been subtly making her suffer at first to now make her feel grateful. She pressed her lips together and nodded to herself. She could play this game too.

A few minutes later, when Lenah was back in the interrogation room, a man dressed in something other than a white robe walked in. This must be an ambassador. Lenah sat silent and upright in her chair and took the time to size him up as he shuffled in with his sweeping robes. After seeing so much white, he made quite an impression with his colorful attire; patterns, stylized animals, and plants intertwined on the piece of elegant cloth, each different motif separated by tiny silver borders.

"Nathan Dreistein, pleased to meet you," he said, smiling at her under bushy eyebrows that seemed to almost cover his eyes. If it weren't for the calm and erect way in which he held his shoulders—broad for someone in an ambassador position—the man could have been described as the harmless, grandfatherly type.

As it was though, she could see a man used to being in charge. And used to being right, no doubt. He was still smiling noncommittally, but in a way that tried to put her in her spot. Lenah couldn't hide her annoyance as he sat down at the table opposite her. She was separated from him by a wall of potentially deadly laser beams. They were still holding her friends hostage in a cell, and this man looked like he was going talk about the weather. Tentatively, she reached out with her talent, but once more, she found nothing. No hint of Nathan Dreistein's mind.

"I apologize if your stay here has been unpleasant. I fear we must take utter precaution in this matter. I understand you are part of the Callo family?"

So that was how this was going to play out? Why was he asking, anyway? They had already addressed Lenah by her name and still put her in a cell.

"Yes, Lenah Callo," she said, trying to not show her true emotions.

The ambassador nodded. "Timothy Callo's only daughter. Even here in orbit of Arcadia, we've heard of your family."

Lenah smiled sweetly at him, a practiced motion her face had performed many times. Astur, her home planet, lay in the fringes of UPL space, and even though it was the local metropolis, it was over a week away by warp bubble to humanity's main settlements like Galtaca or Arcadia. Astur was backwater. Something people from these planets never hesitated to point out.

Nathan Dreistein nodded at Lenah. "With your family's destiny tied so closely to Cheung Corp, I see why you wanted to step out of the shadow. I understand you are attempting to reach corporate status. However, that cannot be done by stealing and kidnapping. You did steal the Mapstone from your father's house, took it all over the galaxy, and when Miss Cheung caught up with you, you kidnapped and mistreated her." His tone made it clear it wasn't a question. "I have spoken with your father, and he has assured me this wasn't done on his command. While your enthusiasm to become part of the elite is honorable, you have clearly overstepped your boundaries, Miss Callo."

"I... *What?*" Lenah inwardly cringed at her lack of finesse, but what she hadn't expected was for the conversation to take this route. She was here to talk about the Mapstone and the Cava Dara. Now she realized the foolishness of that expectation. She'd been part of this world her whole life and only been away from Starwide Research for a month. She shouldn't have so easily forgotten their way of constant scheming.

"Ambassador, no matter who stole the stone, what is important is only the message it carries. Besides, wasn't it UPL who posted all over the starnet a request to have the stone brought here—no matter how and by whom? You didn't care about theft when you posted that, and now you accuse me of stealing?"

"I understand your anger. You must be in a difficult situation." The ambassador's voice was calm. If Lenah could have punched some of that friendliness out of him, she would have. Instead, she clenched her fists under the table. Punching a laser barrier most definitely wouldn't help her case. Or her health.

"Trying to make ends meet for the first time in your life. I understand your father has cut you off from all your accounts. And rightfully so."

He knew more than her. She had left her usual wristpiece, the one that was linked to her accounts, back home to be untraceable for the meeting with the informant in Port Dumas.

"Ambassador Dreistein, there are more important things we need to talk about. Very soon, we won't have the luxury to care about who stole what and who got caught in some corporate power struggle. I have seen something, and it is of utmost importance to humanity. Let me show you."

She opened the folder on her wristpiece where she had recorded the video from the Syrr princess. Dreistein raised a bushy eyebrow but didn't interrupt. Finally, a good sign. Maybe she could do this even without mind magic.

They watched in silence as the video started showing how the Syrr king was warned by the Cassidian high priest and moved on to how the king ingested three stones identical to the Mapstone. Finally, the video showed the winged Cava Dara, Cassidian Angels of Revenge, and how they came down to attack the peaceful Syrr population.

"This is the message of the Mapstone?" Dreistein said when the video ended after a short monologue by the Syrr princess herself. One in her native language of hisses and tonalities they couldn't understand. He scratched his chin in an absent gesture. "I have to say, I expected more."

"More? Has Miss Cheung told you that the Cassidian High Priest gave her the same warning?" Lenah realized her voice sounded desperate, but his lack of understanding about the importance of this left her baffled. What else had he expected of this message? "Has Miss Cheung also told you that she planned to handle this threat with just her own army?" Lenah needed for UPL to understand what was happening, no matter the cost. Even if it meant losing Starwide Research its position in queue to receive corporate status.

"This is big, Ambassador. These creatures, the Cava Dara, are coming for humanity. We saw some of them depart Masis III, and very soon, we might see images like this one, but instead of the long-forgotten inhabitants of Masis III, it will be human civilians being killed."

"Miss Callo, you seem to be underestimating our military strength. A few ancient creatures against all the space force that we have? That the Cheung army has? In fact, Miss Cheung has already assured me that her army can handle the situation more than adequately. Such as was her plan from the very beginning."

That at least explained why Lenah had to wait here for so long. They'd talked to Corinna first.

"You already spoke with her? Did she also mention that she has made a big name for herself in the criminal underworld?"

The ambassador didn't react apart from giving Lenah one of his smiles. Did he know and not care? Or did he not believe Lenah, thinking she would now resort to some desperate accusation to have her voice heard? She shook her head. It would seem that Corinna was also better than Lenah at convincing people without using her abilities. It was no surprise that he had spoken to Corinna first. After all, Cheung Corp was a recognized corporation, including the rights to a position in the UPL assembly, humanity's most important political instance, and it had an army.

"Miss Cheung sees that you acted out of the ambition to elevate Starwide Research's status, a feeling she can well understand. She has also assured me that while her trip in your custody wasn't the most pleasant, you didn't maliciously try to injure her."

Lenah, whose mouth had slowly dropped open while he spoke, closed it with a snap, but he continued before she could speak.

"She is willing to forgo any charges against you and Starwide Research. You are free to go. Best to take that ship you arrived on, and that you seem to have grown so fond of, back home, where your father is waiting. But I recommend you attend tonight's celebration dinner in honor of Miss Cheung. Surely, you would like to apologize to her."

"You are throwing a party in her *honor*?"

"Of course, or would you disagree she has gone through some great suffering in her mission to help humanity and to make one of UPL's finest corporate armies shine?" He paused dramatically, apparently waiting for Lenah to chime in with her utmost respect for Corinna. She didn't.

"Because, if you disagree, I might have to keep you and your friends as guests for some additional time."

Even without her abilities, Lenah could clearly hear the threat. *Suck it up and play the game, or lose.*

She had been part of this world long enough to know that it was always better to keep playing. "Of course. I would enjoy attending the dinner and get a chance to speak to Miss Cheung personally." She couldn't say apologize, but it seemed enough for Ambassador Dreistein, who lifted a hand.

Instantly, the door behind him opened, and the same man who had greeted them on UPL station came in.

"Walk Miss Callo and her entourage to one of our guest rooms. And if you could, find them something decent to wear for tonight's festivities."

Both their gazes went to Lenah's ripped, black blazer.

"Of course, sir."

They both left Lenah alone in the room, then, shortly after, the door behind her opened.

"Miss Callo, if you'd please follow me.

5 REUNITED

"MY CREW, WHERE are they?" Lenah asked, and not for the first time. The man's stoic mask fell, and he sighed, turning toward Lenah. Their eyes met. "They're just behind us and their rooms will be right next to yours." He waved around the doors visible every few meters in the white corridor. His gaze lingered on Lenah, and she thought that implied honesty. Still without her abilities, that was the most she could ask for.

"This is your room. The dinner is in one hour," he said matter-of-factly, then held a door open and nodded a goodbye as Lenah stepped into the lavish room beyond.

She barely heard the door close as she took in the floral motif of the tapestry, the equally detailed cloth on the bedspread with its golden borders, and the multiple colors of the couch. Her gaze fell on the outfit they'd apparently given her for the dinner party. At least, whoever had chosen it, hadn't assumed she dressed like her bedspread. A blouse with a dark-red collar and a tight, sleeveless vest of the same color—and of the latest fashion—lay on the couch topped off by black velvet pants with red knee inlays and fine-heeled black pumps. The type where the heel was so thin, it was impossible not to tremble and wobble in them.

Lenah scanned the room again, trying to see if there was anything useful in here, but she had to admit, she didn't know herself *what* she was looking for. A way back to her friends? A map back to the *Rambler*? The stone? No, she had absolutely no expectation of getting it back. And that wasn't the worst of it. UPL wouldn't prepare for what was to come and wouldn't pay Lenah's group for it either. It seemed they had turned out to be less reliable business partners than the Craff smuggler on Lunara Station. He'd paid promptly and as promised upon delivery.

Instead, here they were, all thanks to Corinna Cheung's mercy. A mercy Corinna granted, because she thought she had won. She'd be able to deal with the Cava Dara, thinking herself the next Asturian or even galactic hero, whereas the next thing for Lenah was to leave in bad graces. Did that mean that it was simply over? Would Lenah sit back and watch how the Cava Dara flew down on Asturis I like a swarm of death? She knew her answer to that. Determination started to push away the helplessness.

"No, we'll keep playing the game," she murmured, grabbing the outfit from the couch and making her way into the bathroom. After all, she'd been trained to do this her whole life.

An inadvertent moan escaped Lenah when she stepped into the bathroom. The shower was bigger than the *Star Rambler*'s complete lavatory unit. Just what she needed before a stiff social function. Nonetheless, Lenah tried to not linger under the hot water too long, forcing herself to step out and don the clothes that had been laid out for her. Everything fit perfectly. Adjusting her hair in a tight, high bun and even using some make-up that the bathroom provided, Lenah finally left the tall heels behind and instead grabbed her boots. She wasn't all too sure the evening would go over smoothly. Playing the game or not, she had limits.

She took a last look in the mirror where corporate Lenah, daughter of Timothy Callo, was looking back at her for the first time in a month. Lenah had framed her eyes with dark-brown shadows, the same color as her eyes, inserting just a little bit of gold into each corner. Feeling safe in the familiar look, she stepped back and would have almost tripped despite the boots, when she realized who was standing there, looking amazing.

Cassius turned around to face Lenah, dressed in a combination of black pants and a high-collared blazer. The silver buttons on it shone and sparkled almost as much as his eyes. Deep green eyes, she couldn't help but notice.

"Wow...I mean, you polished up nice." She finished weakly and felt blood shooting up into her cheeks.

His face lit up. "So have you, Miss Callo. Apart from down there, I mean." He gave her boots a significant look, then grinned.

"You should have seen the shoes that came with this outfit."

"I've seen the ones that came with *my* outfit." He shuddered, and Lenah realized he was still wearing his black combat boots, even though he seemed to have taken the time to clean them.

"Well, then you shouldn't judge."

"I wasn't. I was merely making conversation, or isn't commenting on the outfit one of the topics you talk about to your date in these social functions?"

"I think you're supposed to point out your date's perfection, not imperfection. Since you're not my date but my companion in crime, you are entitled to have an opinion on how fast I could run away. Your comment was adequate." She grinned.

He rubbed his chin, looked her up and down again, then let out a long breath.

Had he *meant* to imply they were going on a date tonight? Had she just bombed it? Would she like to go on a date with him? He *did* look handsome and was nice to talk to but also a totally inadequate choice for her. Luckily for Lenah, they had more important things to think about tonight. She shoved the nice image of the two of them on a date to the back of her mind.

"Ready to go?" he asked lightly, as if equally relieved that their conversation had gone back to safe topics. That was probably not a good sign for a future date, anyway. He simply had never seen Lenah in anything different than her worn out and ripped black blazer. No wonder he hardly recognized her in these clothes.

She nodded and moved toward the door.

"The others are already waiting," Cassius commented as she passed him on her way outside and grimaced. *Why?*

She realized why the instant she stepped outside. Lund and Uz were talking to each other in low voices, looking stunning in their all-black outfits, but Persia, who was strutting up and down the corridor, had taken some liberties. She was also wearing a high-collared blouse and tight vest but had left at least four buttons open, showing part of an intricate bra with thin metal chains arranged to resemble lace, no doubt a remnant of her gladiator outfit.

"Uhm." Lenah stopped dead in her tracks, making Cassius collide with her from the back.

"You all look amazing." She forced out. "Persia, did you forget to finish dressing?"

"What do you mean? You don't like my personal touch?"

"Have you been wearing a metal bra all this time?"

Persia touched one of the small chains. "It's the one my gladiator outfit came with. And it's not exactly metal. Most of it is cloth; only the lacey part on top is metal. Makes a gladiator look feral."

"Er, sure. You wouldn't mind closing a few more buttons on the blouse, would you? We're not here to make male acquaintances." She shot Cassius a look. "But to find a way out of this mess."

"Wow, I thought you were all happy to be reunited." Persia pursed her lips. "Seems not. And here I was, almost hugging you," she trailed off, throwing her arms up in a dramatic gesture.

Lenah couldn't hide her smile as she stepped closer to Persia and encased her in a hug.

"I *am* happy to see you," Lenah said, though she dreaded the moment when she'd have to admit that she didn't have the stone or the money.

"Thank the stars you're okay. We were so worried," Persia mumbled into her hair, pressing her so close, Lenah could feel the wires of her bra. Grimacing, she stepped out of the hug. "Yeah, I'm okay. The ambassador and I had a *chat*," she said, looking around the corridor to make sure there were alone. She was worried that their status as houseguests could be revoked into prisoner status again at any time.

"So, does us being free and invited to a fancy gala mean that you have the money? We're rich?"

"No, not yet," Lenah replied, leading the way through the corridor and shooting Persia a warning look that she finally seemed to understand. Luckily, holosigns reading 'Evening Reception' were indicating the way, as if someone had anticipated they'd otherwise get completely lost in the white hallways. She wondered if they were now, even here, being watched by invisible eyes. *Likely*.

"Lenah, what happened?" Uz asked softly as they turned into another corridor where classical music was playing from invisible speakers.

"They spoke to Corinna first, that's what happened," Lenah whispered, stopping and gathering everyone close.

"They totally believed her story, about how she was—and is—trying to save the galaxy, and that we were trying to reach the same fame. She also promised to address any incoming threat using only the Cheung army, something the ambassador gladly believed. I think he really didn't want to be bothered. So, when I showed him our recording of the Cava Dara invasion on Masis III, he told me to chill out and that Corinna Cheung was already taking care of it. The big message is that we're lucky to get out like this."

"And the stone?" Doctor Lund asked, his eyebrows drawn into one sharp line.

"They took it."

"They won't give us a reward at all?" Persia said, her eyes wide.

"No." Lenah shook her head. "After all, we're the thieves who are lucky to get away. In fact, he specifically seemed to ask us to get away on the *Rambler*."

Cassius lifted a scratched his head. "They call us thieves and then want us to keep a stolen ship? Why?"

Lenah took in a sharp breath as she realized how strange that was. They'd arrived to UPL, a galactic authority, on a stolen ship and it hadn't caused any repercussions. In fact, Ambassador Dreistein had seemed very explicit about Lenah staying with the *Rambler*. Wouldn't they usually confiscate a stolen smuggler ship? So why did the ambassador think it such a good idea for them to leave on the *Rambler* instead of taking whatever anonymous shuttle from here? There had to be a reason. As she thought about it, she could only think of one. And that was the same reason that Corinna and her men had always shown up about the same time Lenah and her crew had come out of a warp bubble.

"I think they're able to track the ship," she croaked.

Everyone was silent at that.

"Given how easily they've always found us so far, that would make a lot of sense," Uz finally murmured. "We shouldn't leave on that ship."

6 ALLIES ARE FEW

THEY FINALLY REACHED the dinner hall, and it turned out to be one of Lenah's absolute horror settings. It was a formal dinner *ball*. As in Old Earth days, important guests were paraded through the room like meat for everyone else to bow to. She hated functions like this. It wasn't because the Callo family rarely made it onto the guests-of-honor list, but because they were stiff and pretentious. Today, however, she was part of the entourage of the guest of honor: Corinna Cheung.

Persia, who upon their arrival seemed to have noticed the conservative dress code of everyone else and closed all her buttons, and Doctor Lund were beaming as they queued to enter. Corinna stood to the side, pointedly ignoring them. Her eyes briefly flickered over to Lenah, shining coldly and her face barely hiding a sneer, but then she simply turned away. Lenah dreaded what they would say about her group when they were announced to the room. Was it unheard of to ridicule people? She worried it was not.

After a few long and dreadful minutes, the group made their entrance. Lenah walked in the front row with Doctor Lund holding her arm, while Cassius took Uz's and Persia's arms. They passed the tall doorway and stepped into a world of gold curtains, marble pillars, and something that looked like a ruby chandelier and was the most decadent thing Lenah had seen in all her life. That chandelier must be worth more than all of Starwide Research.

"The heroes who have brought us the Mapstone, Lenah Callo and entourage. Welcome to United Planetary Legion," a male voice announced as the music interrupted. The crowd clapped politely, and Lenah breathed out a sigh of relief. They weren't going to be humiliated. At least not yet. She put a pained smile on her face as Doctor Lund, still beaming next to her, walked her through the corridor that the crowd had formed in the middle of the room. How was she supposed to survive this evening?

As they passed, Lenah felt many pairs of eyes on her. But without her mind magic, she couldn't gauge if she was being met with friendly or angry stares. What did these people know? Everyone's faces seemed neutral and pleased; it could mean anything. Only one face, a lanky young man dressed in brown robes, smiled at them.

Was he a guild mage? The cut of the long robe with the wide sleeves suggested so, but she had never seen a mage dressed in brown; usually, they wore black. Nor a mage so young. He couldn't be older than nineteen.

Finally, and under a lot of nodding, they reached the end of the room, and Lenah took the first opening to step behind the other guests. Hesitantly, Lund followed her. He had been visibly enjoying this, and she was sure that being a member of USO, a not-so-liked cult focusing on scientifically explaining magic, he didn't often get positive public attention.

"Amazing. They are good hosts here." He grinned at Lenah as they watched the others walk through the room. Cassius and Uz were among the tallest people, apart from a regal looking Cassidian, and Lenah allowed herself to take another good look at Cassius. He, too, had changed a lot since she'd first seen him with dreadlocks and a full beard. He shaved everyday now, which showed off his angular features and even his lips. A few people gasped at them, and Lenah wondered if that was because they had noticed Cassius's enhanced arm hooked around Persia's or because of Uz's cut gyrums.

"And now, today's guest of honor, Miss Corinna Cheung, leader of Cheung Corp, innovator, UPL army commander, and High Commander of the Astur II Defense Mission. Welcome to United Planetary Legion," the booming voice announced to the room, and this time, the roar of the crowd was definitely more enthusiastic.

Just as well, Lenah thought. In case something went wrong, her group wouldn't be the center of attention. Somehow, her skin itched uncomfortably as if her body knew something her brain hadn't caught onto yet. She scanned the whole room with more care.

It was stuffed with at least fifty people, most of them men and women in black-and-red dress robes like the one Lenah wore. Colors reserved for members of corporate families. A few people were dressed entirely in red, the color for the most important guests. Both Corinna Cheung and Ambassador Dreistein, who was walking her in, were clad in shimmering red from head to toe. Some others wore only black, like Lenah's friends. These were outsiders, not members of the families, but who had somehow found their way into this circle. Only a handful of guests didn't follow that dress code. Like the young guild mage in his brown robe and the Cassidian, standing tall, and dressed in a purple robe with a white Cassidian silk shirt sticking out at the collar. He was looking around, as if searching for someone, and finally headed in their direction.

He bowed his head when he reached Lenah. "Miss Callo, may the tradition of the Old be with you. A pleasure."

"May the tradition of the Old be with you, Wise —" Lenah answered in the way she had learned to greet Cassidians.

"Ikanobu." He offered his name.

"— Wise Ikanobu."

"It is said you saw the threat of the Cava Dara's return."

That surprised Lenah. She had assumed that UPL would try to make as little a deal out of this as possible, celebrating mostly the upcoming military mission of Cheung army. Preferably, without telling most people what was really happening and painting it like a minor defense mission. But the Cassidian High Priest had known what was coming and warned Corinna, hadn't he? So maybe this Cassidian also knew more.

"Yes, we saw them leave the Syrr temple on Masis III."

"Masis III?"

"A planet in the fifth octant. Outside of UPL space."

"And it's livable, but your people haven't settled on it?" He arched an elegant eyebrow at her.

Right, Cassidians took some offense to the expansive nature of humans, who were always trying to settle on new planets, constantly growing their trillions of population in size. Cassidians, instead, stuck to their home planet Cassidia and the traditions they called the Old Ways. Old Ways, that had cost Uz her gyrums, Lenah reminded herself.

"It's highly volcanic. And not very comfortable to live on."

"Ah." He didn't sound convinced. In fact, Lenah figured that Masis III was not settled due to the secret about the Syrr it had held, back when the first humans thought the race had been destroyed by Cassidians, instead of Cava Dara. Otherwise, someone would surely have started to terraform the world, and it wasn't even far away. Humans inhabited far worse places, like Oscuris, with its eternal freezing temperatures and the short day-night cycle. But the first humans who had discovered Masis III, had suspected that the temple was proof of the Cassidians committing genocide on the Syrr and tried to hide that from the rest of the humans on the Generation Ship.

"Wise Ikanobu," Uz said from behind Lenah, "what do you know of the Cava Dara's return?"

He tipped his head from one side to the other, looking temporarily flabbergasted to be addressed.

"Your Cut is energetic. Surprising, even outside of the home world. I'm relieved that you freed her. No one who was born Cassidian should ever end up in a human laboratory," he finally said, eyes boring into Lenah's. Lenah didn't know what to say. That freeing Uz had only been a coincidence? That it was her own father's lab she'd been kidnapped to go to? Or that she was shocked to realize what he knew. When Lenah didn't speak, Wise Ikanobu slowly turned back to Uz, as if inwardly stealing himself to look at her. "I know only what is taught. Even you will have learned it, or were you cut that early?" His eyes turned back to Lenah.

"And you are sure you don't know anything else?" Uz continued as if his treatment of her was the most normal thing in the world. "You didn't seem surprised about them returning. They didn't teach me that in the lessons."

His eyebrow raised again, and he addressed Lenah as he answered. "Very astute. Yes. There are circles that know, but it certainly isn't intended to become common knowledge and especially not spread among the humans." The way he said humans irked Lenah almost as much as his treatment of Uz. *Worthless beings*, the tone of his words implied.

"Don't you think it's important for them to know if the Cava Dara are posing a threat?" Uz's voice sounded agitated.

Unlike her, Wise Ikanobo stayed entirely calm. "Like you, they have forgotten to follow the Old Ways. Therein lies fault."

"The Old Ways? We are not Cassidians, Wise Ikanobu," Lenah said. "We don't teach following the Old Ways. We teach moving forward, not looking backward." She tried to keep her voice calm. He seemed terribly arrogant, although she didn't think he was trying to be mean. He was naturally condescending like that. Or what humans perceived as condescending. His treatment of Uz, however, was hard to forgive.

"And you still believe you should?" his second eyebrow met the first.

"Wise Ikanobu, it is the way of humanity," Uz said in Lenah's stead. "They don't have old books to follow. Instead, they write new books about technology and progress and are constantly improving their way of life."

The Cassidian didn't answer at first, just frowned at Uz. Then, pointedly, he turned to Lenah, looking her directly in the eyes with a hard stare. It sent shivers down her spine. "You should put your Cut in its place." Just like that, he nodded to her and strolled off.

Lenah turned to Uz.

"What was that about? Is that how they treat you?"

Uz swallowed. "It's normal, he didn't mean bad."

"Didn't mean bad? He treated you like you're my pet, not my friend."

Uz gave her a lopsided smile. She seemed way less shaken by the encounter than Lenah.

"Let it go, it's nothing new to me, and I can take it. But now you know why I had to leave there. Let's go check out the food, okay?" she finished, her tone making it clear that the topic was over. She turned pointedly toward the buffet that was set up along the short end of the room, conveniently located in the opposite direction the Cassidian had taken.

7 DISMISSED

HER PLATE PILED high with antipasti, caviar, and duck, all the Old Earth foods that were only served in the fanciest of environments these days, Lenah slowly walked through the room, looking for Corinna. Whatever Corinna was up to tonight, Lenah was sure it included lobbying with the most important people around. Lenah wanted to either listen in to what was being said or also talk to them.

She almost crashed plate-first into the young mage in the brown robe as he suddenly appeared in front of her, panting. Had he run? How had he managed to do that in a crowded room?

"Is it true you're a spaceship captain?" He blurted as soon as she had stopped in front of him. "I mean, you're from the families, aren't you? How did you even learn that? Um, I'm Lorka Enggaard, by the way. Um, sorry." He stopped talking, ears red and eyes downcast. Lenah couldn't hide a grin.

"Hi, Mage Enggaard. It's not that unheard of. In fact, our very own guest of honor, Corinna Cheung, also flies."

"She does?" His eyes flickered over toward the back of the room, and, indeed, Lenah finally located Corinna there. She was talking to Ambassador Dreistein and another man, also dressed in red ambassador robes but adorned with even more gold and a few years older than Dreistein. Someone important, no doubt. Was that the High Ambassador Corinna had inquired about?

"Lorka."

"What?" Lenah had to bring herself back to the conversation as she'd been staring intently at Corinna.

"You can call me Lorka," the young mage said.

"Nice to meet you, Lorka. I'm Lenah."

"Are you the one with the adventure? Who brought the famous stone they are showing out front?"

"They are showing the Mapstone?"

Lorka nodded eagerly. "Yes, in an exhibition room next to the guest landing bay."

That was news to Lenah. They weren't keeping it secret after all. The ambassadors seemed very confident.

"Did you say the stone is famous? What else do you know about it?" Lenah was intrigued.

Lorka's ears turned red again. "I mean, not famous. Not since recently, at least." He looked around, his eyes darting nervously over the crowd.

"You're a guild mage, aren't you?" Lenah changed the topic. Maybe that would make him more comfortable.

"Guild mage in training, at your service," Lorka answered, giving an awkward bow, accentuated by his lanky build in the wide robe that was no longer covering his shoes. He wore brown sneakers with yellow socks underneath.

"And what are you doing here at UPL station?" Lenah asked. She'd never heard of young mages traveling before they could do actual work for the Guild. As far as she knew, the students were shipped off to train at the Guild's secret location as soon as they manifested powers. That could be anywhere between six to twelve years old. The next time they reappeared to the world, they were fully formed mages, and most of them started jobs on spaceships as transporters: mages dedicated to moving ships through warp bubbles.

"I, um. . ." Lorka studied his shoes. "I'm doing an internship with High Ambassador Pantha." He looked up toward Corinna, and Lenah followed his gaze.

"Is that the older guy talking to Miss Cheung and Ambassador Dreistein?"

"Yup." Lorka nodded. "Thankfully, I only have two more months to go. I can't stand making coffee with whiskey for the old man."

"He has a mage making him coffee?" Lenah asked, amused. "Doesn't he have servants?"

"It's all part of my *educational punishment*. I'm supposed to learn to follow orders, no matter how boring. And leadership skills. And not listen in to conversations I'm not supposed to hear. Like the one about the st—some random conversation I overheard at the Guild."

Had he been about to say 'the stone'? Lenah finally shifted all her attention to the young man. What did he know?

"Lorka, if you think there's something interesting, I might want to know, in exchange for me showing you the cockpit of my ship. I won't tell anyone."

The inner war was written all over his features, and Lenah started to feel bad for having tempted him.

Finally, he shook his head. "Nothing, Lenah. I better hurry on. I'm supposed to talk to as many people as I can without making it awkward. Um, do you think I'm doing okay? And if you wouldn't mind telling the High Ambassador. I think he's coming this way."

With that, he stretched out a hand and almost bumped it into the pile of antipasti on Lenah's plate. He retracted it as he realized she was holding the plate in one hand and the fork in the other. Lenah looked around and saw the older ambassador and Corinna Cheung walking their way.

Just great. When she had imagined talking to Corinna tonight, she hadn't figured it would be in the presence of a senior UPL ambassador. Lenah had things to say that didn't belong in such company.

"Miss Callo, I'm pleased to meet you," the man said as they stopped in front of her. "My name is High Ambassador Pantha." He also stretched out his hand, and Lenah hurriedly put her fork down to shake it. His grip was like iron and certainly not what she would have expected from someone with such narrow and droopy shoulders. His robe, though tailored to his size, seemed to drown him, but that was only until she met his eyes, which were sharp and seemed to see into her core.

"An honor to meet you, High Ambassador," she replied, giving him her most professional smile.

"Corinna." She nodded but didn't extend her hand. By the way Corinna bared her teeth at her in a bad imitation of a smile, she wouldn't have taken it, anyway. Venom poured toward Lenah, and she was for once glad that neither her nor Corinna's mind magic was working.

"Lenah." Corinna finally nodded when she noticed that the ambassador was waiting.

"Well, now that you two are on speaking terms with each other, I want to let you know the threat will be handled, Miss Callo. No one is holding a grudge against you for overestimating what's coming. You only did what you thought was best, didn't you? And Miss Cheung has assured me that you and your crew didn't hurt her."

Overestimated the threat? Of course, that was how they would spin it. But Corinna hadn't seen the Syrr princess's last video diary, and she had been unconscious when the reawakened Cava Dara had flown away from Masis III.

"What do you plan to do about the trigger? The mage farm?" Lenah said instead. She didn't think an angry outburst would help with these two.

Corinna shook her head. "What about them?"

"Are you going to close them?"

"Of course not. The mage farms are far too valuable an asset for Cheung Corp *and* Starwide Research. We'll handle the Cava Dara in space. Cheung army has an excellent space fleet."

"You won't shut the mage farm down even if they could stop the attacks?"

"Miss Callo, there is no need for that tone," the high ambassador said. Overall, Lenah felt that he was scolding her like little child.

"Have you even seen the video that I showed to Ambassador Dreistein?"

Both didn't answer.

"Let me show you. I promise, it will only take a few seconds," she said to the high ambassador in the nicest tone she could muster and trying not to look away from his piercing gaze.

Before they could tell her otherwise, Lenah opened the video on her wristpiece and held it out to them. She studied their faces as they watched the Cava Dara attack the Syrr population, wiping them out. Corinna's face remained stony throughout the whole recording, but the ambassador's eyes widened ever so slightly as he watched the Cava Dara fly away from the planet.

"That's right. That last bit is not part of the ancient recording. I took it myself less than two weeks ago from the cockpit of my ship as we were leaving Masis III. They are coming, and I don't think these are all the Cava Dara. What's recorded here is only one part of their army. As you saw in the video, there were many Bartoc in the last invasion, but we saw none back on Masis III. I think you greatly underestimate what's approaching. This might not be a matter that can be handled just by Cheung army."

"If you are implying that the Cheung forces receive help from Starwide Research Security, we can talk about it. Or rather, your father and I, can talk about it," Corinna answered.

Lenah shook her head. Corinna was bringing up again the topic of Starwide Research's security not being part of the corporate UPL force.

"The point I'm making is not about Starwide Research, but about needing a greater part of the UPL forces. There might be multiple attacks in multiple locations. We just don't know."

"And you think that you can make a better judgment of this than the high ambassador himself?" Corinna shot Lenah a dark grin. "Let capable people handle this. You've already done enough damage as it is," she finished, and Lenah noticed the high ambassador nodding.

Lenah pressed her lips together. She didn't trust herself to speak and instead took a deep breath to calm down. Not trying to get provoked was turning out to be really difficult.

"I see that it might be too early to make peace yet," the ambassador finally said. "Please send my best wishes to your father. I recommend you take that ship of yours and leave as soon as tomorrow."

They both walked away without sparing Lenah another glimpse. She'd clearly been dismissed. And told to take her ship again.

8 NEW PLANS

"I CAN'T BELIEVE they're belittling the threat," Lenah whispered to Persia, stabbing an olive with her fork. They were standing together in a corner of the room, watching Corinna walk from one group to the next, smiling and making perfectly relaxed conversation.

"We won't get any help here," Persia muttered, equally hushed. Her beaming mood at experiencing such a fancy party had visibly become gloomy, and she kept glaring openly at Corinna.

"What do you think we should do now?"

"Do?" Lenah echoed, though the feeling she'd had before—of itchiness to leave—was peaking up inside her again. "I don't know if we *can* do anything," she whispered. "We certainly can't fly in with the *Rambler* and fight the full Cava Dara force ourselves. And I don't think we could go and recruit more corporate armies to join in. Not as long as they don't see the threat as serious enough to hurt their own worlds."

"That will only happen once planets are attacked," Persia said.

Lenah nodded. "Or if UPL told them to, which they won't." She stabbed the olive again before putting her fork down. "However, there is one thing that we could do."

"And that is?" Persia asked.

"We could try to avoid the attacks altogether."

Persia shook her head. "How?"

"If we're right, and the mage farm is what's triggering the Cava Dara attack on humanity, then destroying the farm should stop the attack, right?"

"Right…That's what the Cassidian Elder who came to Corinna thought."

"There's only one mage farm location as of now, and it's inside the Starwide Research compound in Asturis I."

"What do you plan to do there?" Persia whispered, leaning closer to Lenah.

That was the weak part of Lenah's plan. "I haven't gotten that far, but something to turn them off."

"Like shutting down the electricity?" Persia bit her lip and shook her head.

"I meant a more permanent solution."

Persia gaped. "You want to destroy your own company?"

"If that's what can save trillions of lives, of course."

"Well, if you put it that way. But how can we do that? We don't even have the stone to get there in time."

That was a good point. They couldn't warp as long as they didn't have the stone or a mage, but a plan formed in Lenah's mind.

"We don't have it, but I know where it is."

"You do?"

She nodded. "It's being exhibited somewhere next to the guest landing bay. The young guild mage told me. All we need to do is get there, take the stone, and find our way back to the *Rambler*. Then we can warp our way to Astur."

"Well, you do realize there are flaws in that plan, don't you?" Persia raked her fingers through her hair. "For one, the stone will be guarded. Two, we don't know where we left the *Rambler*. Plus, I'm thoroughly lost with all these white corridors. Third, we'll need a weapon of some sort to destroy the mage farm. I don't suppose you can walk in and tell everyone to turn the destroy-all switch. Which brings me to the fourth thing, we need to get into the compound to destroy anything."

"True. There's an entrance inside of Callo mansion. My father hides a key to the mage farm in his office. We could get the key and enter the farm through the house."

"Won't the people in the house know you didn't exactly leave on good terms?" Persia said, shaking her head.

She was absolutely right, of course. Before Lenah could answer, Uz, Doctor Lund, and Cassius approached.

"You two look like you're having secret conversations without us," Doctor Lund said amiably. When neither Lenah nor Persia said anything, his eyes widened. "You are having secret conversations without us."

"Our captain here plans to walk out with the stone, board our ship, sneak into her own house, and blow up the mage farm," Persia grumbled, low enough for only them to hear.

Doctor Lund's eyes widened even more.

Uz looked from Persia to Lenah, then back into the crowd of UPL guests. Frowning, she muttered, "That might be a good idea…"

"*Might* be a good idea?" Persia echoed, sounding incredulous.

"I thought you'd never ask," Cassius said, a determined grin spreading over his face. Lenah's jaw dropped open. Were they serious? Was *she* serious?

"Okay, does that mean we're doing it?" she whispered to the group. It was a severely underdeveloped plan at the very best. But what else were they going to do?

"We're doing it," Cassius said, and Uz nodded.

"Persia, Lund—are you in? If you don't want to come, that's fine. You're under no obligation."

"And leave you and the cyborg here on your own when you get in a fight? You know I couldn't be responsible for that," Persia said.

"That means you're coming?" Lenah asked, feeling hopeful. She had spoken the truth, that she wouldn't ask Persia to come along, but she'd thoroughly miss her company.

"Of course, I'm coming. Who else will keep you out of trouble, eh? Besides, where else would I go?"

Doctor Lund's eyes wandered over the crowd in the room. After a few seconds, he faced their group again. "These people have nice parties, but they are determined to ignore what's coming." His hand touched his throat where he'd worn his order's necklace before the Cava Dara had ripped it off him. "I'll come along as well."

9 ESCAPE

"HOW DO YOU KNOW where they're keeping the stone?" Uz asked tentatively as Lenah stopped once more to turn around and look for holosigns. She had decided to trace their way back from where the other guests had come. Hopefully, that would lead to the guest bay.

"I asked several people just now if they'd gotten the chance to see it on their way in, and they all had. I hope I wasn't too conspicuous." She winced.

After developing their hasty plan, they hadn't left the party straightaway, even though that was what they'd all wanted to do. Instead, they'd spent more time talking and mingling with the other guests. Lenah had even learned a trick on how to orient herself a little better in the corridors. Now, if she paid close enough attention to it, she could make out the slight bend as UPL station's main corridors followed the shape of the sphere. They now knew that they were in the station's main rings and which direction they were walking. Given how hard it was to see the bend, Lenah figured they must already be in one of the outer central rings. That was also where they had left the *Star Rambler*.

"Did you ask them directly where the stone was?" Doctor Lund asked.

"Of course not," Lenah answered. "That would have definitely been suspicious. But since we brought the stone here, I also felt entitled to ask if they had seen the beauty of it."

"And?"

"And most had. Though no one seemed to find it as captivatingly beautiful as me."

Persia snorted. "Rich folks are always bored. It's difficult to impress them. I constantly needed to come up with new hammer moves to keep crowds engaged."

"No wonder you fight like a show star," Cassius muttered.

"I *am* a show star. Or rather, I was before I met Lenah and had to protect her all the time."

It was Lenah's time to snort. "I can fight for myself, thank you very much."

"And who beat most of those smugglers when we first met?"

"We both beat up one each."

"Yes, but I helped with yours while you were inspecting the door from behind."

"You inspected a door?" Uz repeated, looking from Persia to Lenah, then back to Persia.

"No, I got stuck behind one when the two crowded the room where we were hiding. But I quickly made up for it and was able to beat up my share of the thug," Lenah explained. "Aah, I think it's over there."

They had reached a part of the white corridor laid out with a fluffy carpet and an open door leading off it. The only open door—or at least the only visible door—they had encountered in several minutes.

Loud voices sounded from behind them.

"Uhoh, do you think our absence was noted?" Uz whispered.

"Possibly," Lenah whispered back. "Though I hope they'll check our rooms first. After that ordeal in the cells last night, it ought to be understandable that we're exhausted and had to retire early."

Lenah *had* spent the last half hour of the party yawning ostensibly before excusing herself.

"I can't hear anyone inside that room," Cassius said after walking a few steps ahead of them. With his hearing implants, he had detected mere breathing behind closed doors before, and Lenah trusted his assessment.

Nonetheless, they tread carefully toward the room, and Lenah reminded herself that UPL station wasn't only defended by guards but also by advanced technology cleverly hidden inside its white walls. Like those damn smart cells.

They didn't have any weapons; those had been taken away from them before they'd been given their rooms, and with

Lenah's mind magic still not working, their only real weapon, apart from old-fashioned fists, was Cassius.

He was standing in the doorway to the room now, carefully peeking inside. Interestingly, he not only checked what was inside the room but also inspected the walls and the ceiling.

"Looks clear. And the stone *is* there," he finally whispered, though his voice sounded unsure. He took one careful step into the room. When nothing happened, he waved for them to follow.

Lenah took the lead behind him and entered a large chamber. One wall was completely taken up by a giant window, currently showing a panorama of Arcadia and the starry sky expanding next to it. The window was at least four stories tall and had a slight curve to it, amplifying the sensation of being part of the galaxy. Remembering what they had come for, Lenah forced her attention back to the inside of the room. In its center, someone had erected a showcase, and on a blue, velvet pillow rested their stone.

"Can you detect any protections on it?" Lenah asked Cassius who was still looking around. He shook his head and closed the distance to the showcase when, suddenly, his body started shaking violently as if from a lightning strike. For one brief moment, Lenah saw a flash in the ceiling. A small hole had opened up in the smooth surface, emitting a light of something that wasn't bright enough to be laser fire.

Lenah jumped forward, trying to push Cassius, who stood frozen and agony written all over his face, out of the way of the beam, but she needn't have bothered. The fire had ceased.

Instead, stiff as a board, Cassius lost balance and crashed backward. Lenah steeled herself to catch him but was knocked over by his weight while his head connected to the floor with a cringeworthy thump. Still, he didn't react, apart from looking shocked, his eyes open. Lenah crawled toward him, looking up at the ceiling. The small hole was gone.

"Cassius." Lenah knelt next to him, touching his shoulder. He didn't just *look* stiff, he *was* stiff. His muscles were tense to the max and bulging out like strings from his neck.

"What's wrong? Can't you move?"

"I think he got nano-stunned," Doctor Lund said, kneeling on Cassius's other side.

"Nano-stunned?"

"It's a strong stun weapon designed to target cyborgs. The surge attacks the organic material connected to carbon-nano tubes. It's one of the few weapons able to knock out a cyborg, at least temporarily."

"Temporarily?"

"I'm not sure, but it should subside in a few minutes."

"But we don't have a few minutes," Lenah hissed, looking down at Cassius's face. His eyes were full of pain, and he seemed alert, as if he could hear them fine but just couldn't move.

"I hear loud footsteps," Persia said from the doorway. "We should leave."

"Okay. We can do this." Lenah got up, trying to feel as sure of that as she sounded.

"Persia, Uz, and Doctor Lund, you carry Cassius. I'll get the stone, and I'll go first."

"But you don't know if it's protected," Persia said with a worried glance at the display.

Lenah thought the same but couldn't think of another option. They were out of time. Without further delay, she snatched the stone, prepared to be either whiplashed by something invisible around it or from the ceiling. But nothing happened. She turned, glad to see that the others had already grabbed Cassius.

Doctor Lund and Persia were each holding one of his arms, while Uz was struggling to lift him from his feet. He was a big guy, but maybe all those implants made him even heavier. Lenah took the lead back into the corridor where footsteps were rapidly approaching. She couldn't see anyone yet, but judging by the noise, that would change any moment.

She turned and started a quick jog down to where she suspected the landing bay must be. Hopefully, they weren't back in the same corridors that could be turned into prison cells. Or could that be done on the whole station? That seemed a splurge, even for this place.

To her dismay, all Lenah could see ahead of her was an empty corridor. She touched the walls with her hand to discern if she could find a mechanism to open the doors that surely had to be there, but she couldn't feel anything. Even worse, the others were visibly struggling with Cassius's load, and their progress was awfully slow. Lenah turned back to help Uz when figures came into view from behind.

Guards. And they were armed.

"Stop. You're under arrest for stealing UPL property."

Lenah almost pointed out that UPL had stolen the stone from them. But that seemed fruitless.

She stopped and faced them. It was four guards, each armed with a pistol. The weapons had curious top builds, not usual for lasers, and she could see a small dart sticking out of it. A tranquilizer. At least, they weren't going to be injured.

"Drop him." One guard pointed toward Cassius. With hesitation, the others put him down on the floor where he lay still, even though Lenah could see him move his fingers just a little bit. Did that mean he could move again? But by the look of agony all over his features, she doubted he would be useful within the next few minutes. Besides, he'd never get to the guards before they could shoot.

Lenah put her arms up in a gesture of surrender, feeling a lump in her throat. They hadn't made it, and she doubted their punishment this time would be limited to one night in a cell.

"Alright, shoot them," the same guard, apparently their boss, said in a bored voice.

"Wait, we surrender, there is no need to—"

"Shoot them," the man repeated as the other guards hesitated at Lenah's words. This time, they reacted. In a desperate attempt, Lenah tried to feel for their minds. Maybe the adrenaline would augment her abilities and enable her to influence them. But there was nothing. They pressed the trigger, and Lenah steeled herself for the impact.

She watched as small darts flew from the guns toward them, then suddenly turned around, as if bouncing against something in front of Lenah. Pained yells sounded, but not from her group. It was the guards. Somehow, they had been hit by their own darts.

Then she saw it; the watery texture in front of them. Was that a warp bubble? Lenah had been trapped in one only a few weeks back. A guild mage working with smugglers had cast it on her, and she had been similarly protected from laser fire around them. But who was casting it now?

"Quick, come." An urgent voice sounded from behind them, and she whirled around, expecting to be magically attacked next. Instead, the young guild mage from the party, Lorka, stood there, forehead creased in concentration. He was waving frantically for them to follow him.

Lenah processed that for a second. Why was he helping them? What was he even doing here? This was either real help or a trap. But it couldn't be a worse trap compared to staying here, she decided.

"One second," she told Lorka before turning around and running over to the guards who were all unconscious from stunning themselves. She bent to pick up three of the tranquilizers. They also had real laser pistols, but Lenah left those. The dart guns would be handy if they needed to defend themselves. But she didn't want to risk truly injuring anyone here. That would surely have grave consequences. Behind her,

Persia and Uz were helping Cassius to his feet. He managed to take a few wobbly steps on his own, then, with a mask of pain, accepted their help. Lenah was glad he could walk at all.

"Quick, come." Lorka urged as she closed the gap to him. On her way, she handed a gun to Doctor Lund and another one to Uz.

"Why are you helping us?" she asked the young mage as they jogged down the corridor.

"I believe you," he said, then stopped in his tracks. "I don't know if there are more people up ahead."

"There's more from behind us," Cassius said through gritted teeth.

"More guards?" Lenah inquired.

"Yes. Carrying weapons," he said, sounding out of breath.

"You can *hear* that?" Lorka asked, gaping at him but then seemed to catch himself.

"Yup," Lenah answered, unwilling to give away any information about them. She was grateful for the rescue but couldn't understand the young mage's motive for helping them yet.

"Right, um. Can you guys get close to me? I want to create another bubble, but it gets harder the bigger I have to make it."

"Lorka, what do you believe?" Lenah inquired, not moving.

He gave her a pained and impatient look but nodded. "That you're not a trouble-maker. That you're right about the magnitude of the threat."

Lenah regarded the young mage in a new light. This was not just a clumsy youth talking, this was...

Cassius cleared his throat and shook Lenah out of her thoughts. She realized that now was not the time to think about this. "Let's go, everyone," she said, and they all shuffled up behind Lorka after only the slightest hesitation. A few moments later, the whole group was encased in a watery texture. Unlike the last time Lenah had been trapped in a bubble, she was able to move. It wasn't encasing her everywhere but seemed to be a sphere around them. *Very handy*.

They followed the corridor down and toward a sign that read 'Guest Landing Bay'.

Lenah hoped that was the landing bay where they had also parked the *Rambler*. She could imagine a big space station like this having numerous landing bays for its many guests in different areas. Especially, since this place received visits from all kinds of people: family members, elites from the various planets, commoners.

They crept down the corridor, Lenah and Doctor Lund going first, holding their guns.

"Cassius, can you hear if there's someone up ahead in that landing bay?" Lenah remembered seeing a control cabin inside the bay when they had landed.

They stopped, so he could listen. "I hear breathing in there," Cassius finally said.

"Ok. Persia, can you switch positions with Doctor Lund? You and I will go in first."

"Let me, I'll go," Cassius growled, stumbling a few steps forward.

"No way. The worst you'll do is crush someone under your weight by coincidence."

"I'm fine," he pressed out but needed to take hold of the wall.

"Cassius, stay back. Handle the guards coming from behind. We'll go in," Lenah said before turning and nodding toward Persia who had taken the gun from Doctor Lund. Together, they snuck up the final meters to the entrance.

The door was open, and Lenah carefully took a peek. No one was in the bay directly, but she did spot the *Star Rambler*. It felt so good to see it. Then her eyes darted over the clamps still tying it to the station's floor.

"Thank the stars, it's here," she whispered while taking another look around.

Two guards were sitting in a room off the side wall.

Signaling for Persia to follow, Lenah ducked in and carefully walked toward them. Their cabin wasn't directly pointing toward the hatch but instead watched over the parked ships. They'd need to crane their necks to see Lenah and Persia approaching, but luckily, they seemed to be watching a holovideo coming from one of their wristpieces. Lenah and Persia made it to the cabin and, without hesitation, Lenah ripped the door open and stormed inside.

The two guards, both young women of thin build, startled into action. One dropped a coffee cup she'd been holding, spilling the content over her companion's leg who yelped from being hit by the hot liquid.

Before the guard could grab a laser pistol from her belt, Lenah slapped her hand with the butt of her tranquilizer gun. Persia was doing the same to her colleague.

Next, Lenah turned her gun and pointed it at her guard. "Open the clamps on the *Star Rambler*, and I won't tranq you."

The young woman shook her head frantically and lifted trembling hands.

"Just do it. Then I won't have to stun you and do it myself," Lenah repeated.

"Do it, Micky. I've read once that it's a pain like being struck by lightning when you get hit by a stun dart," the other woman finally said.

"And you know how much it hurts to be hit by lightning?" Micky asked.

"Well, no. But I suspect it's a lot."

"Quit talking and act," Lenah pressed, shoving the tranquilizer gun closer to Micky's face. She *would* use it on her if she needed to, but really hoped that wouldn't be necessary. These two had nothing to do with the reason for their escape. Apart from their bad choice of employer, Lenah couldn't blame them for anything. Not that she wanted *them* to know that.

"Okay," Micky said and nodded. Keeping her eyes locked on the dart of Lenah's gun, she moved her still trembling hands down toward one of the screens, only looking away at the last moment.

"The *Star Rambler*. That's the crappy ship, isn't it?"

"It's old and reliable, not crappy," Lenah answered. Though maybe she shouldn't have. Maybe they wouldn't give as much of a chase if they thought the *Rambler* could barely limp away. "Be quick," she added, remembering the noises of armed guards Cassius had heard.

Micky swiped in a command on the screen. "Done."

"Great, now step out of the cabin."

"But you said you wouldn't tranq us if I did this!"

"And I won't. But we'll need to tie you up." She held the door open for them, and they both filed out of the room, distrust written all over their features. Lenah saw some metal wire in the corner of the bay and made her way there, then tied them up. She noticed that Cassius seemed to be more himself again, as he was moving a heavy-looking shelf to block the entrance to the bay, aided by Uz and Doctor Lund.

"Which button opens the station's airlock?" Lenah asked the two guards. The young woman pointed to a red button on the panel in the cabin, and Lenah went to press it. A hiss sounded several hundred meters away from the depth of the airlock tunnel. She shoved the guards back into their cabin and closed the door.

"Let's go, quickly."

10 AWAY

ONLY WHEN THEY were outside of the UPL station's long airlock tunnel, did Lenah dare breathe. They had made it out. They even had the stone.

But her respite was short-lived. Less than a minute out of UPL station, three more ships emerged from a different spot on the round wall. Her scanner identified them as military-use shuttles. *Not good*.

"I think we have company." She winced and looked over at Persia, who was sitting next to her, the stone propped up in her hands to heat it for use.

The others were cramped behind them in the corridor, except for Lorka who was sitting on the floor further back. He looked unsteady and pale, speaking of the great mental effort it had taken to keep them all protected in a warp bubble for several minutes and especially after Lenah had exposed them to the open airlock. As soon as the *Rambler*'s hatch had closed behind them, he'd dropped the bubble and only been able to walk up the stairs and to the cockpit supported by Persia.

At least Cassius looked a lot better. He was still grimacing in pain, but he was standing by himself now, looming behind Lenah like he always did.

"I don't suppose the stone will be ready in the next few seconds," Lenah addressed Persia.

"No, at least five minutes."

Lenah cursed. "That's long. These ships are only seconds behind us. And we still have a tracker somewhere on the ship."

No one said anything. Was it because they also felt the helplessness of the situation, or because they wanted her to concentrate on whatever she was going to do about it? They couldn't start shooting at three ships at once and hope their shields wouldn't fail first. The only thing they could do was somehow get these ships further away from them. Speed was not an option, but what if...

"Everyone, you should go to your cabins and buckle in. This is about to get a little rough," Lenah said. When they didn't move fast enough, she yelled, "Now!"

That jerked them into action, though Cassius gave her a frown before turning and vanishing down the corridor to his room. The internal buffers would catch most movements from the ship, but what Lenah was about to do didn't count as a normal movement.

Taking a deep breath and seeing that the other ships had almost reached them, Lenah dropped the shields of the

Rambler. She'd need every bit of energy going to the engines now. If this worked, they wouldn't need the shields, anyway.

Lenah took a slightly sideways course, then, hoping the others were already buckled in on their bunks, flew them up at a steep angle. This would bring them closer to the approaching ships, but hopefully, not close enough to get them caught. *Or shot down*, she thought as the detectors showed an incoming laser beam from one of the ships. Luckily, it went wild when the other ship also adjusted its course. They certainly wouldn't have expected Lenah coming back toward them.

The *Rambler* groaned from the strain of the steep angle, and the station grew bigger in the view window as she took them closer.

"Er, Lenah, are you sure you want to go back toward the station?" Persia, who was buckled up next to her, whispered, and Lenah felt her worried glance.

She grunted but didn't have time to answer right now. If she messed up the timing of this, she might crash them head-first into the station. Or put them straight into the direction of the other ships' lasers again.

All three UPL ships had followed her by now, their upward angle even closer to the station than hers.

Perfect.

Lenah pulled the back thrusters hard. She had practiced this maneuver in the simulations when she learned to fly but had never done it in real life. Nor with a ship so old. Her stomach lurched as she was pressed hard into her seat, the

Rambler lifting unevenly from her hard braking. The nose kept going up, the body of the ship catching most of their speed until they hung vertically in the air, less than a couple of klicks away from UPL station.

Lenah dared take a deep breath, watching the other ships on her screen. As she had hoped, they hadn't expected her maneuver and were about to overtake them, thinking she'd been aiming to fly across to the other side of the station.

As soon as the back thrusters had stopped the *Rambler* completely, Lenah carefully gave it forward thrust. Just ever so much to tip them forward but not move them from where they hung. If she were wrong about how the ship would react, she could crash them into the station or send them past the other ships and straight into their line of fire. Especially, since the thrusters of the *Rambler* were less than sensitive. But she had learned to use her ship in the past weeks and now found it a lot easier to micro-adjust.

Ever so minimally, she moved the thruster. The ship kept hanging until—suddenly—Lenah felt her stomach lurch, this time forward. A pearl of sweat dripped from her face onto the control board under her as she hung in her harness. Again, timing was of utmost importance.

When the *Rambler* had turned straight downward, she pulled the thruster to its fullest. Despite the downward angle, she was pressed into her seat from the sheer speed of the ship's weight and its thruster power combined.

Lenah took a glance at the control panel. The other ships, like she had hoped, had vanished over the other side of the station and were turning around in a less dramatic way. Nonetheless, she would need to be fast now.

They plummeted past the station, as they continued their downward angle, but just as they passed the thickest part of the large globe, Lenah pulled on the back-thrusters again, this time with less force. The ship shuddered hard, and, for a moment, she thought she had overdone it and would send them spinning uncontrollably into the station. The white sphere came uncomfortably close, but then their flight evened out, until they were facing forward, the ship coming out in a standard position under the sphere.

Lenah went to search for a place to hide immediately. When they'd first come here, she had noticed that while the top part of UPL station was mostly smooth, the white plating only interrupted by the large silver view windows, the bottom half of the station was full of air ducts, vents, and other large machinery. Given the station's size, even the air ducts were huge; huge enough for a small ship like the *Rambler* to hide in between. *Or so she hoped.*

There, a cluster of round towers was sticking out of the station's underbelly. Lenah directed the ship over slowly, keeping an eye on the three crafts up above on screen. They were coming closer again, apparently having managed to turn but must still be far above her.

The place she had chosen was tight, tighter than she'd anticipated and would only fit the *Rambler* leaving minimal space at its side. If she crashed into the station, surely someone would notice. As slow as she dared, Lenah brought them into the middle of the air ducts.

When they were surrounded by them, she turned the ship's motor off. Then she turned everything else off, only leaving on basic gravity and life support. If the other ships didn't have incredible sensors, this would ensure they were no longer showing on their enemy's screens. Given they were still high above in the middle parts of the sphere, they also shouldn't have seen Lenah vanish under the station. Hopefully, they'd interpret their vanishing as them going into a warp bubble.

Immediately, it got cold on the ship. They wouldn't be able to stay like this for long. Lenah waited, staring out of the front window, having to rely on mere sight now as she'd also turned off all the screens. She didn't have to wait long for them to show up.

Two of the shuttles flew by fast, apparently thinking they were trying to escape downward, but the third one was coming in slow. Had they seen through her ruse? She didn't breathe, holding her hand over the 'On' button of the ship in case they started shooting, and she needed to pull up the shields. But they flew underneath them, vanishing out of her window's view. They must be right under them. Lenah even thought that she could hear the motor rumbling only a few ship lengths away.

A minute ticked by, until the ship emerged again, this time in her side window. It had flown past and was going after the other ships now, accelerating away fast.

"Stars, that was tight," Lenah said when they vanished out of sight in the distance. But how long would it be until they discovered the *Star Rambler*, including its tracker, hadn't actually entered into a warp bubble and was instead right here?

Lenah loosened her harness and went to find the others. She had to pull open all the hatches manually, given the ship was not supplying any energy. After a few minutes, her crew was assembled in the dark corridor. Lenah turned on the flashlight of her wristpiece, illuminating everyone's faces and clouds of frozen breath.

"That was some amazing flying," Persia said, patting Lenah on the shoulder.

"They think we've already vanished in a warp bubble?" Cassius asked.

Lenah nodded. "That's the idea. But we don't have a lot of time until they realize we must still be here. We still most likely have a tracker on board. Corinna knows this, and it's only a matter of minutes until the ships out there know it too."

"We all take a section of the ship," Cassius said. "Everyone is responsible for their own cabin, and we'll search the common areas together.

"You think they put it somewhere in a cabin?" Us asked.

He nodded. "That would be the least frequented place."

11 THE TRACKER

"OUCH," LENAH CURSED as she knocked her head against the galley sink from below. She crawled out of the tight space with the urgent need to take a bath. Her crew had cleaned here, yes, but they hadn't addressed the underside. Somehow, the pirates that had owned the *Star Rambler* before them had been very talented at leaving filth behind everywhere. Which included the tracker they still hadn't found.

She blew breath on her icy fingers, watching the cloud of cold air escape her mouth. Without the temperature control system running, the *Rambler* had turned into a freezer within minutes. If they didn't find the tracker soon, they'd have to start up the ship, anyway. Just where was that damn thing?

Could it be on the outside of the ship where they couldn't access it, given that they were parked in space? Or was she being paranoid for being so convinced of being tracked?

In a desperate attempt, Lenah started to pull open the kitchen cabinets in the common room once more, touching the walls for anything out of order.

They'd been searching for thirty minutes already, and everyone was frantically turning over their mattresses and any other belongings the original owners had left. The other ships, miraculously, had not returned. But there was nothing even close to a tracker, apart from a strange clock device Lenah had found in the emergency compartment of the cockpit and an old-fashioned grenade Uz found wedged under her bed. She had carried it out of her cabin with wide eyes, probably thinking she could have blown them all up in her sleep. Doctor Lund, deeming it a real grenade, not a tracking device that was disguised as a grenade, had taken it to the cargo hold for safety.

"Hey, still haven't found it?" someone said from the entrance. Lenah shot a quick look to see Lorka standing there, still looking pale but at least walking on two legs instead of almost crawling on the floor.

"You recovered quickly."

He shot her a lopsided grin. "Not really, but Uzara told me you have a stash of Cassidian marches tea in here. I should be more useful after a cup."

"That's what got you up from your bunk?" Lenah shuddered, remembering the foul smell of the beverage. But then it clicked. "It did get you off your bunk, of course!" She had forgotten the almost magical reviving quality of the tea.

Lorka looked hopefully at her. "Will you show me where it is? Then at least I can help find that tracker."

"Sure, sure. Though you did enough for one day by rescuing us out of that station," Lenah said but interrupted her search to reopen the cabinet with the tea. As things were going, getting another pair of hands involved wouldn't hurt.

Someone, most likely not Uz, had stashed the old box in the very back of the closet, and Lenah had to stretch on her tiptoes to reach it. She couldn't blame the person who'd done it as the whole cabinet emanated an unpleasant smell of ancient bog and rotten water. She moved the box with her fingertips until it got stuck on something. Cursing in a low voice for losing further time in her search for the tracker, she tried to get a hold on the box, but instead, her outstretched fingers felt a small line indented in the cabinet's bottom.

"What?" She fumbled along the line a few more moments, until she got her fingernail in and managed to lift out a chunk.

Lenah handed Lorka the piece of metal and the box of tea, which he accepted with wide eyes, and proceeded to swipe her hands over the hole she had revealed. Her fingers dipped into something slimy.

"Ugh, disgusting." But she stuck in her hand anyway, despite remembering the leftovers of food from the underside of the sink.

To her utter amazement, she soon was able to lift out a small cube that was attached to a key chain. A sticky substance that could be rotting marmalade was covering one side of the cube. Lenah held it out between her and Lorka, and they both stared at it.

"Is that...the tracker?" Lorka asked.

"I think it might be," Lenah answered. "Let me verify." She bolted out of the door and toward the engineering room where Doctor Lund and Cassius were searching in the dim light of Lund's instruments. "Lund, take a look at this."

"What is it? You found it?" He received the small device, pulling out one of his handheld measuring tools.

"I can definitely read a tiny amount of energy coming from this. Cassius, hand me that screwdriver."

Cassius complied and returned to Doctor Lund with a tiny screwdriver. Doctor Lund opened the lid on the back of the cube with trembling hands, though Lenah didn't know if it was because of the cold or the excitement.

"Yes, that's it," he said and nodded rapidly. "A simple but effective tracking device. Do you see that?" He pointed at something shiny and black that was reflecting the dim light in the room. "It has a c-nano component."

"And what does that mean?" Cassius asked.

Doctor Lund looked up, grimacing. "It means that a mage can track this thing even while it's traveling inside of a warp bubble."

"Bloody stars," Cassius rumbled impatiently. "What are we waiting for?" He practically ripped the tracker out of Doctor Lund's palm and squished it with his metal hand as if it were no more than an egg. "Will that work?"

"Um, yes. Yes," Doctor Lund answered.

"Let's also throw it out the hatch," Lenah suggested, holding back a grin. Doctor Lund didn't seem to know if he should be relieved or scared at the display of cyborg strength.

Cassius nodded and opened his fist. "Ugh, what's that sticky stuff?"

"Not sure. I thought it might be aged marmalade, but I really don't want to know." Lenah wiped her own hand on the leg of her pants. "At least we know that the tracker was probably here for a long time."

"You don't say," Cassius grunted and made his way out of engineering and into the cargo hold where the *Star Rambler*'s only hatch was located. Lenah followed him out but took a turn to go back to the cockpit. She planned to leave as soon as Cassius had gotten rid of their unwanted cargo.

Persia stepped out of her cabin as Lenah approached.

"We found the tracker!" Lenah announced and couldn't hide a grin.

"Thank the stars," Uz's voice drifted out of her cabin, accompanied by the sound of her clattering teeth. The cold seemed to be hitting her harder than the rest of them. Lenah hadn't known, but she suspected that Cassidians were less cold tolerant than humans. "Can we turn back on the heat, please?"

"On my way," Lenah answered and squeezed by Persia.

"Where was it?" Persia called after her.

Lenah turned around. "In a false bottom in the kitchen cabinet. Curiously, the one with the Cassidian marches tea."

"Um," Persia said. "Good hiding place. No offense, Uz." She lifted her arms.

"Lund says it even had a c-nano component, so we could be tracked inside of a warp bubble."

"Explainsss…a…lot." Uz trembled, reminding Lenah to get the ship heated and away quickly.

Lenah proceeded toward the cockpit, followed by Persia.

"I wonder who put it there," Persia mused.

Lenah did too. "I guess it might have been the very owners of this ship."

"Prior criminal owners," Persia corrected her.

"Prior criminal owners," Lenah echoed. "Maybe, they wanted to be prepared should their ship ever be stolen. Or taken over. Isn't that what smugglers do? Dump their smuggler boss on an asteroid, take over the crew, and leave with the ship?"

"I don't know what smugglers typically do. We should ask our cyborg smuggler," Persia said as they stepped through the cockpit's hatch.

"He's busy throwing the remaining shambles of the tracker out of the airlock."

"Good."

"When you're done ranting about the habits of smugglers, we can leave," Cassius called up the corridor. He had to yell for them to hear him; the other way around, he'd apparently not needed them to speak particularly loudly.

Lenah cringed inwardly, though it hadn't been her to call him a smuggler. Lorka stepped into the cockpit behind them, a terrible smell wafting in with him. He was holding a cup of steaming liquid.

"Ugh, what is that?" Persia asked, covering her nose. "Did you take off your shoes?"

"Tea," Lorka said pleasantly, nodding toward Lenah. "I already feel so much better. Thank you for letting me have some."

Lenah grinned, not minding the smell. They'd still be looking for the tracker if he hadn't made her get the tea.

"How did you even heat it? Everything is off," she asked as she pressed the buttons for the *Rambler*'s starting sequence.

He grinned. "Friction magic. I used it to heat the water particles."

"Huh, that's practical." Persia looked him up and down.

"Let's go," Lenah said, feeling like she shouldn't be losing any more time. UPL might not have found them yet, but that could change any second. "Do you still have the stone ready?"

"Heated and ready. Been holding on to it all this time." Persia pulled it out of her pocket and handed it to Lenah. She almost dropped it, as a loud metallic wheezing started right next to them. Frantically, Lenah looked out the windows in case a ship had snuck up on them.

She exhaled when she realized that it was only the big air duct next to them turning on. Her gaze went back to her control panel, and she clutched the flight stick, ready to move the ship as soon as all the systems had started up. A sigh escaped all three of them as the heat control turned on and blasted away the cold air. After what seemed like an eternity, the engine light turned green, and Lenah moved the ship forward. They would be detectable again on the screens of whoever was watching. And she was sure that someone *was* watching.

"What's that 11111 comm number?" Persia asked, bent over the communications screen where an incoming message was blinking.

"Sounds official," Lenah groaned, then went back to maneuvering. "Only the highest-paying customers get numbers this good," she added distractedly, concentrating instead on the radar and weapons screen. She wouldn't be surprised if they fired. Unfortunately, they couldn't start a warp bubble right here, this close to the station, unless they wanted to risk tearing off some parts of the station as well.

"Hope no one is going to shoot us in the next thirty seconds," she stated, clutching the stone in one hand and the flight stick in the other. As slow and careful as she dared, Lenah guided the ship out from under the station's belly. Several icons of other ships blinked to life on her screen, but she ignored those too and focused on her other screen that was asking her to enter coordinates to the warp bubble.

As fast as she could, Lenah typed in some coordinates in the middle of nowhere between here and Astur. She wasn't sure what they were going to do next, but at least she knew that was the general direction they wanted to go—where the Cava Dara were most likely headed.

An alarm started beeping, indicating weapons had locked on them. Were they really going to shoot them here? This close to the station? She had to admit that she'd still hoped UPL wouldn't deem them this important. After all, the stone had done its job of delivering its message.

A moment later, the beeping stopped, and the blackness around her was replaced by the colorful swirls of a warp bubble. Lenah flopped back in her chair, becoming once again aware of her surroundings and Lorka behind her, still holding his cup of tea.

Persia let out a loud breath, then pressed play on the message that had come in.

"Stand down. You will not be allowed to leave. You will not meddle in fights that are not yours. Trust me, we will find you." The voice was Corinna's.

"So much for hoping they wouldn't be too angry," Lenah grunted. But she also couldn't hide her wide grin. Without the tracker on board, and with them in the depths of the galaxy, it would be a lot more difficult for Corinna to make good on that promise.

12 LORKA

"WHAT IF WE GOT rid of one tracker but let another one on board with us?" Persia whispered so low that Lenah had to lean forward over the common room table.

"But what was his motive to help us?" Cassius said, furrowing his brow and leaning back comfortably in the chair next to Lenah. "He couldn't have known that we were about to find the tracker."

"How am I supposed to know? What motivations would mage spies have?" Persia looked at Lenah as if she should have all the answers.

"Don't look at me. I've never been to the Guild, nor am I a mage."

"You have magic. That makes you a mage, don't you think?"

"But I have mind magic, not warp magic. Or rather, I had…" Lenah trailed off. She had been so acutely aware of not having access to her abilities and suppressing her instincts to use them while on UPL station, she hadn't even tried to see if they were working again. After all, she hadn't noticed anything off about them before landing on the station. She gathered her focus, and, immediately, the shapes of her friends' minds became visible.

"Thank the stars! I can see your minds again!" she exclaimed, tempted to try influencing them but holding back. Friends didn't react well to losing their free will.

"Can you influence us like normal?" Cassius asked.

"I don't know. May I?" she asked him and was surprised to see him nod.

She sent an image of him as she had met him a couple of weeks ago—dreadlocks and overgrown beard—paired with the emotion of discomfort. Cassius jumped up from his chair, touched the short hair on his head and was halfway to the hatch before Lenah dropped her influence.

Cassius stopped and turned on the spot. "I guess that's a yes," he grumbled but smiled at her, as he returned to his seat.

"Back to Lorka," Lenah said, "I agree with Cassius. He didn't just assist us. He is the only reason we were able to escape."

Cassius shook his head and looked down but didn't say anything. Lenah could guess what he was thinking.

"It's not your fault they have crazy futuristic weapons against cyborgs hidden in their ceilings," she said, patting his forearm. It seemed to lighten him up a little, but he still looked stern.

"There's only one way to find out," Lenah continued.

"You're going to read his mind?" Persia asked. "I thought you'd never suggest it."

"Actually, I meant that we go *talk* to him. As long as we don't think he's trying to trick us, I don't want to invade his privacy."

"But he's a weird guy with unknown motives from a mysterious and powerful organization, and he's on our ship," Persia insisted.

"Unknown and mysterious, not *evil*," Lenah answered. "But I agree that we need to be careful and watch him."

"It'll be too late if he cages us all in a warp bubble and takes the ship back to UPL. Or worse—the Mage Guild," Persia said through pursed lips.

Lenah didn't disagree, though she was hoping that her talents could push back any warp bubble as she'd done with the mage who attacked them a couple of weeks ago. But she was not willing to condemn Lorka before at least giving him a chance to explain.

"He's been resting for hours. I'll go get him, and we can talk."

Persia threw her hands up in a frustrated gesture, but she didn't object again. "Fine, fine."

Cassius, on the other hand, nodded when Lenah got up to walk the few steps down the corridor to the cabin Lorka had claimed. It couldn't really be called a cabin, more like a servant's closet with a bunk. Only half the size of the other cabins, it wasn't much more than a mattress with one drawer on the opposite wall for storage. No table, not even room to walk around. But the young mage had preferred it over the other option Lenah had presented him with: the storage cabin where they had dumped everything inherited from the smugglers that they didn't want anymore.

The *Star Rambler* wasn't a big ship, and with the six people they now were, it almost felt crowded. *The good kind of crowded.* Lenah didn't think she'd be able to handle this new life of hers without the people that surrounded her.

Lorka opened the door a second after Lenah had knocked on the hatch. Had he been able to sense her coming? Or maybe it was so small in there, he could easily reach the entirety of the room within one second. Looking around, that seemed likely.

"How are you feeling?" she asked, taking in the spikes of black hair sticking in all directions and the crumpled mage robe he was still wearing.

"Better. That tea and a nap really helped." He yawned and looked up at her with a lopsided grimace. "I know, a real mage wouldn't need any rest after that little bit that I did, but…"

"Aren't you still in training?" Lenah asked, both wanting to reassure him and curious to hear any detail on how the Guild trained their mages. They were one of the most secretive organizations, and Lenah didn't think any information about their training was public.

"I guess," Lorka said and looked at his feet. "I'm supposed to be able to hold my bubble for several hours at least. Not with so many people in it though." His belly gave a low rumble.

Lenah grinned. "There's food in the common room. If you come with me, I will even let you choose between chicken and urash for your rice dish."

"I love rice!" the young mage exclaimed when he sat up on his bunk to follow Lenah up the corridor.

"I recommend the chicken, it's really not bad at all. Though it's no caviar canapés," Lenah said, remembering the bites she'd had at the UPL party.

"And thank the stars for that. I hate water stuff."

"Water stuff?"

"Yeah, gross things that live in the oceans." Lorka shuddered when they stepped into the common room.

Lenah proceeded to the small kitchen area to heat a chicken dinner for Lorka who timidly stood next to her.

"Sit. And don't worry, Persia looks fiercer than she is," Lenah told him, and he took a few hesitant steps toward the table.

"Um, okay."

"Cassius here is nice too," Persia said, knocking on his metal shoulder. "When he's not too busy kidnapping people."

"Kidnapping?" Lorka's eyes went wide, and he looked like he wanted to bolt out the room again. "Who did you kidnap?"

"Oh, that was Lenah and me," Persia said, grinning widely when Cassius kept glaring at the young man, who settled stiffly into a chair, his robe entangling itself into the leg of

Persia's chair. If he was a spy, he was doing an excellent job at appearing harmless.

Lenah got the heated dish out of the oven unit and put it in front of Lorka with a smile. "Eat. And don't listen to these two. They are just trying to scare you off."

"Not off, we're trying to scare you into telling us the truth," Persia corrected.

"The truth?" Lorka asked, looking up from spooning in large bites of chicken and rice.

"About why the stars you helped us."

"Oh." He shoveled in some more bites.

"Well?" Cassius prodded, flexing his arms in a casual gesture but managed to bring his cyborg fist closer to Lorka's face.

The young man froze midbite.

"Cassius." Lenah warned. She didn't know why, but she wanted Lorka to be comfortable with them. Not that she wasn't curious to know what had driven him to help.

"It just felt like the right thing to do. Besides, I liked you," Lorka finally said, looking at Lenah.

"That's it?"

"Yeah, you were very patient with me and, I don't know, you seemed honest. Not like everyone else around. Besides, ah, it seemed fun. More fun than brewing coffee and making paper copies. I mean, that's not what dad had in mind when he sent me anyways. I think." He waved his spoon around the room in a gesture of frustration.

"Paper copies?" Persia asked. "What in the galaxy is that?"

"It's a figure of speech. Thousands of years ago, humans didn't have wristpieces and every text or image they wanted to duplicate was physically copied on another paper by a machine."

"Back when humans lived in caves?"

"Nah, that was already advanced technology of Old Earth," Lorka answered.

"And what do you know about the Cava Dara?" Lenah said, not interested in learning Old Earth history today.

Lorka turned red. "I…only what is public knowledge: Cheung army handling some ancient creatures coming for the orbit of Astur. And you," his gaze fluttered to Lenah, then to his rice again, "blowing up the danger, threatening to make a mere trifle galactic news. Not my words," he said, nodding rapidly, still staring into his food.

"You're not a good liar, Lorka," Lenah said, sending the slightest influence toward him. The group would react well to hearing the truth.

"Hey, don't do that! Didn't you get lesson one in mind magic?" Lorka exclaimed, and Lenah dropped her influence, taken aback.

"What? You felt that?"

"Yes, it tickled like hell. Don't they teach you manners in that secret cave of yours?"

"Cave? Tickle?" she echoed, feeling stupid and excited at the same time. All these years of looking for someone else with her same abilities and this young mage knew something?

Of course, Lenah had read up on the Guild. That had been one of the first places she'd looked. But all that her search had revealed was what everyone knew already. The Guild trained warp mages. There was no mention of anything else.

"Uhm, you are a mind mage, right?" Lorka asked Lenah, drawing his thin eyebrows together in one line. "Because if not, just forget what I said."

"I…yes. I'm a mind mage. But how did you know that? It tickled you when I touched your mind?"

"Yes, but how do you not know that? You were trained by the Guild, were you not?"

"Well, no."

"What? But why?"

"Er, I didn't know about it?"

"But the test."

Lenah shook her head at him. "What test? The only one I know about is the test they do on newborns to determine if they might have warp magic. I didn't test positive. Because I don't have a smidge of it."

Lorka looked thoughtfully at her.

"I'm not sure, but I think there used to be a test for mind magic."

Lenah sat silently at that. How was it possible that this young mage had so much information? He seemed to know mind magic better than Lenah who had lived with it all her life. Did the Guild train mind mages in secret? Why? And why hadn't she been discovered? Or Corinna? Lenah had read that she'd gone to one of Arcadia's best universities to study business. There was no mention of staying with the Guild for years to train her abilities. Could Lenah believe anything Lorka was saying? Now she wished that she could influence him as Persia had suggested.

"Are you okay?" Lorka asked into the silence when Lenah didn't speak. She looked up to see that everyone was looking at her.

"I…yes." She really wasn't. With all the changes her life had taken in the past few months, this one was the hardest to digest.

"If there's a test, how come I didn't test positive?"

"No clue. I don't know what they test for. I don't really know anything about the mind mages."

"And what does that mean?" Cassius growled. "You just knew a lot." He put his hand on Lenah's shoulder.

The gesture sent a shiver down Lenah's spine.

"I…it's not public knowledge," Lorka stuttered.

"Then how do you know about it?" Cassius didn't sound any friendlier.

Lorka sat back in his chair—possibly to get as far away from the angry cyborg as possible—his meal forgotten.

"It's just something I once overheard my dad say. He and another council mage walked straight to that cave entrance and they didn't realize I was there. The cave is magically protected, supposedly because the caves inside are in danger of collapsing. They started to talk about the mind mages training area in there. How the tests hadn't revealed anyone in ages. That's all I know, and it didn't make any sense to me then, until years later, there was a mention of a different kind of mage in one of the old books they give us. Mages who influence what people do. It also said no one has seen one in hundreds of years. It made me recall the conversation at the cave. All this was an eternity ago. At least ten years." He let out a long breath.

Lenah looked Lorka up and down. He couldn't have been more than eight or nine. He certainly felt like the sort of person who'd make up all manner of vivid stories in their head. But what if not?

"Are there mind mages training there right now?"

"I…don't think so. At least, not that we are told. I'm sorry, Lenah."

She waved her hand dismissively. One, because she didn't think he had anything to apologize for. But also, because a lump had started to form in her throat. Cassius looked at her with knowing eyes and appeared about to protest in her place, when Uz and Doctor Lund interrupted the uncomfortable silence by choosing that moment to walk into the common room.

13 NOW WHAT?

"DID WE ALREADY miss part of the meeting?" Uz asked, pouring herself a glass of water.

"What meeting?" Cassius asked her. "We were just keeping young Lorka company while he had dinner."

"Great. Then we can start now." Uz nodded, downing the glass in one go. Apparently, she had come with an agenda. "We have to decide what to do next. We can't show up at the mage farm and ask them to flip off the switch, right?" She looked at Lenah. "I don't suppose you could do that?"

"No." Lenah forced the word out. She was tired and didn't feel like having the flaws of the plan pointed out to her right now. She already had too much to process for one night. Besides, nothing significant could come out of discussing this. Out of everyone present, she was the person who knew the mage farm best, though even she had never been there—that was striking her as suspicious now—and short of blowing the whole thing up, she couldn't really think of any way to deactivate them. And for that, they'd first need something to blow it up with.

"Okay, let me recap so we are all on the same page," Uz said, giving Lenah a questioning look with raised eyebrows. When Lenah said nothing, Uz continued. "We've seen the Cava Dara descend from the temple on Masis III, and we think they are coming for humanity because of the mage farm. We believe that because the Cassidian High Priest approached Corinna Cheung about it, and we also saw the prophecy, and we agree." She was looking directly at Lorka.

Was Uz this sure that he was honest? Or did she think that she could shock him into a reaction by dumping the scary facts on him? "The Cava Dara were created to come back every six thousand years to punish civilizations that misuse magic. Every time they come, they wipe out everyone."

Lorka was listening to her wide-eyed, but he didn't seem more flustered than he'd been before. What did he already know?

"You don't look surprised, Lorka." Lenah interrupted Uz, wanting to test him.

"I, um, yes, I already knew some of this. I've been serving coffee at the High Ambassador's meetings and may have heard some things from the back room. But did you really see them? Everyone thought they were only a myth."

"Yes, we saw them. There were thousands on Masis III. And that's only in one location. We have no idea how many more are out there."

"What do they look like?" Lorka asked, his eyes going even wider.

Lenah shuddered. "Like Cassidians with wings and purple eyes."

His mouth dropped open, and he didn't say anything else.

Lenah was satisfied. Lorka appeared to have a habit of overhearing conversations that he wasn't supposed to hear. But apart from that, he seemed honest. At least that's what she thought, and it looked like Uz did too.

"We need to intercept them somehow. We don't have an army, so we need to do that at the source: the mage farm. It needs to go." Uz looked at Lenah, an unspoken question in her eyes. As if Lenah were going to veto her suggestion.

Lenah cleared her throat. "Yes, we need to stop the mage farm. For that, we need to sneak into the Callo mansion, steal my father's key, and take the elevator down to the farm," she said loudly. *Better make her loyalty very clear here.* And her loyalty was definitely with the people who'd get killed if they didn't do something about the farm. "There is only one way I can think of in this short amount of time. We need to blow them up," she added, feeling her throat clog up.

Doctor Lund looked up; eyes wide. Lenah focused on Cassius, who seemed to smile at her in approval. It was hard to tell, for his mouth twitched back into neutral after a moment, and only his eyes seemed to still gleam.

"You'd blow up your own family's facility?" Doctor Lund finally said into the silence. "Why?"

"Because I don't think there's an alternative. Though I'm open to suggestions if anyone has any."

"Is there something you could do with warp magic, Lorka?" Uz asked the young mage.

"To destroy a whole compound? No, that's not what warp magic is about. I assume it's a big place?"

"I think so," Lenah answered. "I've actually never seen it for myself."

"Didn't you live and work right there?" Persia asked.

"Yes, but the compound is off limits. It has new technology that is under strictest trade secret and unstable still," Lenah said. "At least, that's what I believed until a few weeks ago."

"What do you believe now?" Cassius asked.

"That it's very suspicious that I, as my father's main assistant, never even set foot there."

"Hah, let's blow it up!" Persia exclaimed, clapping her hand on the table.

Uz nodded as if that were the outcome she had expected from the start. "Okay, issue number one is the most obvious one. How are we going to get explosives?"

"I know where," Cassius answered after a short silence and to Lenah's utmost surprise. She had expected to spend a lot of time on that particular issue.

"Really?"

"We'll be getting out of the warp bubble somewhere in the first octant, close to Astur." It wasn't a question, but he paused nonetheless, so Lenah nodded.

"There is a smuggler trading hub maybe a day or two away. Neeth Station. And explosives are commonly traded. Great way to illegally mine asteroids. We can get enough to blow up half of Asturis I."

"A smuggler hub that close to the planet?" Lenah asked. "How is that even possible?"

"It's not really close to any planet," Cassius said. "More in the gray zone where Astur's authorities, or the ones from Victory II, aren't pointedly looking. Galactic Security Force doesn't come out that far very often. They tend to stick to the more populated areas like Galtaca and Arcadia."

Lenah nodded. From the perspective of UPL station, Astur lay on the fringes of the populated galaxy. A provincial hub, no more. Victory II was even worse—a dust ball with no significant industry.

"Besides," Cassius continued, "it's a flexible set-up."

Lenah looked at him, shaking her head.

He nodded. "Every other tenthday several modified spaceships dock together and form a unique trading station: a canteen, market place, and private bays for bigger or less legal trades. It all can be assembled and disassembled in a matter of minutes. If the authorities ever get a whiff of Neeth Station, then the next tenthday it will simply be put somewhere else. I think it's never in the same spot exactly and can be a hundred thousand klicks more over here or there."

"How are we supposed to find it if we don't know where it will be?" Persia asked, tipping her head to the side.

"I know who to call to pull in a favor," Cassius said.

Persia let out a loud breath, then chuckled. "The benefits of having a smuggler on board." She looked at each of the, triumph written on her face.

Cassius looked sternly at her, but finally he shrugged. "I'll make the call once we exit the warp bubble."

14 UZ'S TALE

HESITANTLY, LENAH KNOCKED on Uz's hatch, unsure if the Cassidian would welcome or condemn the reason for Lenah's visit. That worry increased when she didn't get a response for at least twenty seconds. She knocked again, and this time heard a soft 'Enter' spoken from inside. As Lenah stepped through, Uz was sitting cross-legged on the floor of her cabin. Her immaculate cabin, Lenah noticed. Was Lenah still on the same ship?

"Wow," she said, looking around in astonishment. "I mean, can I interrupt your, err, sitting for a moment?"

"Sure," Uz nodded. "I was just meditating over my accomplishment. Do you like it?"

"Like what?" Lenah asked, still distracted by the shiny surfaces.

Uz nodded toward the wall. "I used a hull brush to go over all the surfaces. They're meant for smoothing c-carbon, so they go into the intely-steel walls easily. What you see is literally the layer under what formally were the walls. I figured I might as well do a deep cleaning and make sure there are no more explosives wedged into secret hiding places."

"Like grenades in the crack of your mattress?"

"Precisely." Uz shuddered. "And then I thought, might as well do a really good job with it." She nodded back to the wall again.

"Right." Lenah followed her gaze. "And can you do that to the whole ship?"

Uz nodded again, her eyes sparking. "Absolutely. She'll be as good as new. Like ours, you know."

"Like ours," Lenah repeated, not missing how Uz's eyes brightened at the words.

"So, what's up?" Uz changed the topic. "You've never come to visit me in my cabin before."

Lenah shrugged and put her hands in her pockets. "Right." Seeing how well Uz looked, maybe she was overblowing this. "I just wanted to check up on you. I thought that the way Wise Ikanobu treated you was really terrible."

To her surprise Uz's lips opened into a smile. "Ah." She got up to sit on the bed and offer Lenah a seat next to her. Since there was no other furniture to sit on, Lenah took a seat on the mattress.

"That's fine, Lenah," Uz said after a short silence. "I'm used to it, really. And over it, too." Her hands went to the scars on her forehead, but her smile didn't falter. "I've handled this for many years of my life, and now I have friends and somewhere I belong."

Lenah looked at her, feeling unsure. Wise Ikanobu had treated Uz like a flea, certainly not like an intelligent being. How could she be okay with that?

"Really," Uz assured her, surprising Lenah by patting her leg. Cassidians hated touch, but Uz seemed to be different in that department as well.

"I suppose you might be more human than Cassidian at this point," Lenah said, looking down at her leg.

"Hah, I like that." Uz grinned. "And I even almost became a human spaceship engineer."

"You are a spaceship engineer. You have your own spaceship."

"Full of dirty walls to polish?" Uz asked, still grinning.

Lenah sobered. "If you want to. Once this is over, I'll gladly drop you off on Arcadia and you can continue your training. Not like you seem to need it."

Uz nodded thoughtfully. "I did it mostly because humans, almost as much as Cassidians, love their protocols. And to get a job as an engineer, you need an engineering certificate. But I think I already read all of the training books and manuals several times by the time I got the position."

"Were you on Arcadia for long before getting the job?" Lenah asked, intrigued to get a glimpse into Uz's past. She didn't know much beside Uz being kidnapped as an engineer-in-training to go into Starwide Research's illegal lab.

Uz rubbed her chin. "Three years on the street or doing toxic waste disposal jobs. Then two years in training."

"Three years?" Lenah asked, wondering how Uz had gotten by for such a long time and realizing what a bubble she herself had grown up in. Her worst worry for years had been how to get to fly a spaceship. Because it was under station in life. What must it have felt like to be an outcast and living in the streets?

"It's okay, Lenah," Uz said, giving her a reassuring look. "You don't need to feel bad for me. Not your fault how you grew up. And you're a good person. I'm just glad we didn't meet inside of a Starwide Research laboratory." She cringed.

Lenah shuddered, then asked. "Are you nervous to be going there now?"

Uz inclined her head. "A bit. But at least I'll be in charge, you know? That helps a lot."

Lenah nodded, understanding perfectly. She was experiencing some of the same feelings. Lenah wasn't thrilled to be going back to Starwide Research and potentially even having to confront her father. Just before blowing up billions of CGC worth of factory. But at least, she wouldn't be the same clueless Lenah this time.

15   A SYRR ALLY

"ARE YOU GOING to check out the drone?" Lorka almost bounced as he intercepted Lenah in the corridor.

"Um, yes."

"I'm coming too. I can come, right? Uz told me she got this ancient piece of technology from the Syrr temple. I'm so curious to see it. I love ancient tech. Don't you?"

"Not particularly, no. I'm more into modern spaceships," Lenah admitted, grinning at Lorka's enthusiasm. At least he wasn't worried what would happen to him now that he had practically united himself with fugitives. Or he was hiding it very well.

They quickly crossed the corridor together and entered the common room where Uz had once again taken over the table for her language-reprogramming project. Earlier, she'd told Lenah that she was ready, and that the drone now spoke fluent G-Standard. But she'd lacked her normal enthusiasm.

Lenah was curious to find out why. Had Uz not managed to fix the error from last time? The drone had seemed to be stuck in an odd greeting protocol back then.

"Oh, hey, Lenah. Hey, Lorka," Uz said as they entered. The drone was hovering in the corner, no longer connected to any cables. It still carried the same disapproving look on its stony features. Maybe that was how Syrr had looked? Their facial expressions might be different from what other races, like humans or Cassidians, found normal. After all, it was rude to judge an alien race by human standards.

"Do you know its name yet?" Lenah asked Uz, who shook her head.

"Wow, this is incredible. What is this amazing piece of ancient wisdom and ingenuity?" Lorka exclaimed as he stepped into the room behind Lenah. "What are you called?"

The drone regarded him for a long moment. Did his stony brows narrow a bit?

"I am called Zyrakath, 79th of my name, in the tradition of Zyrakath the First, known as the Great One."

"Er." Lorka gave a small bow. "I am Lorka Enggaard, second of my name, in the tradition of my grandfather who was known to have a ravenous appetite."

The drone nodded. "Sustenance is very important. At least for those still in their biological form. I bow to your mindful ancestor, youngling."

Lenah realized that she had been staring open-mouthed and hurried to close it. She eased back, wanting to let this conversation unfold.

"I have been taken against my will," the drone, Zyrakath, stated. "I can feel your force, young Lorka, and I will rely on your cooperation to help me in my quest of protecting my temple."

"Oh," Lorka replied, looking at Lenah and Uz with a questioning look, his eyebrows raised and eyes wide. Or was that panic? "I'm not sure I can help you."

The drone nodded. "Have they taken you too? Are you here against your will?"

"I...No, I'm not. These are my friends. Lenah and Uzara." Lorka gestured toward them.

"What is this disrespect? I haven't offered *them* my name."

"Oh, please forgive me, Old Zyrakath. But we do not know your traditions," Lorka said.

The drone regarded him, lips pressed in a thin line. "You speak wisely. I am considering this possibility. They might not have meant the offense they committed. I find almost all the relevant words of respect missing from this language. Is it possible the worlds forgot how to address their elders?"

He didn't seem to expect an answer and continued muttering to himself but too low for Lenah to understand. She looked over at Uz, who shrugged her shoulders.

"I have decided," Zyrakath announced. "I will be lenient and speak to you, Lenah and Uzara."

They nodded.

"Now tell me, younglings. Why did you take me by force from my home?"

"We were hoping for your help in the fight against the Cava Dara. We're sorry if that was against your will," Lenah said, thinking how she hadn't even considered this thing had a will when they'd first encountered it—him—on Masis III. Humans made androids too, but most were purposefully built not to appear too human. This drone seemed to think he was a full-fledged person with an ancient family tree and all. Or was that just the name of his production line?

"The Cava Dara. Yes, I remember. It was a very long time ago, but I recall every detail. They killed all of my kin. In the end even my beloved great-great-granddaughter. She had to commit suicide into a stone before they got to her."

"Is she the Syrr princess from the warning the stone unlocked?" Uz asked, biting her lip.

"Hm?" Zyrakath looked down at her. "Yes, Cassidian Uzara." He nodded. "That was all she was able to save of herself. All of it in order to leave a message to the future. Hm," he said, his brows furrowing further. "She was wise. I suppose helping you would be what she had in mind. No matter how strange and primitive a species you are. Humans, you are called?" He looked questioningly at Lenah.

"Yes," she said, too stunned to have any other reaction. *Had he just called all of humanity primitive?*

"Yes, she would have wanted this." Zyrakath nodded. "Very well, I will assist you but I ask that I be returned to my home once I have shared all my knowledge with you."

"Back to Masis III?" Lenah asked. "I guess we could do that. Elder Zyrakath," she added after a short break, giving a little bow. Now that he was talking to them, she wanted to stay on his good side. "But you will help us before that? The Cava Dara are on their way to my home planet, and even though we alerted our leaders, they do not see the threat and will not mobilize in force. We're on our way to help out."

"The ways of the worlds remain. That does sound like what my people went through," Zyrakath said and regarded her.

"Yes," Lenah whispered, "and your people didn't make it, did they?"

He didn't answer at first but finally said, "I alone was left, but my grief diminished with the passing of time. I wouldn't want this for any other race, not even one with your deficiencies, human."

"What happened to your people, Zyrakath?" Lorka asked, staring wide-eyed at the drone.

Zyrakath focused back on him and flew down from where he'd been hovering above them, over the table.

He took a deep breath, or at least the equivalent of what sounded like one. Machines didn't need to breathe, did they?

"It all started as a gradual loss of tradition. It slipped away from my people and was replaced by what this language calls greed. At least that's part of its meaning. There's no true equivalent. The old rules for respect and authority of the Elder were slowly undermined. There is a word for that in this language: Power."

He paused, hovering down even more to stop at face level. His gray eyes bore into each of them.

"My great-grandson, our ruler, found a way to extract and hoard the intellect of others as part of himself. He sought and hunted the smartest Syrr, capturing their essence and transferring it into him." As Zyrakath spoke, Lenah saw the video they had recorded on Masis III play in front of her mind's eye. So that was what the king had done on that chair. He'd fed the intellect of the stones into himself. And the stones were minds of dead Syrr.

"He used magic to enhance himself. That was the trigger," she blurted out loud. "But was he the only person to do this?"

Zyrakath didn't seem happy about the interruption. He pressed his lips together but answered her. "He was alone, but he consumed hundreds. The most intense minds; all of our future. I was only spared because, for years, I managed to hide from him and his soldiers."

Lenah looked at him in confusion. The king used artificial intelligence to enhance himself? But she was worried Zyrakath would stop talking if she interrupted him again, so she let it go for now.

"This went on for years. The corruption of our ways was slow. Apart from the latent terror of being taken, we lived in peace; we were prospering. Harnessing his immense new abilities, the king developed revolutionary farming techniques. He bent climate, the volcanoes, our crops to his will. It came easily to him, and he felt like a god. He fed us well. He protected us from our world's own dangers. He perfected the temple home I had built to withstand an eternity of earthquakes. Only being born with a desirable mind was dangerous.

"But these new ways had to have a downside. And it came in the form of the Cava Dara. The Cassidian High Priest warned us. But it didn't alarm our king. He had become arrogant, feeling like he could outsmart anyone. But there is no outsmarting an army of soulless creatures with the sole purpose of destroying anything in their wake. The adversary played with brute strength, not intellect, which was *our* only strength. Our little army was quickly diminished, joining the ranks of the Muha Dara."

"Wait, aren't they called Cava Dara?" Lenah asked.

Zyrakath turned to her, but this time, instead of looking annoyed at being interrupted, she saw a deep sadness in his eyes. "Cava Dara are the original creatures. Cassandral's creations. The converted are called Muha Dara."

"Mindless Frost," Uz muttered, and Zyrakath nodded.

"And no one survived?" Lorka whispered.

"Only me. I didn't have a biological body any longer, and that made me immune to the Cava Dara, and the king had already consumed all the other Elders. In the end, there was no one left but my great-great-granddaughter and me. And she took her life to infuse part of her essence into a stone."

"Wait a moment, does that mean you once were a real person?" Lenah hadn't considered that before, even though he did have quite a personality for a machine. What exactly was he?

"What do you mean?" Zyrakath looked at her, confusion all over his stony features. "Of course, I am a *real* person."

He turned to Lorka. "The young human doesn't seem an adequate leader. You should consider taking up the post yourself or letting me. Though I am not sure how this box we are in, works exactly."

"Box? You mean the *Star Rambler*? It's a spaceship," Lenah said, reigning in her amusement. The Syrr seemed an advanced culture, but Zyrakath didn't appear to understand the concept of space travel very well.

"Yes, the space box."

"Zyrakath, I don't understand either," Lorka said, probably trying to change the subject about who should be the leader. "You say you're a real person. Do you have memories of your life?"

Good question, Lenah thought. It was possible memories of his lifetime were saved somewhere in this hard-wired brain. Even if he remembered his life before being a drone, it didn't mean it had truly happened.

"Of course, I do. I might have been old already when my people were wiped out, but I remember everything. From the time before I entered this body to the past millennia which I spent studying the books in the temple's library over and over again."

"You entered this body? What does that mean?" Lenah asked, once again intrigued.

"Young female, your questions are insufferable. Have you never met one of your Elders?"

Lenah, trying to be diplomatic, said. "Please forgive me if my questions appear impertinent to you. I assure you, no disrespect is meant. I've met elderly people. My grandparents on my father's side passed a few years ago, but I grew up visiting them every harvest celebration."

"But they were not chosen to become an Elder?" As small as he was, no more than the size of a two-year-old toddler, Zyrakath managed to convey a condescending look down his aristocratic nose.

"Chosen? You don't choose to age. Everyone just ages. Or isn't that how it works for the Syrr?"

"We age. But only the most intelligent individuals are chosen to pass their soul into an after-body." He flared his nostrils. "There is no adequate word in this language of yours."

"Zyrakath, are you saying you are the soul of a real Syrr who was stored inside a stone machine?" Lorka asked, clapping his hands. "Wicked! You're a living person from six thousand years ago!"

"I am not familiar with the time unit you are referring to."

"Oh sure." Lorka nodded eagerly. "A year is 350 Cassidian days, the day is split into our wake and rest cycle, and six thousand years is the time passed since the Cava Dara attacked your people. Though, if you ask me, with most planets having different rhythms from Cassidia, hanging on to the same time unit doesn't make a whole lot of sense. But the soul of someone from six thousand years ago?" Lorka looked at the drone in awe. "That is the most amazing thing I have ever heard in my life."

"I understand you mean to speak a compliment, youngling, and at the same time I realize you could not have seen many things in your short life span."

Lenah suppressed a snort at the arrogant comment this time. It seemed one of the most natural parts of his personality. Or maybe that was considered normal for the Syrr. An unknown and apparently highly developed culture from millennia ago.

"Humans don't worship their Elders and better their society in the same way? Keeping the knowledge an Elder has acquired is an integral part of creating a functioning society," Zyrakath said.

"I'm sure if we knew how, we'd do it," Lorka remarked.

"I'm not convinced that we should," Lenah said under her breath. Wouldn't humanity just keep alive whoever had the most money? She wasn't sure she liked that general idea.

"I had not considered that possibility," Zyrakath said, sounding thoughtful. "I am reaching the conclusion that you are an even less developed race than you seemed at first glance. I shall look forward to learning more about you and coaching you in the right ways." He nodded to himself, and Lenah caught Uz's gaze. It was alternating from amusement to slight annoyance. Lenah had to agree. When they had taken the drone on Masis III, she had hoped it would be a helpful tool in gaining knowledge about the Cava Dara. She hadn't expected to be lectured on her behavior.

"I wonder," Zyrakath said, looking more serious than ever, "if I could see my great-great-granddaughter. What is left of her, at least?"

"You mean the stone?" Uz asked softly. Her face had turned serious.

"Of course. The fragment she stored there; I haven't seen her in almost 1500 of your years. Not since the first of your kind came to take her from me."

"The expedition that made it to the temple," Lenah said. "How did they not take you either?"

"I hid in the library. But I didn't have the time to fetch her in her chamber. They took her and left me behind. I was alone for a very long time until those brutes arrived, blowing a hole into my temple wall. Such immature and underdeveloped behavior, relying on pure strength." He huffed.

"Well, at least we have that in common," Lenah said. "We don't like those brutes either."

Zyrakath looked at her as if she were dirt spattered all over his floor.

"I'll fetch your great-great-granddaughter for you," she said and bolted from the room before he could tell her that he had nothing in common with a lowly human like her.

16 MIND TRAINING

LENAH TOOK A COUPLE of deep breaths and looked at the full crew lined up in the cargo hold in front of her.

She took another deep breath and started concentrating on their minds. Over the years, she had found that breathing helped calm her down, which made it easier to see a mind with her inner eye. Though seeing was a strong word, it was more a perceiving of minds as a cloud. If she kept concentrating on it, that cloud looked as real as an actual cloud in the sky to her.

She took another breath. More minds to influence, more breaths to ground herself.

Cassius, Doctor Lund, Uz, and Persia stood lined up in the cargo hold. All were looking at Lenah, except for Uz, who had her eyes closed. Doctor Lund was also grimacing and stroking his throat where he'd always worn his order's amulet before the stone creatures on Masis III had ripped it off him. He'd been the one least happy about submitting to this plan. Losing control of his conscious mind went against everything he believed in, he had stated, and he had stormed out of the common room as the others pressured him to join. Everyone needed to do their share in preparation for the plan, they had argued. Doctor Lund only agreed after Uz had talked to him in his cabin. Lenah wasn't sure what the Cassidian had done to convince the doctor, but she was glad. She definitely needed every ounce of this training, and so far, their daily sessions hadn't been very successful.

Gently, Lenah pushed an idea toward all of them. It spread out, but she needed to make it large enough to mingle with each of their minds. Only it hadn't really worked in the last few days. She could now cover two of them at once, but all four…Lenah wasn't sure that was even possible.

It entailed more than making her own cloud spread. She had to think of each mind consciously, otherwise, her suggestion would only pass through them without doing anything.

Doctor Lund and Uz, who were standing in the middle, started to bend down first, reaching for their shoes. Cassius's mouth twitched with amusement, giving Lenah a hint that her suggestion wasn't working for him yet. Lenah concentrated on him. And promptly lost her touch on Uz.

Damn it.

She wiped her sweaty forehead. Mind magic, especially challenging applications like this, took as much out of her as a fight training with Cassius.

Her cloud spread around Uz, who was getting up again. Uz stopped in mid-motion, hesitating and neither bending down again nor fully getting up. Lenah pushed harder, trying to keep Cassius and Lund in focus as well.

Uz bent down and mimicked Doctor Lund, who was in the process of taking off his shoes. One quick glance at Cassius revealed that he was doing the same. Lenah tried to take a controlled portion of her concentration away from them and focus it toward Persia, who was still standing and grinning widely, seeing how the others were behaving.

Her knowing what was going on would make it harder for Lenah to convince her that she needed to take off her sandals, too. Past the cargo hold, only slippers were allowed—rule of the host, aka Lenah.

She had chosen this idea, as silly as it was, for its relative complexity. They didn't have slippers to put on. Nor was Lenah the host here. She didn't think anyone would ever ask people boarding their spaceships to take off their shoes. Though you never knew. In the end, it didn't seem too farfetched from convincing someone to hand over their explosives.

As she poured more energy toward Persia, Lenah struggled not to let Cassius, who was standing on the opposite side of their line, slip from her grasp. He was fumbling with the laces of his combat boots, and to her relief, kept doing so.

Persia's expression, meanwhile, changed from amusement to confusion. Lenah pushed some more and was rewarded with her bending down and untying her gladiator sandals.

The next stop they arrive to, they really ought to do some shopping for themselves. Or fetch clothes in Lenah's room if they returned to Callo mansion. Lenah herself had left her own clothes behind on UPL station and had been wearing the formal red vest and tight suit ever since. At least she still had her shoes. *Unlike all her friends*, she thought smugly, looking at their bare feet.

Slowly, to not break concentration, Lenah bent down and picked up their shoes one after the other. They stood watching, but no one objected. It seemed to be actually working. Finally.

One arm full with four pairs of shoes, Lenah backed away toward engineering. While she moved, she also had to expand her influence to make up for the added distance. Lenah couldn't yet sprint away to do it, but easing away slowly, she could hold her influence.

Reaching the door that lead to the small engineering room, Lenah dropped the shoes there, then walked back toward her friends, trying not to feel too triumphant. The next part would be even more difficult.

When she was standing in front of them again, she changed the idea. Instead of a shared vision for each of them, she concentrated on them as two groups. She sent Cassius and Doctor Lund the memory of how Uz and Persia had taken their shoes by force and thrown them out of the airlock. To

Cassius and Lund, she sent the inverted idea: Uz and Persia taking the men's shoes and spacing them.

Doctor Lund was the first one to move. He made a jerking movement, lifting each foot off the ground for a moment, then grimaced. At the same time, the other three looked down at their feet. Lenah kept pouring into them the vivid imagery of the two ideas, spurred on by the success she'd had so far.

"Why did you throw my shoes away? What's wrong with you?" Doctor Lund asked, storming over to face Uz and Persia and making a lot of trampling noise for someone standing only in his socks.

Persia looked down at those socks, looking perplexed.

"That's not true. You threw *our* shoes away. I saw it."

"Don't lie, I saw you throw away my shoes," Doctor Lund insisted through clenched teeth, even though he seemed confused why Persia would be without hers as well. Lenah realized she had forgotten to explain that little detail in her vision.

"What's going on here? Don't pretend." Cassius stalked up to stand next to Doctor Lund. "And your own shoes? Did you hide them? I saw you just now throw mine out, but you were wearing yours." He furrowed his brow. He turned around in the room as if to look for the women's shoes behind the crates stacked against the wall. Lenah scrambled to adjust, but no good idea came to her mind. Cassius spun and finally stopped to stare straight at Lenah. "Wait a second. We're training."

Lenah struggled to hold her influence, but Cassius's comment had broken her concentration. Her influence retracted back toward her, freeing their minds.

"We are training!" Uz exclaimed. Then she looked around. "You didn't really throw our shoes out, did you?"

Lenah grinned at them. "No, they are there by the door of engineering."

"Does that mean it finally worked?" Cassius was beaming. With outstretched arms, he closed the distance to Lenah. *Was he going to hug her?* But when he'd almost reached her, he hesitated and cleared his throat. His arms dropped and he patted her on the shoulder. The touch of metal felt cold through her thin blouse, and she wished he'd hugged her instead. Or had used his other hand.

"That's amazing! All four of us?" he asked, apparently unaware of Lenah's discomfort. That was a good thing. She wasn't sure what to make of her wish to be hugged by him. Especially in front of everyone else.

"Yup." She nodded, focusing on his words. "At least for a little bit." She couldn't stop grinning, and Cassius returned it, showing nice and even teeth surrounded by even nicer lips.

Lenah shook her head. *Where had that come from? Did she want to kiss him?* What would that mean? He wasn't really dating material for someone of her station, but did that even matter any longer? Did she still have a higher station?

"I'm tired. I'm going to go rest in my cabin," she told the group.

Everyone nodded, though Cassius's eyes opened in question. Ignoring him, Lenah turned around and walked up to the main corridor. A few seconds later, she found herself in the safety of her room. She went to sit on her bed, trying to calm her busy thoughts.

What was wrong with her? She should be elated right now, celebrating with her friends who had offered their free will multiple times over the past few days. She was sure these daily sessions hadn't been easy for them. Surrendering control over their minds to Lenah was a huge tribute of trust. And she had accomplished it now. What had seemed unobtainable only a few days ago, influencing four people at once, had become a reality. *They were one crucial step closer to getting their explosives.*

Yet, here she was, with nothing else on her mind other than kissing the cyborg? She must be mad. Or deprived. It had been a long time for her since she had a relationship, the last one being with Mason. Lenah nodded to herself. *There it was.* Her infatuation was merely biological. After all, Cassius was an attractive man, cyborg or not. Lenah got up again to make a trip to the lav unit. She'd told everyone that she was going to sleep, so she'd better get her teeth cleaned and tuck herself into bed. Maybe she'd play a mindless game on her wristpiece to distract herself.

17 SMUGGLER CODE

"SHOULDN'T THEY HAVE answered at this point?" Lenah asked as she watched Uz, who was bent over the *Rambler*'s dashboard. Cassius had comm'ed his friends hours ago to ask about the station's coordinates. Why weren't they answering? "Maybe they aren't so loyal after all. Who knows with smugglers."

Uz tapped her chin, looking up. "It's only been a few hours. They might be far away, and the transmission takes time. Did Cassius say where his friend is?" She squinted at the proximity scanner.

Lenah shook her head. "I don't think he knows."

A soft bing interrupted them, and their eyes turned to the comm panel.

"That's it! Yes! We have the coordinates." Uz beamed at Lenah, who let out a relieved breath. Their whole plan would have fallen apart had they not gotten the coordinates to actually reach the smuggler's market. Now it seemed that they would get to execute their plan. Lenah felt her eyelid twitch nervously.

She was more anxious about this than anything else they had done before. It wasn't just the general risk they were taking, but also because she always seemed to stick out in these kinds of environments. The last thing she wanted was to get them all into trouble. She hoped that her time spent outside of the society of families and with Cassius and the others had rubbed off a little. She'd definitely made an effort.

Don't walk with your head high, always try to catch every detail that's around you. Act like you don't want to be seen, even by someone who happens to pass right by you. So far, Lenah hadn't been able to use her newly acquired movement patterns in public. She'd only practiced in her cabin. And she also couldn't ask anyone here, not without admitting that she didn't know how to behave like a commoner.

"It's not too far away, less than half a day without a warp bubble," Lenah said, looking up from the screen that had calculated their distance to the indicated coordinates. "If the market is tomorrow, we should probably not bother with a warp bubble. That will be better for our fuel reserves, anyway." She shot a worried glance at the fuel meter. Less than half, and they still didn't have money to replenish it comfortably.

This was the worst side of her new life.

"I still find it funny that smugglers open their market at 5 a.m.," Uz said. "I always imaged them being night owls."

"Creeping around in the dark hours?" Lenah raised an eyebrow.

"This is business not pleasure." Cassius's voice came from behind. A few seconds later, he squished himself into the cockpit to take up his usual spot behind Lenah. Her belly gave a little jump as she remembered how he'd almost hugged her after the training session. "If you want to be a smuggler in this time and age, you have to be a businessman or -woman first and foremost," Cassius said.

"Just with slightly altered values?" Lenah asked, happy about the distraction.

He frowned. "Not necessarily. Families steal from poor people all the time. It's wrong that their status gives them the right to do that."

"I guess…if you put it that way," Lenah muttered, never having thought of it in that way.

"Do you think you might meet your old colleagues?" Uz asked into the heavy silence and managed to make it sound almost like a normal question.

But if families and smugglers were alike, then the latter could also be called colleagues, Lenah supposed. She turned to see the reaction on Cassius's face. She'd been asking herself the same question.

Was he worried he might run into his father? His criminal father from whom he had escaped? After all, Cassius had indicated that the man frequented this place on a regular basis. That's how Cassius—and now them—knew about it. Only that

Uz didn't know it was his father that Cassius had left behind, not just some *colleagues*.

Cassius shrugged, but before answering, Lenah saw his gaze flicker sideways nervously. Was it possible that he, a cyborg stronger than any non-enhanced human, was afraid to confront his father? Though, as she thought about it, wasn't she too? She was a mind mage and worried at the thought of going back home and blowing up their company's most lucrative laboratory. And she shuddered at the thought of meeting her father, who hadn't stood up for her at all, not with Corinna and definitely not with UPL authorities. How often had she fantasized to just randomly find that access chip to the mage farm in the last few days instead of having to go get it from his office? A hundred times? Two hundred?

"The *Trader's Anne* usually comes by only once per month," Cassius said. "To the last market of the month and we have the first one tomorrow. I don't think they'll be there."

"I hope not. Do you think they would be mad at you?" Uz asked.

"Mad?" He barked out a laugh. It sounded slightly strangled. "Yeah," he said with a creaky voice.

"Oh. I'm sorry to hear that. But why would they? Wouldn't it be possible that you're innocent? That instead of you kidnapping us, you could have been kidnapped? Maybe Lenah controlled your mind and took you." Uz gestured toward Lenah's head.

Always seeing the good in people, Lenah thought. For someone who had experienced great injustice herself, Uz actually tended to be overly positive.

"Me being kidnapped?" Cassius lifted his enhanced arm and made a fist. "Are you sure anyone would believe that? Unless it was someone with a nano-stunner, and those are really hard to get."

"Mmh, I guess not," Uz trailed off. "I'm sorry. I hope we don't see your colleagues. I'll go check on that temperature control issue you mentioned, Lenah." She got up and squeezed by Cassius to leave the cockpit. "Then I'll try to sleep some. I spent way too much time trying to make that drone speak." She yawned.

"You don't like Zyrakath much, do you?" Lenah asked.

"Oh, he's barely even talked to me. He seems to think that a cut Cassidian is even worse than a primitive human."

"He doesn't seem to like anyone if that's any consolation. Maybe with the exception of Lorka who happened to be sufficiently awed by his presence," Lenah told her.

Uz sniffed. "I think he was more impressed by Lorka's bow than my ability to revive such an ancient piece of technology. In five seconds, Lorka received more gratefulness from him than me after fixing him up for two weeks."

"True. But the rest of us are grateful. In any case, I think it will be useful to have him here. He does know a lot more than we do about the Cava Dara and the Muha Dara."

"He does," Uz said nonchalantly. "Which is why I didn't press together his two off-cables."

"He has cables?" Cassius asked. "I thought it—he—is made from stone."

"They are stone cables. Gem nodes strung together," Uz answered before turning and leaving.

"She really doesn't like him, does she?"

"You weren't there," Lenah said. "He is a handful to listen to. I have a suspicion that he wouldn't like you either. He kept mentioning the value of elderly wisdom and seemed to imply the worthlessness of physical strength."

"Mmh," Cassius said, folding his long limbs into the copilot's chair Uz had abandoned.

"I guess I'm glad I wasn't there."

They sat silently for a few moments, Lenah feeling her belly flutter once more.

"How sure are you that you won't run into your father?" Lenah finally asked. He had looked very worried earlier.

Cassius sighed. "He's a stickler to his routine. I don't think he'd change his schedule if he doesn't have to."

"But you're worried he might have to?"

"I'm not sure. He used to rely heavily on me. Not me, specifically, but this." He lifted his cyborg arm. "And probably making deals got harder for him without it. So, it's possible he'll have to frequent the market more often, try to make more deals. Less dangerous deals with less profit."

"If he saw you there, what would he do?"

"Not sure, but something between trying to mock me for failing my mission and kill me." He grinned, and when Lenah didn't join him, he bit his lip. "He'd probably nano-stun me and try to get me back. I was *expensive*."

"And what mission was that?" Lenah asked softly. He'd never mentioned one, and she'd never found out why he'd specifically wanted to go to Oscuris. Maybe this was the explanation.

Cassius shrugged. "More complicated family stuff." His constrained tone made it clear that he didn't want to discuss it.

Lenah was about to comment that no one got their own child killed, but the memory how her father's smuggler allies had tried to shoot the *Star Rambler* kept her from doing so. "Family is not easy. I hope we don't see him," she said instead. And she meant every word.

18 NEETH STATION

CAREFULLY, LENAH NAVIGATED the *Star Rambler* into the cargo hold of Neeth Station. Or rather, the *parking lot*, given the whole interior seemed to have been taken out to accommodate two decks of marked parking spots. Cassius had recommended they come late, to be last in line, and Lenah could see why.

If they had to leave abruptly, it would be impossible to do so parked in the first row with four lines of other ships tucked behind. It was probably a good mechanism to control misbehavior.

As the makeshift station had come into view, Lenah had marveled at the ingenuity of it. It was a pretty massive place but entirely made out of specially modified spaceships. There was a large center ship, with the market and entertainment areas Cassius had explained, then four wings attached from it. The parking wing was just one of the areas. Two others were for private trading bays—their destination—and the final one held a canteen with decent beer. At least, according to Cassius.

Lenah wouldn't mind having a second sample of the beverage, but that wouldn't happen today. She grimaced to herself. Her hands were sweaty, and she thought she could hear her heart racing. Tonight was going to be a challenge.

She turned off the engine, got up from her seat and made her way into the cargo hold. Cassius and Persia were waiting there, and by how Persia was clutching her hammer, she felt at least as nervous as Lenah. Laser weapons weren't allowed on the station, to avoid violent incidents that could potentially lead to hull breaches. Though selling weapons apparently was an everyday activity, so they'd be bringing their more primitive weapons today.

Cassius was sporting his big knife, almost like a machete and one of the tranquilizer guns from UPL station. Both were tucked into his belt loops. Lenah knew that he had other knives on him too, but those were hidden away somewhere. Lenah herself had also brought a tranq gun and a thin, but long-bladed knife. Not that she truly knew what to do with it.

Cassius had tried to show her, but without dummies to practice on, she hadn't advanced far in the last few days. Lenah didn't even have the nerve to stab his cyborg arm, despite his insistence that she couldn't do him any damage, and that the knife was much more likely to break than penetrate. To her, it was still his arm.

"Are we ready?" Lenah asked, and both nodded. Cassius took one of his favorite relaxed stances, all emotion wiped from his face, and Persia clutched her hammer harder.

"You're leaving already?" Uz's voice came from behind.

"Better get it over with before someone else buys all our explosives and leaves with them," Lenah said, turning around.

Uz nodded. "Good luck. We'll be waiting, ready to depart."

"Comm me if something comes up," Lenah told her, lifting her arm with the wristpiece. Then she turned again and opened the hatch without letting her fear get the better of her.

They had to make their way around several rows of closely parked ships, and Lenah stumbled, practicing her new mannerisms intended to avoid notice while trying to pick up as much detail around her as she could. She hadn't paid attention to the ground in front of her.

Lenah cursed under her breath, and Cassius gave her a curious once-over. Lenah pulled herself together and looked around again, this time focusing on where she was walking.

The ships in here were a curious mixture of modern cruisers and older models, similar to the *Star Rambler*. This might be the first time she had landed her ship somewhere without drawing attention to how old it was.

What all the ships had in common was a wide array of weapon upgrades. One was a civilian transport shuttle, but someone had modified the sides so they could stick one laser cannon next to the other. Compared to all the weapons power displayed, the *Rambler* was still the crappiest ship in here. It only had front lasers; the back ones had probably fallen off at some point.

Reaching a large hatch that opened on a motion sensor, they passed through and into a short tunnel that ended in a similar hatch. The crossing from one ship to another, she realized. They must be in the center ship now, the one that held the market and entertainment facilities. Sure enough, smells and loud voices soon started drifting toward them, and as the second hatch opened, they were immediately swallowed by the intense noise from up ahead.

Like the parking ship, most of this ship had been hollowed out. The market lay situated in one large and several-story-tall room with gangways leading up to the higher levels. Tables filled the area, with large holosigns praising the offered goods. Lenah saw knives, clothes, food, and even toys on display.

The loud and rhythmic voices of merchants praising their products filled the air. Lenah looked curiously at the mix of people. To her surprise, not everyone around was a shaggy-looking pirate. There *were* a good number of uncombed figures, both male and female, and mostly human; but they didn't outnumber the well-kept ones, and even more surprising was the large number of parents holding hands with their children. A woman passed them, deep in discussion with her two sons why they couldn't get another pair of toy water guns. The normality of it struck Lenah.

"I'll go and find out about the special trades being offered," Cassius said next to her. He almost had to yell for them to hear him. "Will you two be alright here? Walk around and pretend to be shoppers."

"We won't need to pretend. This place is amazing," Persia said and beamed. "I already saw a place where they can polish my hammer. I've long lost my polishing tincture."

"And here I thought you'd be more excited about the fashion being offered," Lenah said but nodded her okay to Cassius. He left them a moment later, making his way to the back of the hall. He'd draped his coat around his arm, and she was sure he was worried about being recognized. His imposing size alone drew some looks.

"Let's go see about your hammer," Lenah said to Persia, as Cassius vanished in the crowd.

"Absolutely. I'm not sure if I'll be able to afford it. But it can't hurt to go and look."

"Let's do it," Lenah agreed. "And let's get some more rations, too."

They spent the next thirty minutes slowly making their way through the market. After initially feeling very uncomfortable and fighting the urge to look over her shoulder every few breaths, Lenah started to relax. She knew the people around her were criminals, but with laughing kids and lively merchants, it was difficult not to get into a shopping mood herself.

In her old life, Lenah had gone shopping regularly and always enjoyed the alone-time away from work. The new Lenah didn't have time for that. Nor did she have the same amount of money.

They did, however, have money for urgent things, like food, and Lenah managed to convince Persia to purchase some decent shoes. They were used but sturdy black boots that would go with just about anything while being comfortable enough to allow her to get into all sorts of trouble. She'd been wearing her knee-high gladiator sandals for weeks, and their hike through the jungle of Masis III had been especially uncomfortable—and not the most hygienic—to her bare toes.

"How much are these?" Lenah asked the merchant, a middle-aged woman with a big chest and a big belly whose table sported everything from clothes to dinner plates and even paintings. The only common theme seemed to be that all of it had seen better days.

"That's ten CGC for the pair," the woman said.

"For these shoes?" Lenah stared at her, then realized that she was probably supposed to haggle. At least that's what people in movies always did when they were in a market such as this.

"We'll give you five," she retorted to the vendor, trying to sound very sure of herself. *Was five a reasonable price? Was she being rude?* She had no idea.

"They cost more than that to purchase from the previous owner," the woman said, chewing loudly on pink gum and blowing out a lazy bubble which finally popped close to Lenah's face.

"Then how much?" Lenah asked, backing up as another bubble burst violently, then vanished back into the woman's mouth.

"Eight."

"That's too expensive. I'll give you seven."

The woman regarded her, then Persia. "Fine."

"Seven, those socks, and that hair kit over there," Persia said, pointing to a box promising scissors, a hairdryer, and pale-white hair dye. `Moon Princess Kit` the label read.

"Otherwise, we're picking up the shoes from that other shop over there. They have nicer ones, anyway."

"What?" Another gum bubble was violently pulled back into the woman's mouth. "Old Wagner don't have nicer stuff. His things'll fall apart the minute you're out of here'," she huffed, eyeing Persia while chewing on her gum. Persia tapped her fingers on the table but didn't say anything.

"It's a deal, but only because you're new customers. Special price," the merchant finally grumbled.

"Yeah, right," Persia said and grinned while Lenah pulled out the seven chips. After they paid, the merchant packed up the hair kit in a bag while Persia put on her new shoes.

"Persia, what's up with the princess hair kit? Was that because I was that bad at haggling?" Lenah asked as they stepped away from the booth.

"You *were* being ripped off," Persia said, tying her laces. "Really, these shoes shouldn't have cost more than three CGC. Besides, didn't you say you wanted to dye your hair? New look, new Lenah, or something like that?"

"Oh." Lenah shook her head. "I mean, yes. That was very observant of you," she added, realizing what Persia had been up to. "I guess I'll need it even more once I blew up my father's lab."

"Thought so." Persia stood up and took a few steps in her new shoes. "They're not as awesome as my sandals, but it does feel good not to have freezing toes for a change."

"I bet."

They spent the next few minutes browsing more stalls and picking up some rations when Lenah spotted Cassius's tall figure walking toward them.

"I found us a deal," he gravely said when he reached them. Then his eyes darted down to the bag Lenah was carrying in one hand.

"You went shopping?" He peeked into the bag. "Moon Princess hair dye?"

"It's a whole kit," Lenah informed him, feeling stupid. She hadn't thought that now she'd need to tote it around with her.

Cassius made a face that seemed to say: *Women, can't be left alone in a market, not even for a few minutes*, but he gallantly took the bag from her and didn't comment further. Was he pissed? Or amused? She couldn't tell with his face having gone back to the mask he liked to put on.

"It's that way," he said, pointing to a hatch on the far side of the hall. "We're expected there in twenty minutes to inspect their children's toys."

That meant they had only twenty minutes to find their explosives without being missed somewhere else. Cassius had argued that, in order to be less conspicuous, they shouldn't be asking around for weapons. After all, there was a small chance that their plan worked out so well that no one connected the departed customers of toys with the weapon thieves.

"It's one thousand tablets. Fresh from the factory," he explained as they made their way across the room.

"Oh great, just what we wanted," Persia cheerfully said. And loudly.

It sounded so fake that Lenah hoped no one had heard them. She shot Persia a warning glance.

They reached the hatch where two guards looked them over.

"What's in the bag?" the one on the left asked Cassius. He took a peek inside and then proceeded to pat Cassius down. "You're clear." Satisfied, he repeated the same procedure with Persia and Lenah, who was surprised that Cassius, with his tranquilizer gun and knives, qualified as clear. The guard's hand touched over Lenah's knife in her pocket, then continued.

"No illegal weapons. You can go through."

The hatch opened for them, and they stepped into the corridor beyond. Bright blue lights illuminated it, and large signs numbered the multiple doors.

"It's this way," Cassius whispered, pointing to a small side hatch with a sign reading "Entrance Restricted".

He quickly took in the surroundings, and, apparently satisfied that no one was around, opened it and ushered them through. They ended up in a large and empty corridor. It was icy cold.

"We need to be quick here. This is the transportation corridor, and the drones transferring the loads can pass by at any moment. They'll sound the alarms if they see us."

"Why is it so cold?" Persia asked, her breath puffing out in a cloud.

"This corridor is only meant for the transport drones," Cassius whispered. "Humans are not supposed to come here, and I guess they don't want to encourage it. Using drones ensures anonymous transport of the goods from the parking bay to the trading bays."

"I have no doubt," Persia said, hugging herself.

"I couldn't figure out what other goods were being offered here today, not without being suspicious," Cassius whispered as he started walking. "We'll have to check each bay."

Lenah nodded. They had expected this much. "Is it far?" she asked him, shuddering. It was really cold in there.

He shook his head. "Just a few dozen meters until we're in the next ship of the station. It's heated in there."

They walked in silence, and Lenah started to feel nervous again. So far, everything had gone to plan, but they hadn't really done anything yet.

"The only guarded post is right ahead," Cassius softly spoke as they reached the end of the tunnel and stopped a few meters before a closed hatch.

"This hatch should open by a motion sensor. We'll have to be quick with the guards."

He removed his weapon, and Lenah and Persia followed suit. Cassius waved for them to stay close to the walls while he took the center. He walked forward, and the hatch opened.

Lenah peeked her head out in time to see three guards pulling out their laser weapons. Cassius was already shooting his tranquilizer gun. He got two of them, and Lenah aimed at the third. All three went down unconscious.

Lenah inspected the new corridor. It was very different from the last one: pleasantly heated and with hatches every few meters. A view window on each hatch provided basic visibility to what was going on beyond. They also didn't seem sound protected because loud voices traveled over to them from the closest one.

Carefully, Cassius approached, taking a peek through the window. Lenah stayed behind, reaching out with her senses. She could make out the presence of five people in the bay.

"If you can't pay my price, you shouldn't have bothered to take up my time." An angry male voice drifted into the corridor. "These are good quality woods, freshly cut from the very trees of Cassidia. If they weren't here, a Cassidian would be building a house with it by now. You can't find this anywhere else."

"The wood still looks wet," another voice said, this one with a high-pitched nasal sound to it.

Cassius stepped away and motioned to them. They quickly crossed the hatch, and Lenah got a glance into the room beyond. A group of men stood around stacks of beautiful purple wood beams, the likes of which she had never seen before. Luckily, none of the five men were paying attention to what was going on behind them, and Lenah and her crew passed on undisturbed.

19 BAD SURPRISE

THEY CREPT FURTHER down the corridor until they reached the next open hatch. Here, whoever was talking inside, was doing so in a low voice, and Lenah couldn't pick up more than a faint murmur. Following Cassius, she inched closer to the opening to take a peek. She stumbled into him, not realizing that he had abruptly stopped an arm's length away from the hatch. Lenah had to suppress a yelp as she collided with his metal arm and shoulder. Cassius didn't even react. He continued to stand frozen.

Maybe he was listening to what was being spoken out there? Curious, Lenah edged around and managed to stick her head out next to him.

The crates that were being sold here definitely weren't what they had come for. Wrapped in transparent plastic, she saw rounded, white shovels. Lenah stared at them for a few moments before recognizing them for what they were: ivory from three shovel tuskers, and extremely illegal. The tuskers, native to Galtaca, had been hunted for centuries, their shovels made into trinkets and jewelry. They were grand beasts, as tall as a two-story building with exceptionally long life spans. And a very slow reproduction rate. Now, there were so few left that hunting them was absolutely forbidden. Was Cassius an animal protector? Lenah looked up at him and found him still transfixed on the ivory, fist clenched and gripping a knife with the other hand.

She followed his gaze more closely and noticed that he wasn't actually looking at the crates but at the group of merchants. The sellers, it seemed. There were three of them, but a tall, burly man with green eyes and long, blond hair in a ponytail looked like the leader. He stood wide-legged with an air of authority. Next to him was an equally tall, younger man, with the same eyes and same hair, who must have been his son. The last one was a slightly shorter man with dark eyes and the broadest and most muscled of them all.

Lenah sucked in a breath of recognition as she looked back at the two tall men. Someone with another pair of those green eyes was standing right next to her. The young man—*could that be Cassius's brother?*—was talking, holding a data pad in his hand, while his father was standing next to him, staring down the buyers with an air of importance. Unlike she'd expected, he was well dressed in a purple shirt with shiny silver buttons.

Lenah touched Cassius on the arm, trying to pull him away.

He had gone completely still; the only thing moving was a vein pulsing at his temple. His arm, though not the cyborg one, felt hard as steel under her hand. He looked like he was about to rip open the door and attack his father and brother. *But hadn't he run away from them? Had something happened before that?* He had mentioned a mission.

She put her arm around his waist to remind him that she was here, that he had friends now, and that they were on an important quest. Lenah turned her gaze back into the room. Her hand touched his enhancement, and she shivered looking back at Cassius's brother.

Cassius had told her that his father was responsible for his enhancements, wanting a loyal bodyguard and had made Cassius undergo the surgeries when he was barely an adult. Seeing his brother now, not a cyborg, but instead working as his father's business aid, put a splinter in her heart.

"Cassius," she whispered as she tugged at him again. His mouth worked, and his eyes still bore into the room, but, finally, he looked down at her. He shook his head, taking a deep breath.

"What's the matter?" Persia whispered, coming back toward them and taking a peek through the hatch window for herself. "Those assholes. Smuggling tusker ivory." She shook her head.

Lenah ignored her and tried to pull at Cassius. Her arm was still wrapped around his waist, and this time, he let her guide him away from the hatch.

"No way! That guy looks just like you, but without the cyborgyness," Persia hissed from behind, recognition widening her eyes.

Cassius stopped dead in his tracks, and Lenah firmly gripped him, turning her head to give Persia a warning glare. Persia blushed and came over to them without a further word.

"Time to go," she muttered as she reached Cassius's other side and tugged at his arm.

He looked at both of them and seemed to come to some inner conclusion as he nodded to himself, took a deep breath and started to walk away on his own accord. He walked briskly ahead of them, barely stopping to check the next few hatches and making it very obvious that he didn't want to talk about what had happened. Lenah, still seeing the pain and anger emanating from his tense shoulders, felt like catching up and giving him at least some moral support, but now was not the time. Nor did he seem to want it.

They reached another hatch and could hear loud voices discussing the price of the goods. "Thirty thousand and not a single CGC more," someone said in a thick accent that Lenah couldn't identify despite knowing she'd heard it before.

Cassius was already peering through the window of the hatch. A moment later, he turned around, giving a thumbs-up.

Had they found explosives? Lenah crept closer to take a look for herself. Instantly, she realized why she'd found the strange accent familiar. Two Craff stood in the room, both clad in thick parkas that covered everything but their clawed fingers and reptilian faces. Both had their claws painted in iridescent rainbow colors. Were they female? The parkas were neutral, and Lenah couldn't determine. The last time she'd seen one had been on Lunara Station. The Craff had been in his office, a boiling sauna, probably reminding him of his volcanic home planet. But out here, on a human-dominated station, these Craff had to adjust to the temperatures made to please the other species.

The buyers discussing with the Craff were a trio of humans, each of them wearing a glistening, black combat suit. The carbon-nano material tightly encased their bodies, but they would be immune to almost anything, including laser beams as long as they weren't shot in their exposed faces.

Finally, Lenah looked at the merchandise. The lid of one crate was lifted, revealing small round spheres, mostly silver, with red stripes on them.

"Are these explosives?" Lenah whispered to Cassius, unsure what she was looking at.

He nodded. "These are perfect. The EJ 67s are very modern, lots of destruction in a small explosive, and they also have a timer."

He paused, looking down on her. "Are you ready?"

Lenah's heart started pounding. She wasn't. She'd managed this only twice and with the already familiar minds of her friends. She hadn't anticipated alien minds. What if her powers didn't work on the Craff? But she'd never find out if she didn't try, would she? She took a deep breath and nodded to Cassius and Persia.

Cassius stepped aside, giving her the best view of the room behind the hatch. Lenah took some time to start seeing the minds in front of her inner eye. At least, she had no issue making the Craff's minds visible. In fact, they didn't feel too different to her than human minds. Just as with Uz, a mind was a mind.

She looked at each one for a short while before sending out the first tentative thoughts. The group, who was still discussing prices, stopped talking. Lenah pushed more, worried that someone would realize how unrealistic it was that they had gone from fighting over prices to being overbid by another party. She sent a memory of Cassius and Persia walking through the front door on the other side of the room and offering the double price.

To the Craff, she enforced that image with a feeling of smugness and triumph.

To the humans, she added defeat and the hope that they'd be able to make their deal in one of the other trading bays. One of the humans whirled around, looking straight at them through the window, and Lenah wavered, struggling to hold her image. Next to her, Cassius and Persia lifted their weapons, and Lenah had to force herself not to drop her influence and do the same. She concentrated on the man, pushing harder. A few moments later, he turned around, his shoulders slumped in disappointment.

Lenah nodded to Cassius and Persia. At the same time, she pushed the memory of agreeing to the immediate delivery of the goods into the room. Cassius moved first, protecting Persia behind his body.

None of the Craff or humans acted surprised when Cassius and Persia entered into plain sight. Lenah breathed out in relief, but it was not time to relax yet.

Cassius picked up a crate of the silver and red balls and turned with it. Persia followed suit, lifting her own crate and turning to come back. Lenah saw one of the Craff wrinkle her forehead in doubt, then clench her fist with the painted claws. She concentrated on that one and sent her a feeling of triumph. She'd made a great deal today. At first, the Craff didn't seem susceptible to this idea. She took a step toward Cassius, who was returning for a second box. Cassius froze but didn't reach for his weapon, which Lenah appreciated. If the Craff saw Cassius act in open hostility, Lenah's suggestions would have to be even stronger, and she was already maxing out her ability.

Lenah poured more of the suggestion in the Craff's direction. The merchant stepped back, looking relaxed. Cassius inched forward and grabbed the second box, then quickly transported it out of the room and into the corridor.

"That's all we need," he told Lenah in a low voice.

She gave one nod but otherwise didn't acknowledge. Cassius stacked his two crates and gathered them into his arms, and Lenah assumed Persia was doing the same, but she didn't turn around to look. Instead, Lenah stayed where she was and focused on keeping both the Craff and the humans happy.

She heard Cassius's and Persia's footsteps walking away behind her. Triumph threatened to interrupt her grasp of the minds she was controlling, but she was able to snap back into it. Somehow, and to her surprise, she found it easier with these minds that were unknown to her. Maybe, because she had fewer moral regrets about controlling them? Or were they just easy minds compared to her crew?

Lenah gave Cassius and Persia about a minute head start before starting to move after them. She crept away backward while trying to keep connected to the images for as long as possible until she felt them slipping away. She stopped and changed the image.

The Craff got a memory of the humans stealing the boxes of explosives right in front of their eyes. The humans, on the other hand, received the image of paying and being denied their merchandise.

Instantly, Lenah heard yells inside the room. Someone—a Craff—roared. Then, what sounded like a body crashing into the metal wall of the bay. That was her sign.

Mission accomplished, Lenah turned around and broke out into a full run. Hopefully, she'd given her group enough time to make it back to the ship. As she ran, sounds of clanking reverberated in the corridor, behind the first door they'd passed. She jerked up her tranquilizer gun but hardly slowed as the hatch automatically opened in front of her.

20 THE DRONES

AS LENAH STEPPED through the open hatch, a fight came into view. But it wasn't the station guards as she'd been anticipating. Instead, several transport drones were shooting at Persia and Cassius, and Lenah had to dodge to the side to avoid being hit by a streaking laser.

Stars, hadn't Cassius said laser weapons were forbidden because of the danger of hull breaches? But maybe that didn't apply to the drones. Judging by the crates of ivory lying about, Cassius's father had made a deal. Lenah puffed out a breath that came out as an icy cloud in front of her. *By the stars*, this was making a lot of noise. She really hoped that Cassius's father had already left the trading bay.

Assessing the situation, she tucked away her tranquilizer gun. It would be of no use against drones. Nor would her mind powers. She got out her knife and crept closer to the fight.

There was a total of four drones, each a towering two-meter figure, roughly imitating the shape of a humanoid body.

Cassius was lifting one and actually managed to throw it at another drone nearby. They landed inert on top of each other in a heap of wheels and load-bearing arms. At the very least, they were programmed to not damage each other. It definitely looked like they were programmed to shoot at intruders.

Cassius used the short respite to jump after them and violently pull the square head off one machine. Another drone that was standing in the corridor rolled after him.

Lenah caught a look at Persia trying to crawl over to the final drone as it turned to shoot at her. Making a quick decision, Lenah sprinted after Persia, swinging her knife. It connected to the metal hull of the drone, and the impact reverberated through her whole arm, but apart from that, Lenah hadn't done any damage. The drone stopped shooting at Persia and instead turned toward Lenah. She danced around, trying to evade its laser mounted from an attachment on the block-like head.

A loud alarm started beeping in the corridor, and an equanimous computer voice announced, "A hull breach has been detected".

Lenah ducked and flanked the drone, which was slow to turn around on its four wheels.

Cassius showed up in her periphery, employing the same strategy as he had before. He crashed into the drone from behind and started violently pulling at its head. Lenah could see his muscles straining and thought his enhanced arm might have even squeaked. Though she had probably imagined that. Or maybe the squeaking had come from the drone as, with a sudden release, its head came free, cables flying all over.

Silence fell in the corridor around them.

Cassius turned, breathing heavily—and froze, focused on the corridor behind Lenah. Slowly, she spun.

Cassius's father stood there, together with his guard. The brother was nowhere in sight.

"And this is how one encounters a freed guard dog. I thought I'd heard a commotion." His father sneered. "Didn't you want to turn over new leaf with your granddaddy? So high and mighty. Now look at you. Stealing from smugglers." A wide, showy grin splattered all over his hateful face.

Next to her, Cassius had gone utterly still.

"Shut up, you have no power over him," Lenah hissed.

Cassius's father seemed to see her for the first time. "Found yourself a woman, heh? And a rich one at that," he said, taking Lenah in, from head to toe. "Girl, you better run as far away as you can. My son ain't no good."

"I should have killed you," Cassius growled more than spoke. He paused after every word as if having difficulty keeping his calm.

"You couldn't have," his father answered. "You're too good for that. But you should have helped your grandfather."

"You heard news?" Cassius asked.

His father rubbed his chin. "Nothing at all, actually." Then he gave a quick nod to his guard who had moved to inspect their crates. "I'll want to be paid for the damage done to my fine ivory. And the surgeries. Then you may consider yourself free."

"Let's go," Cassius said between clenched teeth and thinned lips. With his cyborg speed, he pulled up his gun, shooting a tranquilizer dart into his father. Before the guard could get up from where he was inspecting the explosives, Cassius had shot him as well. Both went to the ground, unconscious.

Without a further word, Cassius walked to pick up the crates. Persia, who had been staring open-mouthed at the exchange, caught herself and lifted the other one, leaving Lenah to carry their shopping bag.

They trotted as fast as possible, Persia sweating under her load, and Lenah looking around everywhere with her gun at the ready.

The corridor had gotten even colder and also drafty. Lenah assumed they were losing air through the hull breach they'd left behind. Luckily, gravity control was still working.

The alarm kept ringing, making it impossible to hear if someone was coming closer. They passed first the hatch to the market and then another one. According to Cassius, the next hatch should lead them right back into the parking ship.

Energy bolts fired as they passed through. Cassius dropped his crates and sprang forward, connecting his enhanced shoulder into a single drone that was carrying something packed in pink boxes. It toppled, releasing its load, and several boxes fell onto the floor, spilling plastic dolls.

Even toys were smuggled here? Right next to weapons? Lenah suppressed her surprise as she watched Cassius tumble to the floor with the drone, a single laser beam still shooting out.

"A hull breach has been detected," the same computer voice as before announced over the noise of alarms now blaring also in this section of the ship.

"Wonderful," Lenah muttered as Cassius got up from having dismantled the drone. "So much for leaving undetected."

"Let's get out of here. I hear footsteps," Cassius said, lifting his crates.

They picked up speed again when Cassius abruptly turned. "What's that beeping?"

"What beeping?" both Lenah and Persia asked at the same time. Over the ringing of the alarm, Lenah couldn't hear anything. Cassius, however, seemed alarmed enough to put down his boxes again. He cocked his head, listening hard. "Persia, drop your box. Right now!" he yelled, jumping toward a startled Persia who, after a momentary hesitation, let go of her box.

Lenah realized that a red light was blinking inside the crate and watched as Cassius fetched the small sphere and hurled it back down the corridor. Then, she went blind from an explosion of bright, white light. A wave of heat and power slammed into Lenah a moment later, and she was lifted through the air. She crashed onto the floor, landing hard on her back. Something sharp cut her skin painfully close to the spine. Pain shot through Lenah, disorienting her even more. She tried to move, but blackness threatened to engulf her sight, and the room spun. She only saw a pinprick of a tunnel in front. Someone groaned nearby. Belatedly, she realized that it had come from her.

Footsteps sounded from where her head was resting on the ground, and she could see Cassius's combat boots entering her limited field of vision.

"Lenah, how hurt are you?" He sounded genuinely alarmed, and combined with the shocked look in his eyes, she almost giggled thinking how terrible she must look. Certainly, not date material for a lake-side rendezvous with a few beers. She suppressed the giggle. Even her muddy brain realized this was not the time for such thoughts and that she might be in shock.

"I'm fine," she croaked, trying to sit up. Cassius helped by pulling her gently at the shoulders, and, this time, Lenah found that she could sit up without feeling dizzy.

"Persia?" she asked, looking around.

"Over there, I'll check on her." Cassius left and ran over to where Persia was trying to get up from the floor. She was bleeding from a wound at her temple and grimacing down to one of her legs.

Lenah winced, putting all her energy into getting up and trying to ignore the nauseating smell of acrid fumes.

A hatch opened a few dozen meters down the corridor.

"Over there," someone yelled in a nasal voice, and she realized it was Cassius's brother who was waving more people forward.

The sight of the newcomers—station personnel—gave Lenah the adrenaline needed to get up. Cassius was half pulling, half lifting Persia to her feet, and she took a few wobbly steps.

"Lenah, can you carry a box?" Cassius yelled, scooping up his boxes again. She nodded, bending down to where Persia had dropped hers.

"No more ticking time bombs?" she asked Cassius as she tried to lift it. It was heavy, and her back protested violently at the exercise. Something had cut her there deeply and she could feel it wedge its way further inside.

"No. Just run." Cassius heaved, making his way to a hatch a few meters away. If he had seen his brother, he chose to ignore it.

Behind them, footsteps thundered closer. Cassius led them through the hatch, and Lenah saw that they had reached the parking lot. The explosion had happened in the small space between two ships.

She ran behind Cassius, rounding other ships and trusting him to find his way. All she could do was carry her box and concentrate on running as fast as possible.

The *Star Rambler* came into view. It gave Lenah the strength to break into one last sprint. Just as they were reaching the cargo hatch, her stomach was lurched out of balance, and she went flying. Sounds of crashing accompanied the movement, and the station alarm beeped more frantically.

"Loss of atmosphere detected. Ship will detach in one minute," the computer voice announced. Shouts sounded from behind, but Lenah didn't think it was about them.

She could make out yelling voices of "Get to the ships!" or "Get the ships out!" Had she understood that right, they were going to detach the parking ship from the rest of the station? These people were worried about getting their ships out in time. She looked around, seeing everything lopsided. The gravity and spin control systems were giving out. All of a sudden, Lenah was facing up a steep incline to reach the *Rambler*.

Cassius appeared in front of her, taking the box she was still cradling and the bag she had slung over her shoulder. "Take my arm," he yelled over the noise around them.

Lenah did so, and together they made their way through the open hatch of the *Star Rambler*. Uz and Doctor Lund loomed there, rifles drawn. But when Uz saw Lenah, she dropped the gun and came to her aid, supporting her on the other arm.

Did she look that terrible?

"Where's Persia?" Lenah asked.

"Already inside," Cassius said.

"Lund, get your bandages out," Uz yelled as the hatch closed, and they were left in the relative silence of their own ship. Everything jerked again, and their path suddenly faced downward.

"What happened? Did you cause this?" Uz asked as she steadied Lenah against the movement of the ship.

"Indirectly. Ran into Cassius's old colleagues, and they activated one of the explosives," Lenah said and heaved a deep breath. At least that was what she thought Cassius's father's guard had been doing at their crate.

"They're flying ships out around us," Lorka's voice traveled from down the corridor. "The station's hatch is already open."

"Good." Lenah panted. "Help me to the cockpit."

"You're injured," Cassius said, looking down at her.

"I don't think anyone else can fly the ship. It'll have to be me. Just until we're in a warp bubble."

Cassius hesitated, and Lenah wondered again how bad she looked. She didn't feel that bad.

"Cockpit." Cassius finally agreed and nodded. He put down the box he was still carrying and swept Lenah up in his arms. He was careful not to touch the wound on her back, and his embrace was soft as he broke into a jog. Lenah, too stunned to complain and glad for his help at the same time, leaned her head against his shoulder. *He did smell nice.*

They quickly reached the cockpit, and he gently put her down in her chair. Lenah reached for the controls while trying to find her bearings.

Looking through the front window, she realized that chaos had broken out all around them. Everywhere, ships were trying to get out of the cramped parking ship and into the safety of open space. But the way the parking was organized created bottlenecks all over. One of those bottlenecks was the *Star Rambler* that was still parked in the last row blocking the exit. She gripped the manual control, hoping that their position would mean they'd be easily let into the queue of departing ships.

To her relief, that turned out to be true. As soon as she turned on her lights, the ship behind realized the convenience and gave her room to navigate. She lifted the *Rambler* and was momentarily dizzied as the parking bay around them started to spin.

"They're out of control," Cassius commented, his voice tense, and Lenah wondered if he felt bad for leaving such havoc behind. She certainly did, cringing as she thought of the children she'd seen earlier in the market. They might be the kids of smugglers, but they were just kids. Hopefully, the rest of the station was faring better than the parking ship.

Lenah adjusted the *Rambler* to avoid crashing into any of the other shuttles and carefully made her way out through the open hatch.

No one seemed to have identified their ship as the culprit for the chaos. Or they just weren't shooting until they were outside. Unlike the transport drones that had clearly been under a command to shoot at people in the corridor—even though shooting was forbidden on the ships for good reason—humans would be able to make a more informed decision. Lenah held her breath as they flew through the hatch and made their way into space behind a bunch of other ships. She tried to trail a bigger shuttle as close as possible in order not to present a viable target. To her relief, more ships started to accelerate out of the hatch right after them, and they were not the last in line any longer.

"You didn't remember to have the stone ready? Or can Lorka put us in a bubble?" she asked.

"The stone is ready," came Uz's voice from the corridor.

Lenah looked on her screens for the fastest path away from all the ships. They couldn't start a warp bubble flying so close-by. Luckily, in space even dozens of ships would quickly spread out.

She programmed in the coordinates to Astur, relieved as the colorful swirls of the warp bubble swallowed them.

Her back was screaming in pain, and with the help of Cassius, she made it to the common room where Doctor Lund had already freed the table to make into his makeshift infirmary. *If they kept going at this rate, they'd have to make a dedicated infirmary room*, Lenah thought as Cassius lowered her on the table.

21 BICEPS

LENAH WAS LYING in her room, playing the only flight simulator game that her cheap wristpiece had available. The ships weren't even real models or imitations of such. More like cartoonish illustrations. But at least it was something she could do while in bed.

Healing was costing her the little patience she had. There was nothing to do, no exercising until the quick-heal bandage on her back had finished its job. Doctor Lund had ordered Lenah to stay in bed for two days and promised that she'd feel better and be healed by that time.

That had better be true. Otherwise, the sacrifice wasn't worth it. Lenah grunted as she maneuvered her in-game ship through a maze of buildings. Ruins, she thought. It looked just like Asturis I might look if the Cava Dara got to it. *Pathetic*, Lenah shook her head, swiping away the screen of her game. The holodisplay vanished.

Everything these days reminded her of what was coming. She closed her eyes, and in front of her inner eye saw the video from the Syrr temple on Masis III. In her version, however, instead of the Cava Dara swooping down on the Syrr, she was seeing Syrr killing humans.

Was there even time enough to avoid that? Was it really true that no other corporate army was preparing except Cheung Corp? Lenah couldn't be sure, but it would certainly fit into her impression of the ambassadors on UPL station.

And there was something else nagging at her. The thing Lenah least wanted to admit. She was afraid to see her father again. He spent a lot of time in his office, and that's where he also had the access card to the mage farm. If Lenah did run into him, what would she say? *'Hi dad, I'm just popping by to blow up our company's greatest asset. Never mind me, but can you give me the access card?'* didn't seem to cut it. He had promised that he'd explain himself the last time they'd talked. Had he meant that? Did she still believe her father was just a man who'd gotten himself into trouble with the wrong people?

"Some trouble," she said under her breath before pulling up the flying game again. But instantly, the images reminded her of the Cava Dara, and she ended the simulation. It was no good. If her father had known, even suspected a little bit about what was coming, he should have gone and talked to UPL. Or some of the powerful corporate armies. Or even the Cassidians. Anything but having his daughter pursued and shot at by his criminal associates. All because of under-the-table business deals? What had Corinna said on Masis III?

That she was only doing this to have the matter placed in capable hands. Lenah snorted, throwing her wristpiece down on the blanket and stretching out on the bed.

"Capable hands. Nonsense."

"I see you're already entertained," a voice next to her said. Lenah turned to see Persia in the hatch, carrying a steaming cup of tea. Of foul-smelling, Cassidian marches tea. Lenah sniffed and sat up resigned to accept the cup.

"Sorry, I'm just…"

"Cranky, miserable, and weird?" Persia offered when Lenah didn't finish the sentence.

"Maybe a bit cranky. But weird? I'm not the one carrying a hammer around everywhere."

"That would be weird for you, but it's not weird if you're a professional gladiator."

"Are you saying that weird is only what's not normal to a specific person?"

"Pretty much," Persia said and grinned. "Uz likes this disgusting tea. That's normal because she's Cassidian, and she grew up with it. Now, why you like it, I don't know. That is weird."

"You should try it, too," Lenah said, steeling herself for the first sip. "It's really reviving."

"So they say," Persia said, looking at the wall to get her nose away from Lenah's beverage.

The hatch opened once more to show Uz carrying another cup of tea. "Hey, Persia, you forgot your own cup," she said as she held it out. Persia gave Lenah a desperate look.

"You really should have it," Lenah said, trying to hide a grin.

Hesitantly, Persia accepted the cup from Uz, but she couldn't hide the frown on her face.

"Thanks, Uz," Lenah said in her stead.

The Cassidian smiled and turned to leave when Lenah interrupted her departure. "Hey, do you know about any purple wood from Cassidia?"

Uz's shoulders squared, and she turned around with a sudden movement. "Why would you ask that?" Each word was forced out with a sharp tone.

Lenah was taken aback by her reaction. "They were selling it at Neeth Station. I thought it looked really beautiful. Uz...?" Lenah trailed off as the Cassidian gasped, then clutched her heart.

Persia put her cup on Lenah's desk with a determined clunk and went to check on Uz. But before she could close the distance, Uz shook her head. "I'm fine," she said in a croaked whisper.

"What is it with that wood?" Lenah asked.

Uz clutched her chest again.

"Uz?" Lenah inquired. She was starting to worry. She made to get up from the bed but stopped as Uz started talking.

"That must have been Cascra wood." Uz shook her head more vehemently. "I can't believe humans are smuggling that."

"Why? What is so special about that tree?" Lenah asked, intrigued and confused at the same time.

Uz looked at her. "On Cassidia, we consider these trees sacred and in no way would we ever destroy one. Or transport any part of it off-world. You could say they hold the secret to Cassidian magic. They grow extremely slow. Even the small branches will be centuries old."

"What do you mean they hold the secret to your magic?" Persia asked the question that had also been on Lenah's mind.

"I…They have something to do with our vertex," Uz said slowly.

"With the vertex?" Lenah echoed. "How?"

Uz shook her head. "I already said too much. Any human—any alien—caught with Cascra wood is considered to have committed high treason and would receive grave punishment. The High Priest might even declare war over such a matter."

"War? Over a few logs?" Lenah asked.

Uz nodded. "It's not just a few logs. It's so much more than that." She turned around and opened the hatch. "I'm sorry. You better forget I ever said anything. Even knowing this is dangerous." The hatch closed behind her, leaving Lenah and Persia to stare at each other.

"That was unexpected," Persia finally spoke.

Lenah cleared her throat. "I can't say I expected a reaction like that. I just thought that the wood was really pretty."

Persia nodded and picked up her teacup once more, but instead of drinking, she just swirled the liquid around.

"You should really have it. I promise the experience is better than the smell," Lenah told her, swallowing from her own cup. She watched Persia slowly taking a sip, her face morphing from disgust to surprise.

"Ooh."

"Good, right?"

Persia nodded.

"How are you feeling?" Lenah asked as she watched her empty the whole drink. Persia had been even closer to the explosion than Lenah. It was almost a miracle that nothing worse had happened to her. She'd fallen hard and twisted her leg, but nothing that couldn't be fixed by a day in bed with a quick-heal bandage. Lenah had been less fortunate. Her injuries—a big piece of shrapnel had wedged its way several centimeters into her lower back—were taking two days in bed to heal.

"Still sore, but I'm feeling fine." Persia looked down on her leg. "It could have ended differently."

"It could have." Lenah agreed. "Thank the blazing stars for a cyborg with hearing implants."

"Yeah. He's been very useful," Persia said after a short pause.

Lenah lifted an eyebrow. "If that was your attempt at a compliment, are you sure your ex left you because of your age?"

"I'm neither old nor bad at compliments. But the cyborg did kidnap us. You seem to have forgotten that when you started to admire his muscled bicep."

"His bicep?"

"Yep, the fleshy one. Of which he has only one. I've seen you ogle it. Several times."

"Er." Was that true? Was she ogling over Cassius? Maybe she had *looked* a few times. She had also come to appreciate him for the honest person he was. But ogling?

"I haven't forgotten that he kidnapped us," Lenah said. "But I've also forgiven him for it. He's a good guy and a friend."

"I hope so. We keep accumulating weird people. And things." Persia rolled her eyes.

"If you mean Lorka and Zyrakath, I agree. Is Uz still trying to get a full retelling of the events on Masis III out of Zyrakath?"

"Yup, when I last checked, he was still barely talking to her."

Lenah smiled. She could only imagine how those two were making each other unhappy. No wonder Uz was providing them with tea instead of spending time on her project.

"Lorka has joined up with her to help out," Persia said.

"Well, at least Zyr likes him."

"Zyr?"

"Yep, I've decided to give him a nickname. I'm sure he'll love it."

22 FIGHT TRAINING

CASSIUS SLAMMED INTO Lenah before she could gather her concentration, and she tumbled onto the floor of the cargo hold, now affectionately called their training arena. Since they were not hauling any cargo, they should probably rename it formally.

He doesn't treat me like a girl, Lenah gratefully thought as she jumped up in one smooth motion. He had also shown her how to fall well. A lesson she had mastered, thanks to ample practice. Her back was healed, and she was active again.

As soon as Lenah got up, Cassius came at her once more. She danced out of his way at the last moment, constantly staying in motion with her feet and moving from one side to the other. He came storming after her, and she had to avoid becoming trapped against the wall by shoving a quick image toward his mind of her slipping by on his right side. She didn't have enough time to plant a complex suggestion while trying to evade and dodge, but something reached Cassius as he shifted his course over to the right. He corrected again after one step, but that step was enough for Lenah to slip by on his left side and free herself from becoming pinned. Cassius caught on quickly, reaching her with a few nimble steps.

Lenah couldn't duck out of the way; instead, she launched a fast kick toward his shin, and, at the same time, she tried to implant an image of momentum. Before her idea could stretch out sufficiently, her butt connected with the metal floor. Her suggestion evaporated, having never reached him.

Cassius stepped back, giving Lenah the chance to find her footing. This time when he came at Lenah, she was better prepared and more determined. She found his mind early on, a cloud she had become very familiar with, and sent him the image of slippery ice instead of the metal plating that they were standing on. Cassius waved both arms, trying to make up for the perceived imbalance. Lenah added the sensation of falling and his stomach lurching. With a crash of metal against metal, he went sideways and fell onto the floor. Lenah stepped up, grabbed his neck, and imitated applying one of the grips he'd shown her. The one that would make an opponent instantly unconscious.

Cassius grunted, lifting his arms in defeat. "Tomorrow, we train without your mind magic," he finally said, getting up from the ground.

"Why?" Lenah asked, her breathing heavy.

"Because you need to know what to do even if those abilities of yours aren't working."

Lenah grumbled but didn't object. In the last few weeks, she'd already temporarily lost her abilities twice. She still had no idea what had been going on that second time on UPL station. "Fine, but less hauling me to the ground."

Cassius grinned down at her. "And less stumbling over my own feet for me." He bumped her shoulder with a friendly gesture.

"That was pretty awesome on my end," Lenah said, grinning back at him. "Not only does it keep your attacker off their feet, but it also distracts any companions while they try to figure out what happened or if there is something slippery on the floor that will make them fall as well."

"You should have inserted the image of a pile of banana peels."

"Good idea! I'll keep it for next time."

"Can't wait," he moaned, grabbing a towel from a crate stacked against the cargo hold's sidewall and wiping his face. He bent to fetch a second towel and offer it to Lenah, who accepted and wiped her face. She was drenched compared to him, who was barely sweating. But at least he had broken a sweat. Now and then, she might stand a chance against him, but she'd been doing it less gracefully than he. And only thanks to her magic.

"Let's go for another round," she said, taking a sip of water from a bottle she had brought.

Cassius nodded and took her bottle, taking a sip for himself. They drank in comfortable silence for a minute before walking back into the center of the room.

Lenah took a position opposite Cassius. This time, she tried to reach him with a full-on kick, a technique he wanted her to become better at, anyway. She could manage fine from a standing position but couldn't wrap her head around the right timing when they were actually fighting. Cassius stalked up to her, fists raised. Lenah lifted her arms but in a defensive gesture, not to actually box with him. Even if he weren't a cyborg with an enhanced arm, she was no match for his skill.

She started to side-step him, a movement he copied, even though she knew that he was holding back. They continued like that, with Lenah waiting for her opening. The movements were almost like a dance, and she felt good in those moments. No time to ponder her fears of confronting her father. *Or Cassius's bicep*, she thought, looking at the very object. *Damn Persia for having pointed it out*. Now Lenah *was* looking.

She must have looked a moment too long, because Cassius jumped forward, closing the distance between them before she could even step back. Frantically, Lenah targeted his mind with the first thing that came into her head. She pushed the image of her wearing nothing but a thin black negligee with a deep, plunging neckline and walking into his cabin toward him. Cassius's eyes popped wide, and he gasped as he came to a sudden halt in front of her.

Lenah, realizing what she was doing, pulled back from his mind as if she were burnt. What had she been thinking? Why was that the first thing that came into her mind? Blazing Persia and her talk about biceps. Cassius looked at Lenah, his green eyes locking onto hers.

Was he mad? Or disgusted? He had never overtly shown any interest in her, apart from a few touches that might also have been in friendship. Nor had she. Though she had admittedly been thinking about him—just a little bit—and maybe wishing that he would think about her too.

They stood in front of each other for several seconds, staring into each other's eyes, until Cassius's arms reached for her, his real hand finally closing in around Lenah hair on the back of her head. Awareness tingled in Lenah, and she knew that she wanted to kiss him. She nudged closer, lifting her face and met his lips.

His kiss was not tender; he was kissing her hard, his tongue asking permission to explore her mouth almost immediately. Lenah let him take charge, then, a while later, she asked for the same privilege. Triumph roared through her. Maybe he *had* been thinking of her. Her arms came around his neck in a possessive gesture.

His hair was softer than it looked, which surprised Lenah, especially belonging to a man where everything else seemed to be either metal or muscle. She didn't know how long they kissed, but finally—reluctantly—Lenah let Cassius's lips part from hers. He didn't step away, and she didn't let go of him either, holding his gaze, unsure what to say in words, but hoping that she could say it by keeping her arms locked around his neck. He stepped even closer, both his arms coming around her, and engulfed her in a hug.

A very nice hug, Lenah decided, throwing away all worry about being with a cyborg or an ex-smuggler. He was a man. A nice looking one at that, and she felt safe in his embrace.

"I would ask you out for dinner, which I'm sure you're used to, but I fear I don't have anything to offer other than instant urash and rice meals."

"Is there no beer left?" she asked softly against his chest.

"I don't think so. I didn't buy enough to last us several occasions."

"Hah, so you do admit that it was you who put it on the shopping list. I knew it."

He chuckled, then looked her in the face. "I was afraid you'd figure it out sooner or later."

"That you cheat with your shopping list?"

"That I was interested in having a beer with you."

"And that's a bad thing?"

"Not necessarily," he said, lifting his hands in a diplomatic gesture. "I'd call it a risky move."

"Huh."

"Hmm…" Cassius said, struggling with his words. "That image that you sent me, do you actually…" He cleared his throat, looking almost shy.

Lenah cut him off immediately. "Well, it did distract you from hitting me."

"It looked…" he cleared his throat again, "very good. Do you really own it?"

"I do," Lenah admitted, feeling smug. "Though I don't have it with me."

"Too bad. I wouldn't mind seeing it sometime." Cassius flashed a boyish grin.

Lenah's cheeks flushed, but she grinned back at him, avoiding his eyes, not feeling the weight of the worlds for the first time in a while.

23 WHO'S CASSIUS?

LENAH AND CASSIUS WERE alone in the common room where Lenah was heating instant meals for them both. She was getting that date after all, she thought to herself, trying not to outright grin at Cassius who was sitting at the table, wiping his implanted arm with a blue cloth. Not the most romantic, but it was also going to be their last meal before reaching Astur and her home—her former home.

The heating unit beeped, and Lenah pulled out the two meals, setting one in front of Cassius and the other one opposite him.

Their eyes locked briefly, before he nodded his thanks and put the cloth aside.

"Are you glad you have them?" Lenah asked as they both started to eat. He didn't pretend not to know what she was asking about.

"Yes, and no."

"They do make you strong, and you hardly have to worry about anyone."

He looked at her, curious. "I'm not sure if that's true. Sure, I'll be able to best almost anyone in a fight. Not just best them, I could easily do much more than that. But that's also all that people ever see…" he trailed off, staring down at his arm.

Lenah put her spoon down, feeling guilty. A cyborg was all she had seen in him a few weeks ago. Though that had also been because he happened to kidnap her and the others and not given his name.

"I see more than a cyborg," she whispered, looking away from his implants and into his green eyes. Did he know that she had fallen under exactly the prejudice he'd described for probably more than half of their relationship? Was he going to think less of her now?

"So, it seems," he grinned, and it was obvious that he was again thinking back to the image of her sparsely dressed figure entering his cabin.

"Dating has been tough. Usually, women are not interested in a cyborg." Cassius continued more somberly. "It's been a thing in the past."

"A thing?"

Cassius squared his jaw. He seemed very serious about it, so Lenah decided to be too. Besides, she could identify with the other women. She didn't think anyone liked snuggling up to metal bits. She didn't particularly like them either, but the rest of him more than made up for it. There was even some beauty in how the strings of almost black c-nano fibers connected to his skin at the shoulder. It made for quite a contrast to his much brighter skin, almost like an intricate tattoo.

She reached out toward his metal arm that was still sitting on the table and grasped his hand. She had seen him do almost everything with that hand, be it mundane tasks like lifting a cup of tea to ripping things apart in a display of superhuman strength. Now she decided that she would not be scared of its power and how it could crush her. There was a big difference between could and would.

At her gesture, Cassius's face brightened, and his eyes flickered to her face. His gaze dropped onto her lips.

"They're here!" Uz's urgent voice burst through the ship-wide speakers.

Lenah jumped up, dread filling her, even though she wasn't sure who Uz meant. UPL? Corinna? The Cava Dara? Had they already left the warp bubble? Had she been so distracted by Cassius that she hadn't even noticed? That was the only way Uz would know.

Lenah ran the short distance to the cockpit in only a few seconds with Cassius right on her heels. Behind, Persia was coming out of her cabin.

"What did she see?" she asked, sprinting up the corridor.

"Not sure," Lenah answered before reaching the cockpit's hatch and pulling it open. Uz was sitting on the floor, a few panels from the cockpit's wall lying on the pilot's chair and Zyrakath hovering over it all, wearing his usual look of disagreement. Low voices were talking rapidly over a speaker, but almost too low for Lenah to understand.

"Who's coming, Uz?" Lenah asked as she squeezed into the tight interior and came to a sudden halt because there was nowhere to go.

Uz looked at her, wide-eyed. "The Cava Dara; they've been sighted."

"Most of their numbers will be Muha Dara," Zyrakath said with an impatient voice.

Lenah ignored him. "Where?" she asked Uz.

"I've managed to dial into the frequency and pass the security clearance of the Cheung army comm system. They're stationed in orbit around Astur, waiting for the arrival of thousands of small flying objects. They are only six hours away from the planet."

"Objects?"

"That's what they were saying. They've never actually seen the Cava Dara. Or Muha Dara," Uz said, throwing a look at Zyrakath.

"And they will be here in six hours?" Persia asked from behind.

"Stars, will we even have time to execute or plan?" Lenah's stomach plummeted; the urash rice she'd eaten threatening to come up.

They might be too late.

"We've left the warp bubble and are a couple of hours out. We're actually *behind* the Cheung fleet in orbit. Closer to the planet," Uz said, pointing at the scanner.

"At least that's one good thing," Lenah commented. They couldn't deal with Corinna's army and the mage farm at the same time.

"If they want us, they'll have to catch us first." She slid in next to the pilot's seat, skimming her eyes over the proximity scanner. There were a few ships on the radar toward the planet, but it was very little traffic for a populous planet like Astur. Probably, everyone who could, was hunkering down at home to wait out the coming battle. Behind them, large dots on the radar represented dozens of warships guarding the planet.

"We came out quite far from Asturis I. A little under two hours from the Crescent Hills. And then we'll need to hike there," Lenah said, thinking out loud.

"You still think your father wouldn't understand?" Uz asked.

"Oh, I'm sure of it," Lenah answered. "He won't give up his most profitable business for an event that hasn't even started. It would never be his fault even until the very last moment. When it's too late."

Uz didn't acknowledge, instead she cranked up the volume of the comm transmission.

"...High Commander will arrive. Unit 12 and Unit 13, accompany the High Commander down to the planet."

"Unit 13, acknowledged."

"Unit 12, acknowledged."

Lenah concentrated her attention on the far scanners behind them. Two big dots were pulling out of the defensive position the fleet had taken around the planet and moving closer to Astur. A small dot had appeared there. A shuttle coming in via a warp bubble.

"The High Commander," Persia mused from the corridor. "Does that mean Corinna is here?"

Lenah nodded. "That's the CEO of a corporation with army status in a scenario of war."

"What's she up to? Do you think she knows about our plan?"

Lenah rubbed her chin. "It's possible she has very strong suspicions. But as High Commander, she's supposed to direct the attack. I'm not surprised she's here."

"That doesn't change anything for our plans," Cassius said grimly. "We still need to go and blow up that farm."

24　HOME, NOT SWEET

LENAH POWERED DOWN the *Rambler* after landing it next to a large Vicco tree on the land around Callo mansion. She'd liked this specific clearing as a child, mostly for its remoteness. It had been her favorite place after her mother's death, and the afternoons spent here were some of the few memories she still had of the time. Lenah didn't recall much of the days before and following her mother's sudden passing. She didn't even remember the last time she'd seen her. She'd been young, only seven years old, and the guilt of simply forgetting never fully went away. Coming here automatically triggered that feeling.

Lenah pushed the sad thoughts away as she got up and made her way through the *Rambler*, running her fingers along the walls of her ship as she walked to the cargo hold. *Her ship. Her new home.*

"There you are. That's your pack. Hope it's not too heavy for your highness," Cassius said as Lenah reached the cargo hold. He had distributed the load of the explosives between them, though he himself carried a huge backpack that stuck out tall over his head.

"I'm no richer than any of you," Lenah grumbled but accepted the fairly light backpack he'd assigned to her. "That's your idea of redistributing? I thought we were making sure each of us had some explosives in case we lose someone's backpack."

"Everyone has some explosives. I'm also bringing a bunch of Uz's tools. In case we don't get the key card and have to break our way in. And lots of explosives," Cassius answered, patting the pack over his head.

"You better not get lost. I want those tools back," Uz said, walking into the room and accepting her own pack from Cassius. Doctor Lund came in behind her in what Lenah thought must be his best shirt. He was the only one here that had a change of clothes. The rest of them, like Lenah, were wearing the same thing day in and day out. In Lenah's case, that was still the UPL suit, now ripped in the back where the shards from the explosion had cut her. Lenah had to admit that she was looking forward to going to her rooms and wearing her own clothes again. And not just for the sake of having adequate attire to walk into the mage farm without looking severely misplaced.

"Are you sure we can't have tea and talk to your father, Lenah?" Doctor Lund asked, patting an invisible wrinkle out of his sleeve.

"Tea?"

"Doctor Lund wants to dine with the rich and famous," Uz said, patting the doctor on the arm.

"I see," Lenah said. She shook her head. "No, I don't think we could go and ask him. Not if we actually plan to accomplish our mission."

"Especially, in under four hours," Cassius added.

"Right, let's do it."

One after the other, they filed out of the open hatch and stepped into the late afternoon sunlight. Lenah took a deep breath and looked up to the blue sky.

Everything was so familiar: the Vicco trees provided partial shade, their large hand-shaped leaves having started to shed for the winter season. The ground was covered in brown leaves that crunched under Lenah's boots. She remembered spending time here, barefoot, jumping around in piles of leaves. As always, blue parrots cackled overhead, probably complaining they'd already eaten up the last of the Vicco berries, a white and juicy fruit that was their favorite. It smelled warm and dry, and of home. It was good to have earth under her feet again.

"Alright, the mansion is less than a thirty-minute hike that way," Lenah said, forcing herself back into reality. "I'm not expecting anyone in these woods, not until we're very close to the house."

"All this land belongs to your house? I saw it was a big house last time I was here but didn't realize you own half the planet around it too," Persia said, looking at the surrounding forest.

"Not *my* house really. But my family's. This has been the home of the Callos for over 300 years."

"That's crazy. The crappy container unit my mum was living in when she got me is probably already rusted to pieces. Though I really liked it. You'll have your first home forever," Persia said.

Lenah shook her head. "Let's see how today goes. I might never be able to come back." While she said it, despite thinking about it regularly over the past days, the words seemed more real now that they were spoken out loud. Her throat clogged up, and she fell silent.

Uz joined her at the front of the group, giving her a worried glance but didn't say anything. Lenah was glad for both: the company and the silence. She wasn't worried about losing her old life or her father's approval. She was worried if her friends would still see her the same once they realized where she came from. Lenah figured that actually *seeing* was different from *knowing*. Persia might have accepted it, but what about the others? Would Lenah turn into a faceless corporate class member to them? She knew that none of them had grown up with the luxuries Lenah had. And family members categorically had a bad rep with commoners. Something that she couldn't blame them for thinking.

Lenah shoved the thought away. It felt petty to worry about it when thousands of Muha Dara were approaching the planet. Her crew already knew, at least theoretically, and had forgiven her for not being open from the start. She couldn't avoid it, anyway. Cassius had stopped calling her 'rich girl' weeks ago. Now, he kissed her instead. With the exception of 'your highness' from earlier.

After a hike that Lenah remembered to be much longer, maybe because she'd still been a child when she used to make it, the house came into view. Their path would bring them close to a side entrance just a short distance from her room. She'd had great success sneaking in unnoticed all her life and hoped that today would be no exception.

"That whole house is yours?" Uz asked, staring at Lenah.

"Yes," Lenah answered, feeling again the same worry from before.

"Not even our High Priests have cones that big. I don't' think you could actually hang a cone this size from trees. Not even in the oldest section of the purple woods where the trees are really tall."

"Er, cones in trees?" Lenah looked at her with curiosity. "Like those things that fir trees have?"

"Of course not. Like the things we live in."

"That's what your houses are like? They hang?"

"Yes, I guess you wouldn't know." Uz looked away. "Never mind."

Lenah looked her up and down but didn't ask further. She'd never actually seen the houses Cassidians lived in on their home planet. The only video footage from Cassidia was taken outdoors in the public areas. She tucked her interest to the back of her mind.

"This house is amazing. The architecture flawlessly blends several Old Earth styles together but uses local materials,"

Doctor Lund's excited voice sounded from behind. "I see Renaissance as well as Gothic, and even Fifth War. But then a high use of the green schists from Astur. What do you know about the history of the house, Lenah?" He caught up to her, closely followed by Zyrakath.

"The building seems adequate to withstand eternity. If you don't have elders, who came up with this?" the drone asked, hovering high over Lenah's head.

"I don't know. I actually never thought too much about that," Lenah admitted. She'd always been too interested in space and flying to pay attention to the architecture of the house. "I know the Callos didn't build this house; they bought it from an older family that went bankrupt, supposedly because of the Callo's scheming."

"So typical for humans," Uz muttered.

"I agree with the Cassidian. Displaying such behavior is in any case—" Zyrakath started saying.

"—Anyway," Lenah interrupted, ignoring both him and Uz, though not disagreeing. "There's the door that leads right into my rooms, between those two windows with the red planters."

"You're sure there won't be anyone watching us?" Cassius asked, peeking through the last of the foliage and across the lawn surrounding the house.

"I've done this many times and never been caught."

"Mmh," Cassius said thoughtfully but didn't further object. He shifted his backpack. "I go first, in case we encounter any…obstacles."

Lenah let him pass, and together they made it across the soft grass. *So familiar.* This part of the lawn was where Lenah did remember her mother. Viola had loved to picnic here with her daughter. Preferably, without a blanket, sitting together on the grass. Her mother had loved to sing, and Lenah could still hear her rhythmic chanting in her memory. Hocus-pocus, her father had called it, and Viola had laughed. Sometimes, Timothy joined them for the picnics, though he'd always bring a blanket.

After a short while, they reached the back door, and Lenah ducked under a curtain of ivy where she kept a keychip hidden under a stone. It was still there.

"How much time do we have left?" she whispered to Cassius as she came back with the chip in hand.

"Three hours and twenty-three minutes," he replied.

Stars, the time had gone by fast. She nodded and swiped the key.

The corridor beyond was cool, much cooler than the outside. Thick stone walls would do that. Lenah walked in first, followed by Cassius who hesitated before giving up his post at their front.

There was no one here, as per usual. Lenah was the only one living in this specific part of the house, her father preferring the stuffier rooms in the northern wing. This wing, however, was converted to assistant quarters, dating from a time when the Head of a corporation had hosted their most senior staff and their families in their house. It was much simpler—the walls mostly white and undecorated—but there were apartments with several rooms meant for whole families, and Lenah had repurposed one for herself. She walked up the stairs and made a turn at the first door in the upstairs corridor.

Lenah's heart beat fast as she held her finger in front of the door reader. Her father hadn't revoked her access or changed anything already, had he? But with a little chime, the door swung open. She stepped through and ushered the others in, then closed the door.

It felt strange having them all stand there, in her rooms. A place where she'd spent most of her free time in the past decade. When Lenah had started earning money, she'd invested her first few salaries in decorating the apartment in accordance with her personal taste. Such as the desk chair that looked like a pilot's seat. She had balanced it out with some cozier elements. A fluffy gray couch and a dark wooden media table. That's where she'd played her flight simulations, sitting in the pilot's chair and using the media table's holoscreen.

Lenah turned toward her closet, and as she approached, the door slid open automatically. "Persia, Uz, feel free to grab stuff for yourselves to wear while I get dressed. I think almost everything in here should make you look less suspicious and more like a guest or an investor."

Persia shuffled in after Lenah, an eager look on her face, followed by Uz. The Cassidian cocked an eyebrow at Lenah, who had pulled up the holodisplay of her work outfits and was choosing one of the most comfortable ones: stretchy brown pants, a matching blazer, and a white blouse. And thick-heeled, brown boots.

"You're not one for following shoe conventions, are you?" Persia asked, peeking at the display.

Lenah shook her head. "I hate those thin heels. Can't walk in them all day."

Persia sighed. "I understand. I always loved that a gladiator could wear her sandals even for official events. No heels for me either."

"Do you have a pair of shoes for each of these outfits?" Uz asked, having turned to Lenah's selection of casual clothes. "Really, Lenah, that's just decadent," she said before Lenah could answer.

Lenah turned away. "That's what the designers always give you, what can I say?"

"Uz is just jealous." Persia smirked, stepping in to help Uz pack the casual clothes into her backpack. The Cassidian was almost two heads taller than Lenah, and Lenah's selection of big, comfy sweaters for relaxed winter evenings was the only thing Uz might fit into.

"It's going to be amazing to have clothes to change into and wash in between," Persia moaned as she pulled one of Lenah's blouses over her head.

Meanwhile, Lenah packed clothes for herself and went to put on her business outfit, then adjusted her brown hair in a strict top bun. When she was done, she stepped in front of the mirror, feeling strange and familiar at the same time. Today, at least for a little while, she'd be corporate Lenah again.

Maybe for the last time. When she was done, they made their way back outside.

Doctor Lund was wandering around, touching everything, while Cassius stiffly stood where he'd stopped when they first came in. Lorka sat lounging in Lenah's pilot's seat with Zyrakath hovering close-by. Cassius looked her up and down as she walked out but glanced away before meeting her gaze. *What was wrong?* He almost looked as if he were seeing her for the first time.

"That it, rich girl? If you're done giving us the grand tour, let's go blow up your corporation," he said when they had all assembled in the front room.

"All done," Lenah pressed out, trying not to sound hurt. Or angry. They'd all agreed to the plan, and looking less like thugs and more like they had business here would be solid help in reaching their destination. So why was he like that now? It was bad enough she'd potentially have to confront her father next. Lenah was not letting herself feel rejected by Cassius. She walked out in front of everyone without taking a further look. She might never see these things again.

Persia came after her and touched her shoulder lightly. Lenah walked on. If she let herself feel, she might cry. How would that look for a captain leading her team into a mission?

"He doesn't mean it," Persia whispered as they walked down the stairs and back onto the first floor. Lenah shrugged and forced a grin. "Sure, no worries."

The look Persia gave her made it obvious she didn't believe Lenah one bit, but she also seemed to realize that now was not the time. Instead, she turned her attention to the corridor in front of them.

25 CONFRONTATIONS

"RICH GIRL, STOP, someone is in the corridor ahead," Cassius whispered. "Footsteps are coming." He turned his head to listen for a few moments. Then he slipped by Lenah, his hand resting comfortably on the handle of his tranquilizer gun.

Persia fidgeted nervously next to Lenah.

"Wait," Lenah also whispered, touching Persia on the arm to keep her from getting out her weapon as well. What was Cassius doing? They'd decided together to make use of Lenah's familiarity. And hope her father hadn't shared with most people that his daughter had gone rogue. Lenah approached Cassius as she stretched out her senses.

Whoever was coming was still too far away for her to see their minds, so she looked up at Cassius and shook her head. His arm twitched, and he flexed and fisted his enhanced hand a few times before reluctantly falling back. Lenah got the impression that he was itching for a fight. She shook her head at his behavior. He'd chosen the worst moment. She needed to focus. They all needed to focus.

Lenah turned her attention back to the approaching group, hoping her father wasn't going to be part of it. She'd never been able to control his mind, and she wanted to run into him from a position of power, not sneaking through the house like a burglar. By now, she could make out approaching footsteps and faint voices. From the regular rhythm of the footsteps, she suspected it was part of the house guard.

They were not far from their destination—her father's offices, located close to the mansion's main entrance and the most guarded part of the house. The faint conversation grew closer, as the other turned into the corridor up ahead, and Lenah could now see the dim outline of several minds.

"There are four of them," she whispered to Cassius and Persia. Persia's posture stiffened as she nodded, while Cassius didn't acknowledge. He'd likely already known with his enhanced hearing.

Lenah resisted the urge to influence the approaching minds. The plan was not to disrupt regular house activity if possible. She steeled herself with what she hoped was a warm smile as figures appeared around the corner. All four stopped when they saw her.

"Lenah," the Head of Guards, Marcus, said as he took her in from head to toe.

"Hi, Marcus. It's good to see you again," she said with a smile, trying not to remember how he had collaborated with

Kahoot the last time Lenah had seen him. He might even suspect the truth; in fact, he probably did know some of it.

"Hi, Danilo," Lenah greeted the other guard she knew by name, then nodded to the remaining two.

Danilo nodded back, but his eyes widened as his gaze swept behind her to the rest of her group. Lenah wondered if it was about Uz, Cassius, or Zyrakath but didn't turn around to check.

"I didn't know you were back from your *vacation*," Marcus said, his eyes turning to slits.

"I just came back," Lenah answered, maybe a little too quickly. She couldn't believe he was calling it a vacation when he'd sent armed thugs after her. Her heart started to beat quickly, and she had to force herself to not lash out at him. Or tell Cassius to do so.

"Who are your friends?" Marcus finally asked.

"Oh, not friends. These are potential new investors. No one you should concern yourself with," Lenah managed to force out, trying for her best authoritative tone and lifting her chin high. She was the family member here; he was only the house guard. "No worries, I'll get them security clearance soon. They are not armed." She smiled sweetly, hoping that Cassius was hiding his cyborg arm as they had discussed. Danilo and the other two guards gave her a friendly smile and made to move on, so she figured he was doing a good impression of looking harmless.

"See you around, Marcus," Lenah said, then waved for her group.

"Oh no. Not so fast, little one." Marcus stared at her with cold eyes, so different from the man who'd taught her self-defense moves when she was a child.

Lenah stopped, bracing herself. This couldn't be good.

"Arrest them," Marcus said in a clipped tone.

There was some commotion behind Lenah, and she turned her head to see that Cassius and Persia were reacting faster than the guards and detaining them instead. Cassius's arm was slung around Danilo, who struggled without any chance in the metal hold. Cassius had one more guard similarly secured under his other arm. Persia held the tranquilizer gun to the third guard's temple. Out of the corner of her eye, Lenah saw Marcus move. Before she could jump away, she felt the cold metal of his gun at her neck.

Their eyes met, and she snarled at him, then reached out with her mind, injecting an image of him bleeding from a terrible wound in his leg. His arm with the gun trembled, and he went down with a groan, sitting on his butt to clutch his leg. Lenah kept pouring the thought at him, then kicked away his hand. This man had almost gotten her friend and her killed. She rammed her boot against his leg, then his belly. She had trusted him. She grinned as he yelped. "You asshole." Lenah kicked his belly again and he curled into a fetal position on the floor. "Are you aware that right now thousands of lives are in danger because you decided to band with criminals?" She kicked once more. "Instead of straightening out my father, you helped him, you —"

"Lenah. Stop," Cassius said, right next to her.

She ignored him. "—you probably helped him make the contacts. Did you know Kahoot before?" A thick leg blocked hers as she kicked at Marcus again. Then Cassius's arm shoved Lenah back, away from the man. Within seconds, Cassius touched him on the neck, and he lay unconscious.

Cassius turned to Lenah. "What's wrong with you? We have a mission here. Instead, you yell around the house like a spoiled brat." He was whispering, but his words cut sharply into the silence of the corridor. Lenah shook her head. She'd been right to accuse the guard. Marcus was the bad guy here. He probably thought he could get promoted if he helped her father. He deserved what she'd done to him.

"You. Need. To. Chill. Out," Cassius hissed.

Lenah looked down at Marcus, then up at Cassius. He was staring back intently, his eyes cold. Lenah shook her head, trying to calm down and control the raging anger she felt welling inside her. Cassius was right. No matter what Marcus deserved, she was here for something else. What had gotten into her?

"Stars." She breathed out. "I'm sorry." She looked away from Cassius, no longer able to bear his accusing face. What must he think of her now?

Persia stepped next to Marcus and gave him a good shove with the butt of her tranq gun. "That's for setting your smuggler dogs on our trail. He does deserve it," she said and nodded to Lenah. "But we have to move on."

Lenah took a deep breath, grateful to Persia for breaking the tension. "I could not have said that better." She managed a weak smile at her friend.

"We'd better hurry," Cassius said, finally stepping away from Lenah. "Where can we hide these bodies?"

"In here." Doctor Lund held open the door to a rarely used sitting room, and Lenah didn't object. Cassius bent down and made quick progress heaving all four bodies into the room. Somehow, all the other guards were slumped unconscious as well. Lenah suspected this was Cassius's doing and cringed at the thought of what Danilo would think when he awoke. Then she reminded herself that her friends were right—this was not what they were here for. It didn't matter.

"It's not far now," Lenah said as she retook the lead. She still felt angry and shaken. But at least for now, she was in control.

26   TIMOTHY CALLO

THEY ALL FOLLOWED LENAH as she made her way around the turn in the corridor. Cassius walked next to her, looming protectively but not speaking. Now and then, he'd glance at Lenah through cold eyes as if scanning her to see what was the next appalling spoiled-brat-thing she'd do. Or was she interpreting that? Was it because she felt shaken and was nervous? He had called her rich girl. And he had seen her flip out over Marcus. As if he'd always been in control of his emotions. She snorted to herself, causing Cassius to turn his head toward her again. Lenah looked away, determined to not let this get to her. It was best not to care what others thought of her. This was one more of those situations.

Lenah made the last turn that would lead to her father's office. No one was in the corridor, and she jogged the last few meters, swiped the Starwide Research access card she'd picked up in her room, and stepped inside. Lenah wasn't expecting her father to be in here. At this time, he usually read his business correspondence in the library while enjoying a coffee. Indeed, the spacious office was empty. Maybe she could avoid meeting him altogether.

Lenah quickly made it to the center of the room, scanning the familiar surroundings with new eyes. Where would her father store his visitor's access card to the mage farm? A mysterious place where he'd take investors and scientists but not his daughter, who was his right hand at business. How could Lenah have ever believed that? She'd gone down to the underground lobby of the farms and nodded in understanding when her father hadn't allowed her to go inside.

Now she wondered what really lay behind those doors and why the mages were working there if it was so unstable. Did they know the risks? What were those risks exactly? Or was there something else entirely going on that her father was hiding from her? No matter, Lenah was determined to find out today.

Her gaze traveled over the neat, invaluable mahogany desk; an antique made centuries ago from an ancient wood that since had ceased to exist. Humanity had brought all kinds of seeds on the generation ships all the way from Old Earth. This desk had been made on New Earth, but no one had thought to take more seeds when humanity had to abandon their new home. It might well be the last of its kind.

The desk was freestanding in the room, its thick ornamented legs accentuated by the space and the modern, almost invisible chair her father's interior designer had paired it with. It didn't have any drawers though, so she decided to move on after only a quick sweep. Lenah walked further into the room and toward the bookshelves. They were stacked with a combination of useful things, like holobooks with Starwide Research's projected figures, and decorative items, many of which were also antiques. The most valuable was a display with a few coins—little metal buttons—that dated all the way back to Old Earth. Some, like the U.S. dollar, were from the later centuries of humanity's home planet, others, like a Roman centaur, dated a few thousand years back in Old Earth history.

Lenah couldn't imagine what it would have been like to carry heavy-weighted coins like these. Her limited, and recent, experience with physical coins had solely consisted of handling the lightweight, plastic chips CGCs were made of. Paying with a wristpiece was way more practical.

Her eyes scanned the displays, trying to determine if there was a place to store a key card. Her father used it for guests, presumably guests who were already in here with him. That meant it couldn't be hidden too far away. Or be inconvenient. He wouldn't climb on a chair to fetch it from the top of the shelves. Or go get it in his bathroom. Unfortunately, that still left plenty of space. She swept her hands over the displays, lifted books and figurines, but couldn't find anything out of order.

Lenah turned and saw that Uz and Persia were searching the coffee table her father used to hold intimate meetings with clients. A good choice. Doctor Lund was clanking around in the bar area, lifting carafes and touching behind the glasses on the shelf. Cassius was nowhere in sight.

A commotion sounded outside, followed by the door banging open. A moment later, Cassius walked in, holding Lenah's father in his relentless grip.

Timothy Callo tried to walk with dignity, but Cassius was making that impossible by the way he forced her father's head sideways in the grip of his metal arm. Lenah knew from personal experience how scary it was to be suddenly gripped by that cyborg arm. She felt sorry for her father but pushed away the feeling. Cassius was doing this for good reason, and he wasn't hurting him. When he saw her, her father stumbled, and his eyes widened in shock.

"Based on his looks, this is your father?" Cassius asked as he deposited Timothy into a seat in the sofa area.

Lenah nodded. People said that a lot. They shared the same brown eyes and long nose. Looking at him now, she thought he appeared aged even though she'd only seen him four weeks ago. Otherwise, he was the same—spotless black suit, white shawl elegantly draped around his neck. Standard corporate wear. The only oddity about him was the yellow stone ring he always wore. It had been a gift from Lenah's mother, and he never took it off.

"Didn't want to hurt our *host*," Cassius said, taking up a heavy accent, presumably to shock her father into cooperation. Her father would have a heart attack if he knew Lenah had kissed a man who talked like that.

"Yes, thank you," Lenah choked out before turning to her father and coming to stand next to Cassius, who had let go of Timothy but was still standing so close to him that there was no doubt her father would regret trying anything foolish—like screaming.

"Lenah, this is how you come back? Stealing your way into my rooms and surrounding yourself with these people?" Timothy stared at her. The incredulity in his eyes seemed real.

"These *people* are my friends, and they've been on the right side—the side that thinks of defending our species. Meanwhile, you've been banding with criminals." Lenah said and swallowed, even though her mouth had gone dry. No matter the consequences or means, she would find out what her father knew.

Her father flinched, but he didn't deny it. He looked up at her, shaking his head almost unnoticeably.

Lenah ignored it. "You said you would explain once I came home," she said instead, glad that her voice sounded even. "Well, here I am."

He sighed, then looked around. "This is information that should stay in the Callo family. Send your *friends* away, and I'll tell you everything." His gaze swept to Zyrakath who was searching a shelf with Uz and his eyes widened.

Lenah shook her head. "No, Father, we're doing this on my terms now. Do you even know what's about to happen to this planet? Because of your mage farm?"

Her father watched her for a few seconds, and Lenah stared back. With a sigh and a nod, he seemed to come to the conclusion that she was serious. "All right. Your terms. But, Lenah, you seem to think that something terrible is coming for us. You forget that Astur is not defenseless. Cheung army is up there as we speak, protecting the planet. And they will not be alone. Starwide Research's ships are with them. In the end, it might be us who win the day. And the glory."

"You're trying to abuse this situation to become a corporate family with army status." Lenah stated.

"Not abuse, no." He shook his head vehemently. "All I'm saying is we'll be there, should the threat prove too much for Cheung's army to take on. We have a lot of fighters now, in large part thanks to you securing us investments over the past years."

The comment landed like a fist in Lenah's stomach. "I didn't realize you put that much into our security force," she pressed through clenched teeth, though she had to admit this was perfectly acceptable behavior. Predictable too. She shook her head, frustrated with herself for not seeing it before. She'd been thinking the investments she secured were mainly going into expanding the mage farms and make intergalactic travel a lot smoother for everyone.

"You know our forces are respectable. Even though we weren't the ones to discover the threat, we can still benefit from it."

Lenah snorted; he sounded just like the UPL ambassadors. "So that's it? You were working on our corporate status when you had your smuggler friends chase me for the stone?" She didn't care that she sounded like a child. She was angry.

"How could I know it was you on that ship with the stolen stone?"

When Lenah remained silent and stared down at him, he continued. "Lenah, why didn't you share the information you gained with me? Is the company worth so little to you? This is your future too."

Lenah barked out a laugh. "You lied to me. You manipulated me. You had your people hunt me down. Meanwhile, I had no idea what was going on until we found the temple on Masis III. You were the one who betrayed me."

"I'm your father and you can trust me. I'm sorry all this went so much out of control. I really am. I did everything to make sure that you wouldn't get involved in any of this. I regret that I put you at risk. And as your father, I was very worried about you." His words rang of truth, but Lenah was too angry to accept them.

"Stars be damned, Father. It's not that easy. You can't just say sorry and then have it your way again." Lenah almost stomped her foot, but caught herself at the last moment. She took a shaky breath, then continued with determination. "We're doing this on my terms. Once this is over, and only if it ends well for us—for humanity, not Starwide Research—I'll consider forgiving you."

Her father seemed surprised—truly surprised—at her outburst, and he shrunk a little in his seat.

Cassius softly cleared his throat and lifted his wrist to look pointedly down at it.

Right, they needed to be quick.

"Father, where's your access card to the mage farm?"

"The mage farm? What do you want down there? You know it's dangerous."

"No, I actually don't," Lenah answered. "I've never been down there."

"Sure, you have…"

"Not in the security section."

"Because it's too dangerous."

"But why? Aren't the mages who live there supposed to have good lives? Apartments, plans to expand them to add lake views. Something is awfully wrong down there."

"Like trafficked test subjects," Uz growled from behind Lenah.

Lenah's father looked over to Uz, and his eyes widened as he took her in, though Lenah didn't know if it was because she was a cut Cassidian or because he recognized her as one of his appointed lab rats. The one to replace someone who had died in there.

He shook his head. "Why would you want to go down there?"

"I don't know, maybe to try stop the incoming attacks? Our farms triggered the Cava Dara on us. You know that, right?"

Her father continued to shake his head slowly, deep wrinkles standing out on his forehead. "That's why we're fighting it off with the armies. Mindless monsters can't stand in the way of magical advancement."

"Millions of lives are in danger."

"We have military strength," her father insisted.

"Father, this is not a matter of fighting off a few lame spaceships. It's a serious threat. People might die. People will die. Who's going to buy those warp drives then?"

Her father shook his head. "A few common lives, but it will serve a greater good." Ignoring Cassius's snort, he continued and said, "If Starwide Research became an official corporation, it could improve so many more lives with its mage farms."

Lenah stayed silent, not knowing what to say. The worst was that she knew she was being the odd one out. Ruthlessly pursuing business goals was not uncommon, and she knew it had cost plenty of lives over the centuries. All for the greater good that a corporation brought to a world's economy.

"Lenah, check this." Uz's voice came from near the shelf. "I think I found a hidden safe."

With one last look at her father, Lenah turned to see what Uz was pointing at.

It was part of an exposed wall behind the statue of a horse, but as Uz touched the spot with her long fingers, an outline became visible. Only a faint glowing line, but Lenah had seen these before in this house. That's how the treasury safe looked too.

"Father, open this for us," she said, turning back to him. Cassius went to help her father up in a less than gentle fashion, then ushered him over toward Uz.

"You can't be serious," Timothy whispered, but when Lenah pointed at the safe again, he reached out his hand.

Touching a seemingly random spot on the wall with his index finger, a small door opened. Lenah stretched her hand in, not seeing any obvious content. There were only two things inside. An envelope—an actual physical piece of paper, printed with a symbol that looked like a vertical line with two branches coming out of it—and a small access chip, the item she had come looking for. Lenah took the chip and left the envelope behind. She didn't really want to know.

"That's it." She announced to the others, holding up the chip. "We can go."

"What do we do with him?" Cassius asked, still holding her father by his arm.

"He…" Lenah trailed off. "Tie him up in the bathroom back there. Lock the door."

Cassius raised an eyebrow but did as told. On a last whim, Lenah stopped him, touching his arm and turned to her father.

"What do you know about mind magic?"

Her father frowned at her. "Mind magic?" he repeated.

"Why can't I influence you, Father?"

He shook his head. "You know that I have no idea." For the first time today, he sounded completely genuine.

27 DOWNWARD

THE DOOR TO THE Starwide Research offices, Mage Farm division, swung open in front of Lenah. She stepped through the door and into the familiar space beyond. Would anyone question her presence? Or the people she was bringing? Passing the group behind her as investors was a stretch, but if anyone asked, she'd spin a tale of them being a group of quirky sponsors and their toy drone, along with a little sprinkling of mind magic. They wouldn't be the first ones. The eccentric semi-naked trillionaire with the indigenous costume that Lenah had once brought here had definitely been worse. People would just stare and shrug.

The room was emptier than expected for a normal mid-week afternoon. But today was not a typical day for anyone. People might have left early to be with their families in anticipation of the upcoming fight in space.

Nonetheless, around fifteen pairs of eyes followed them as they crossed the room, loaded with their backpacks and with Lenah in the lead. She gave a friendly nod to the familiar faces and held her posture upright, as corporate Lenah would when trying to give off an air of authority. The room was long, with rows of desks on both sides of a corridor and a silver elevator door that led to the mage farm on the far side.

Lenah saw people frown at them, then quickly move their gaze away when they met Lenah's eyes. She wondered who they'd seen. Uz? Maybe not, since the Cassidian was trying to hide most of her face behind her hair. Zyrakath? He was hovering low to cover most of himself up between Lorka and Doctor Lund. Maybe the presence of a mage as part of a group of investors looked suspicious. Whatever people saw, it didn't seem to alarm them enough to take any action. Lenah reached the elevator, and the cart instantly opened when she swiped her stolen access card in front of the panel. As the doors closed, she smiled confidently back into the office, then let out a big breath as the elevator started moving.

The cart would take them not only underground but also several klicks further west toward Lake Astur. A soft slide sideways indicated they were traveling toward the lake now. It also reminded Lenah of the moving prison cells on UPL station. Not a good memory, and she couldn't help but tentatively reach out to her friends' minds. She was glad to find she could still feel them.

"He's an ass for not wanting to help," Persia said softly from her side, apparently mistaking Lenah's broody mood for worry about her father. Lenah grunted, not wanting to be reminded. The encounter with her father had drained her, and if she could, she'd be curled up somewhere right now by herself. Maybe in the cockpit of the *Rambler*.

"You made the right decision. Sometimes we have to lose something for the long-term good," Uz said when Lenah didn't speak. Lenah looked at her, nodding. Uz would know all about that. Lenah might have lost her family and status, but Uz had lost her sense of vertigo, then her people, and finally the life she'd painstakingly rebuilt for herself.

"I know," she whispered. "But I still feel terrible."

"I think that's normal too," Uz said. "But it'll get better once you find something to distract yourself.

"I'm not short of tasks." Lenah groaned, thinking what they were about to do.

"Then focus on that right now. And deal with your father later. One step after the other."

"You're right. I just need this elevator to get there." Lenah glanced over at Cassius, who was standing stoically in one corner of the cart. By this time, she was sure he was angry with her. Nodding she was okay to Uz and Persia, Lenah stepped closer to him and put her hand on his forearm. After a few moments, he shifted, dropping his arm as if in a natural movement and let her hand slip.

Without thinking further about it, Lenah reached out to his mind, prodding him with the idea that he urgently needed to tell her what he felt.

"You and I, we're incompatible. Look where you come from," he sputtered out before catching himself as she pulled back her influence. He looked at her in shock that turned to anger. Lenah felt a jolt as if he burned her with fire. The cart had gone silent—apart from the ringing in Lenah's ears. This was exactly what she'd been afraid of. But how could she have made him say it like that? She stared up at him, unsure what to say when the elevator chimed to a stop. Lenah whirled, checking for the display.

"We're not there yet. This is someone getting in at the entrance close to the city. Zyr, Uz, try to hide," she hissed out of pressed lips.

Lenah stepped in front of her group, and Doctor Lund who was the most respectable-looking stood at her side as the door opened.

Two men in suits nodded politely and entered the cart. If they were surprised to see them, they hid it well. Businessmen. Lenah put on her look of confidence, trying to appear like she was not only meant to be here but that she was the most important person around.

"Miss Callo, right?" one of them asked, and the other one nodded a greeting.

Lenah returned the gesture. "Yes."

They continued their journey in silence, and Lenah's ears started ringing again. She wanted to get rid of these people and apologize to Cassius. She glanced over toward him, but he stared straight through her, eyes locked on the metal doors. If he'd been distant before, he must be fuming now. She couldn't blame him. Lenah usually knew better than to cause people to have outbursts like that, and she was regretting this one deeply and, especially, doing it in front of the others. She hadn't lost control over her power like that since her teenage years. Now, it couldn't be taken back. Not the manipulation and not what everyone had heard.

"Wasn't your father going to attend the test results session?" One of the suited men, a middle-aged with a mustache, interrupted her thoughts.

"You'll have to excuse me, but I've never seen you down at the meetings before."

"Ah," Lenah answered, forcing on a nonchalant smile. "My father couldn't make it today and sent me in his stead. Of course, he filled me in on all the details." She kept up her smile and met his gaze. At the same time, she sent out a burst of sympathetic feelings toward them like she'd done hundreds of times before with investors.

"Wonderful," the man with the mustache said. "I'm pleased to meet you. I'm Doctor Whiteham. This is my colleague Doctor Lagun. We're regulars at the Innovation Roundtables."

"Pleasure to meet both of you." She shook hands with them, continuing to smile. But inwardly, she worried. Were there going to be a lot of visitors down there today? They had expected to rescue mages but not to deal with a large group of probably unwilling scientists.

"If you're regulars, then you surely know how many innovators usually participate in the roundtables?" she asked, trying to sound like an insider throwing around the same words they had.

"Oh, we're a small circle," Doctor Whiteham said amiably. "Usually just half a dozen of scientists and doctors." He looked at the others curiously. "Are you bringing more people today…?" his voice trailed off as he regarded her friends one by one.

Before Lenah could answer his question, the elevator chimed again, this time announcing their arrival at the mage farm entrance hall.

"Please, go ahead." Lenah extended a hand. "I will follow once I've shown our new staff their workplaces." She nodded toward her friends. "Where will the Innovator meeting be held again?"

"As always, in the amphitheater. What kind of new staff are they? They're quite the mix," Whiteham said and looked curiously at Cassius who was looming in front of the others, presumably trying to cover them.

"Are you in need of more security down here again? I thought it had already been considerably bumped up thanks to Cheung Corp."

Lenah was scrambling for an answer and trying to decide if she should try to influence these two again when Cassius answered.

"Not at all. I'm merely the new cook." He grinned his most stunning grin.

Lenah, thinking that the comment hadn't helped ease the men's suspicions at all, shoved an image into their minds of Cassius pleasantly working on delicious-smelling steaks.

Both looked up at Cassius in surprise, then smiled. "In that case, let's hope we'll get to taste one of your meals sometime. Good luck with the new position."

Before they turned to go, Doctor Whiteham touched Lenah on the arm and pulled her aside. He gave Lorka a grave look. "I know you're new to these meetings, but tell your father that getting young mages like that one is absolutely against the roundtable's recommendation. He should know better, and I will be bringing this up later."

"Oh…" Lenah said, at a loss for words. "I'll let him know."

Doctor Whiteham seemed content with the answer and turned away.

"What was that about?" Uz asked as soon as the scientists had vanished behind a door that was labeled Tract A.

"It's obvious. They didn't appreciate being told that a youngling is sharing their prestigious table," Zyrakath said, hovering higher.

Lenah rolled her eyes. "Then it's good for them I won't actually be attending. But no, I think they meant Lorka."

"You shouldn't be so disrespectful," Zyrakath said, apparently wanting to continue the subject.

"Just be quiet, Zyr. We have more important things to discuss." Lenah sighed. "Like which of these tracts to go to first."

Zyrakath sputtered as if her disrespect was causing his cables to malfunction.

"She means it as a compliment, Elder Zyr," Lorka's voice interrupted the drone. "For humans, calling someone by a nickname is a great sign of respect. As is mutual silence." He reached up and patted the drone on his small arm.

Lenah was grateful that someone was patient with Zyrakath. And trying to tell him that her mocking was a sign of respect. If he bought into the idea, she could live with that.

"I say we take Tract C," Persia suggested. "It's opposite from where these scientists went. If I wanted to hide illegal operations, I'd put it as far from official rooms as possible."

Lenah nodded.

"Do these stairs lead somewhere outside?" Lorka asked, looking around the room.

Lenah turned to see the emergency exit sign. "It's a safe assumption. I say you and Zyrakath scout out those stairs. See where they lead and if we can evacuate the mages there. The rest of us will go into Tract C."

"Young human, I don't—" Zyrakath started, but Lorka interrupted him once more. "I think that's a great suggestion. Thanks, Lenah." Then to the drone, he said. "Let's go, Elder Zyr." Zyrakath pressed his lips into a thin line, but he seemed to come to the conclusion they were right. Without another word, he followed Lorka.

"I don't suppose I could go with them." Uz spoke softly. Lenah regarded the Cassidian. She was fisting the straps of her backpack hard at her shoulders, and the blue of her bones was visible at her knuckles.

"Relax, Uz. You're here on your own free will." Doctor Lund tried to comfort her, but he too looked nervous. Sweat was streaming down his forehead, and he rapidly tapped his foot. Lenah couldn't imagine how it must feel for them to be here. After getting kidnapped to come to come to the mage farm, it was probably the last place in the galaxy they wanted to break into.

Uz nodded. "I know," she said quietly. "I've just feared this place for the longest time. It's really strange to be here now and think nothing will happen. At least not to me personally."

"Something will happen. Just not what they had intended for you two." Cassius's tone was serious as he patted his backpack.

28   THE MAGE FARM

CASSIUS TOOK THE LEAD toward the entrance to Tract C, motioning for everyone to be quiet as he put his ear to the door. After a few seconds, he shook his head.

"It's thick metal. I can't hear anything," he told them. Then, he pointed to the wall next to the door. "Stand back."

"If someone's there, it's better they see me," Lenah interjected. "I could have a reason to be here."

"For being a fancy Callo?" Cassius remarked, and it didn't sound like a compliment.

Lenah shrunk back but nodded. "Precisely. Besides, I can defend myself." She tapped her head.

Cassius regarded her, then made space. At least he was talking to her in some capacity. Maybe he'd be able to forgive Lenah at some point. There was still the issue of him believing them to be too different. Admittedly, she had also thought that herself. She shoved the thoughts down. Now was not the time.

Lenah stood in front of the door and tensely watched as Cassius turned the doorknob. To her surprise, it wasn't locked. There was no one in sight, though Lenah could now hear faint voices, and she took a moment to take in the room. They were in another atrium, this one significantly smaller and less decorated than the first one. A counter sat in the middle, equipped with a medical station. Overall, it felt like she had stepped into a hospital. Lenah's stomach plummeted. A hospital was very far from the apartments promised to the independent mages who supposedly lived here.

A wide corridor with a long glass wall led away to the right. Plants in pots stood against the transparent panels, and, behind the glass, rooms were visible. As if someone had made a feeble attempt to make the place homier.

Several more rooms, these hidden behind solid walls, lay to the left. The door to one of those rooms stood open, and that was where the voices were coming from. Trying to walk as silently as she could, Lenah made her way over to the entryway. Cassius wanted to overtake her, but she held up her hand and sent her influence toward the three minds in the room. They would be expecting Lenah.

She only stepped through when she was sure her influence had reached them. The smell inside was like hospital disinfectant, and a young man lay stretched out on a gurney in the center of the room. Two women, both in medical coats, attended to him but looked up as Lenah and her group stepped inside.

"Hello," Lenah said, trying to sound friendly and harmless. "Please, don't let us interrupt you. We're only here to take a look as we had discussed."

"Miss Callo," both women greeted, their faces pleasant. One of them was younger, and a tag proclaimed her a doctor, the older woman's tag read nurse.

"Just keep monitoring his heartbeat, will you? Alert me as soon as you see changes," the doctor said to the nurse, who nodded and stepped close to a machine.

"What happened to him?" Lenah asked, approaching the man on the gurney. He couldn't be much older than Lorka and was wearing a mage necklace. His chest was exposed, showing several tubes connected to his body. Was that one of the young mages Dr. Whiteham had warned about?

"He's not yet used to the drain," the doctor answered willingly under Lenah's influence.

"The drain?" Uz asked, stepping closer, eyes wide and her voice quivering audibly.

The doctor took a long look at Uz, especially taking in the scars on her forehead, before answering.

Lenah enforced the idea that she'd been expecting them all, including Uz. Nonetheless, Uz shrunk backward at the doctor's scrutiny, her hands going to her forehead.

"Yes, transfer of too much magical energy into the reservoir." The doctor hesitated. "You remind me of someone," she said a bit stiffly, still looking at Uz, and furrowing her brow. Was it because she recognized her promised lab subject?

Uz flinched into a corner while Lenah tried to relax the doctor, sending a more dominant idea into her mind.

"We don't usually allow visitors in here." The doctor said slowly.

"I'm Lenah Callo," Lenah said in her best authoritative tone. "We exchanged communications about this just yesterday. Don't you remember, Doctor?" Along with her words, she sent the image of them receiving an official message from her father and the request to answer any questions.

"Yes, yes, of course." The doctor shook her head. "I remember now. Please, accept my apology, Miss Callo."

Lenah nodded. "I don't know much about the farms and would like to have a thorough introduction."

"And we'd like to see that reservoir," Doctor Lund added.

"Yes, if you don't mind, could you give us a quick tour?" Lenah asked.

"Of course," the doctor said, looking down at the man on the gurney. "Just know that his regeneration process will not be optimized if we leave him. But I suppose that's your money lost."

"Will he suffer alone here?" Lenah asked.

The doctor shook her head. "No, he will sleep."

Lenah breathed out in relief. "Let's start the tour here," she said. "What happened to him? Is this normal?"

The doctor looked up at her in surprise and with some anger, though Lenah didn't know why. Her influence was working, wasn't it?

"The mages experience complications from the transfer. It's very taxing on the body, and the maximum amount someone is able to give depends greatly on the quality of rest they were able to take. Mage Proles," she nodded down to the man, "probably didn't sleep well—we've caught him before not taking his sleep medications—and now his immune system is flaring up."

When Lenah gave her a questioning look, the doctor continued, "Imagine yourself getting the wrong blood infusion. Flu-like fevers, aching joints, chills. And there is the burn on the injection site…" The doctor's voice trailed off, and she pointed toward a red and swollen part on the mage's neck. He had a port there, sticking out of blistered and bleeding skin.

"That's what happens to them? They get sick? Always?"

"Not always, no. It's a fine line to know how much magic you can filter out of someone's blood or overdoing it just a bit. But you don't need to worry, Miss Callo. Mage Proles will be hooked up to the reservoir again by tomorrow night."

Lenah didn't say that that was exactly what she was worried about. Apparently, the impression down here was that the Callos wanted to get the reservoir filled to the maximum, no matter the suffering it brought to the mages.

"Let's move on," she said, her voice sounding raspy. Her throat suddenly felt very dry. "I'd like to see the rest."

"Of course," the doctor answered, clicking several buttons on the machine connected to the mage, then briefly touching his forehead. "The fever is still very high," she said to the nurse. "We need to monitor that." Then she turned to the door, waiting for Lenah to walk out first.

"Over there," she said and pointed to the next door, "is the ICU. State-of-the-art. We've saved lives in there. Luckily, we haven't had a patient in a few weeks." The doctor walked toward a window that revealed a room with three beds inside and lots of machinery.

"Tina was released less than two weeks ago from her total overdrain." The nurse spoke for the first time.

"Mage Tata," the doctor corrected. "We don't address our patients by their first names."

"Yes, of course."

Lenah saw in her mind a woman spread out in one of those beds and almost lost her grip on the influence she was still sending toward the two. Total overdrain. That's what the farms could do to the mages? They'd signed up to lead a better life, not to spend a lifetime on spaceships and away from their family. Instead, they ended up in an ICU down here where the only nice thing seemed to be the potted plants lining the corridors. Like that would help.

29 FREEDOM

NEXT, THEY SAW THE apartments behind the glass wall down the corridor. Studios with a kitchen unit and one door that Lenah assumed led into a lavatory. There was zero privacy in the living area, thanks to the glass wall.

"That's to make sure no one faints or experiences any negative side effects without our notice," the doctor explained when Lenah inquired.

"Why wouldn't you use tracking implants for that? What's the need to have these people live in glass boxes?" Lenah clearly remembered the initial designs she had seen of the mage farms that had included studios with a view of Lake Asturis. Had all that been a lie to calm investors? Or to manipulate people like Lenah? She certainly had not agreed to this at any time in her life.

"With the degraded blood and weak body signals when the patients come out of their shifts, the scanners are completely useless."

Lenah didn't answer. She became distracted by an older mage in his unit, shuffling from where he'd been lying on the bed toward the kitchen. He shot them a few hostile glances as they passed. Lenah couldn't blame him. She wouldn't want anyone gawking at her under no circumstances, and especially when she wasn't feeling good.

"Then why are they still here?" she said more to herself, trying to remember the employment contracts made for the mages. "I do remember that it was a two-year contract, but our lawyers surely gave them an out-clause."

"If they can pay fifty thousand CGC, yes," the nurse answered, looking Lenah up and down. You are the asshole who created these conditions, they seemed to be saying. Lenah certainly wouldn't disagree.

Her job had always been securing investments, but now she felt she should have paid attention to this. She had always prided herself on being a skeptic. Or was she really the spoiled girl Cassius saw in her? She glanced at where he was walking, in the back of their group. He hadn't spoken at all since they entered the facility. Was he trying not to call attention to himself, or did he want to get as far away from Lenah as possible?

They passed a dozen more units before reaching the end of the corridor where an orange sign over a door announced the area as restricted. Just in case, Lenah sent the doctor and nurse a more detailed version of the message requesting a tour, now specifying to include the restricted areas and the reservoir as well.

The doctor stopped, turning toward Lenah with narrowed eyes. "We won't be able to show you the reservoir. It's only accessible for the chemists and their security." She suddenly looked doubtful. "Who wrote that message again?"

"It was my father, Mr. Timothy Callo," Lenah said, further fleshing out her image of the message with her father's name on it.

"Ah, that's right. I remember now," the doctor said and nodded. "He doesn't come here often; he probably forgot. You big guys up there can't be overly bothered with our little rules and problems down here, right?" She barked out a short laugh.

"Er, right," Lenah answered, feeling terrible. She didn't care to be known as the big guy up there.

"Can we at least go past this door, or which way is the reservoir?"

"Oh, sure. The reservoir is in Tract B. But here, we have the transfusion facilities. I assume you'd want to take a look?"

"Yes, please." Lenah smiled at her. That sounded like they would find mages behind this door. "Just a quick one." She added, thinking about how time must be running out.

They walked through the door and stepped into a large room that looked even more like a hospital than the one they had come from. There was a large area with special gurneys surrounded by a station of machinery on each side. Several mages were hooked up to the machines by IVs. Most of them looked up as the group entered.

Lenah saw the mage closest to her take in her face, then her badge as his gaze lowered. He sneered. Fighting her feelings, Lenah stepped closer to see the station better. Two tubes filled with blood were sticking out of the man's neck and led into the machine. Lenah remembered that one tube would pump a certain amount of blood into the machine where the Cheung Corp technology filtered out the magic and sent it into the reservoir where it was stabilized and saved to the warp drives. Finally, the drained blood was pumped back into the mage's bloodstream.

"What else is in this tract, other than what we've seen?" Lenah asked the doctor.

"Not much. There's a laboratory back there, but it hasn't been used in months. I heard that the colleague who was going to staff it never showed up to his first day," the doctor answered, and Lenah shuddered. Behind her, Doctor Lund let out a strangled moan. He'd been the candidate to staff the lab, unwillingly. As an expert in warp magic, he'd been taken from his archeology mission on New Earth to be forced to work here. The assumption presumably was that that he would not be missed for vanishing from an inhospitable place like the abandoned wasteland of humanity's old settlement. By taking off the *Rambler*, where he and Uz had been held, Lenah had left with him before he was able to show up for his first day of work.

"The mages are either in the hospital, their rooms, or here?"

The doctor nodded.

"No recreational facilities? Lake view?"

"Lake view? We're several hundred meters underground," the doctor said. She and the nurse gawked at Lenah.

"Never mind," Lenah said, before turning slightly and trying to get her friends' attention. If nowhere else was filled with people, then the next step was clear. It was time to act.

This time, Cassius picked up her gaze and gave a small nod, touching Persia lightly on the arm. Persia's hand went inside her jacket where she had her weapon. Lenah held up her palm in a calming gesture. They needed to get the mages off these machines first. The doctor had seen Lenah's gesture too and froze. Lenah took a few moments to collect her concentration. Then she shoved the idea of shift end and the resulting unhooking of all mages toward the nurse and doctor.

"Shift end?" the doctor said, incredulity dripping out of her voice. "But we don't have shift end. What are you doing here, exactly? Did Mr. Callo really send you?" She stepped closer to Lenah. "If you get me in trouble…"

That made Lenah stop. She didn't want to get these women in trouble.

"You need to unhook all the mages. Now." Lenah sent urgency with the words but felt like she was doing a sloppy job. She was tense, frustrated, and felt like hitting something rather than concentrating.

"Unhook? No. I'm not going to risk my job for a business puppy."

Lenah huffed out a breath. Had she gotten too impatient? The mages watched the discussion with interest, but none of them moved. Could they even move with those tubes stuck inside their necks? Someone cleared his throat behind Lenah.

She turned, seeing Cassius and Persia standing there, weapons pointed at the doctor and nurse.

"You'll do as she says," Cassius said, coldness in his voice. He lifted his metal arm in what Lenah knew was a gesture for added effect.

The doctor shrunk from him, full alarm spreading over her features. "Who are you? Why is a cyborg down here? Are you military? Why didn't I realize something was off before?" She fumbled with a black band on her wrist.

Lenah dropped all pretenses and jumped for her. She grabbed the woman's arm to yank it toward her but was only in time to see her press a tiny button attached to a bracelet.

"Show me that," Lenah demanded at the same time the other woman said, "Who are you really?"

Lenah got hold of her arm, and the doctor didn't object as she started inspecting the bracelet. "A Cheung-branded security alarm bracelet," Lenah said.

"That probably means there are guards down here, but I can't hear them coming yet," Cassius said, his tone worried. He was holding the nurse tightly in his metal arm.

The nurse gave him an incredulous look like it was impossible to hear anyone through these doors, but she probably wasn't thinking of cyborg hearing implants.

"Good. That means we at least have some time," Lenah said, before addressing the mages in the room. None of them had moved away from their chairs, even though several looked like they really wanted to. None had attacked either.

"We're here to free you. This facility is about to be attacked. I am Lenah Callo, the daughter of the owner, and my friends and I will help you get outside and drop you off in a safe location." She looked at the faces staring back at her. Upon closer inspection, she wasn't surprised none of the mages had attacked. They all looked exhausted. Maybe their resources were drained?

"Unhook them from the machines," Lenah said to the doctor in her best commanding voice. "We won't harm you, and you'll be evacuated as well." She put the feeling of truthfulness toward the woman. The doctor eyed her for a moment, but when Lenah's emotion touched her mind, she shuffled to do as asked.

"Why are you not defending yourselves?" Uz asked, stepping closer toward a female mage who eyed her suspiciously but didn't otherwise move.

"They can't," the nurse answered. "They can't use their abilities during the filtering process, and it's really difficult to unhook yourself when you're stuck in that chair."

"What would happen if you used your abilities?" Uz asked the mage softly.

It was again the nurse who answered. "The filtering process is difficult. It's like getting a bunch of dirt deposited in your veins."

The first mage had been unhooked by the doctor and got off his chair. Lenah sent the emotion of getting help toward him. Then extended it to his companions. He didn't attack, just stood there, waiting. Maybe he didn't feel a tickle like Lorka had?

"I can hear the guards coming now," Cassius said. "Five or six pairs of footsteps. They just entered the Tract C door and will be here in under a minute."

Lenah nodded. "I can take care of everyone else in here. You take these guards."

Cassius dropped his backpack in the corner, followed by the others. Then he, Persia, and Uz took up positions by the door. Doctor Lund guarded the backpacks, but even he drew out a gun. As always, he looked uncomfortable even holding it, and it was only a tranquilizer.

"They're here and pulling out weapons," Cassius whispered and yanked the heavy door open. Uz had to sidestep to avoid being hit, but she recovered quickly. Cassius succeeded in surprising the six guards outside and was already in the middle of them, swinging his cyborg arm. Two of them were struck and stumbled toward Persia and Uz, who each shot them with a dart from their tranquilizer guns.

Cassius turned, repeating the gesture with two more guards, but they withstood the attack. Trying not to lose focus on the minds she was still calming, Lenah saw the guards were wearing strange suits with a Cheung Corp logo on the chest. The suit fit their bodies snugly and was made out of iridescent material. Fighting suits. That probably meant these guys couldn't be stunned or get hurt by a tranquilizer dart. *Unlike Cassius*, Lenah thought, as she watched him dance around his four adversaries. He managed to push two more guards in normal uniforms toward Uz and Persia, who took care of one each.

Persia lurched for her adversary and actually brought them both down to the ground where they started struggling. Metal clanked against the floor as Persia tried to wrangle the laser pistol out of the guard's hand. The other guard was too late to react when Uz crashed into him. Apparently, she had approved of Persia's plan.

Next to them, Cassius confronted the two remaining guards, but despite his enhanced strength, he wasn't having much effect. They seemed as fast and as strong as him and matched each of his attacks with ease. He took a blow to his chest and stumbled back. Were they cyborgs under those suits or was it something else? With a hand on her own tranquilizer gun, Lenah was about to turn to help when a movement out of the corner of her eye caught her attention.

The doctor moved away from the second mage and was running toward Lenah, a syringe filled with a red liquid lifted high. *Shit*. Lenah had dropped her influence while worrying over Cassius.

The doctor's actions seemed to animate the two free mages, for they also came toward Lenah, a look of concentration on their faces. A second later, something translucent appeared between Lenah and them—a warp bubble.

"I'm not going to hurt you," Lenah said urgently, trying to reason with them. At least the warp bubble was also keeping the doctor and her syringe from reaching Lenah.

"Then why are you attacking us?" the female mage asked.

"We're not the ones attacking. What I said before, I meant it. We're here to get you out. All of you."

"Nonsense. No one is coming here to free *us*. Least of all a Callo." The woman spoke through clenched teeth. Meanwhile, the doctor who was also trapped behind the warp bubble was giving the mage a shooing motion. She wanted to attack Lenah with the syringe.

Behind her, Lenah heard a surprised gasp coming from Cassius but was unable to turn around and look. She hoped that he was fine.

The female mage stared hard at Lenah who resisted the urge of using her powers to push back on the warp bubble. Though she did stretch out her senses to be ready for a surprise push at any time. She sensed that this woman, though overly thin, pale, and barefoot under her robe, was strong beyond her frail look. All Lenah needed to do was convince her that they were really being rescued.

"Let me pass, Mage Sureika," the doctor urged. "I can disable this freak." Then she looked straight at Lenah. "I don't know what you did to us and how you got us to show you around, but you're out of luck now. Whatever drug you gave me is not working any longer and—"

She stopped abruptly. The sounds of the fight behind them became more agitated. Someone yelped, and this time, Lenah was sure it had been Cassius. But she still didn't dare look back. The mages were pushing the warp border toward her, and the doctor still held the syringe pointed at Lenah. This wouldn't do. They were out of time.

Lenah pushed hard against the mages' border. She was surprised by how easy it was. Then, she sent the sensation of extreme tiredness toward the doctor and the nurse. The doctor sat down on the floor instantly, never finishing her sentence. Lenah saw another, weaker warp border flare up in front of her and replace the prior one. Looking at the mages, she saw that Mage Sureika was trembling, her look one of utmost concentration. Softly this time, Lenah pushed back. The warp magic was so weak that it collapsed at first contact with her mind magic. The other mage went to the doctor and took the syringe out of her weak hands while Mage Sureika gaped at Lenah. "How did you do that? It's impossible to penetrate a warp wall."

"I didn't penetrate it," Lenah said softly.

"But how?" The mage shook her head.

"Your magic is weak. It wasn't hard," Lenah said, hoping they would drop the subject.

"An Other," one of the mages, an older man still connected to the chair, whispered.

"A what?" Mage Sureika frowned at him. Behind them, the fighting continued.

"It only means that my magic is different. Now is not the time to explain," Lenah answered. "Are you able to free them?" she asked instead, nodding toward the two mages still hooked up to their chairs.

Mage Sureika's eyes were wide, and she didn't move. "You're a mage just like us?"

Lenah nodded.

"And you'll really free us?" Mage Sureika asked.

"Yes, we will," Lenah said without sending any further influence toward them. They might be able to tell as Lorka had, and that might destroy any trust they'd tentatively started to feel. Besides, Lenah wouldn't be able to mind control a dozen mages out of the facility. They would need to come by themselves.

"We have friends waiting outside who can bring you to our ship. From there, we can drop you wherever you want in Asturis I.

"Police Central," the older mage firmly said. "I have family there. My son. He'll help us get justice."

Lenah held back her grimace. That couldn't be good for Starwide Research, but did she honestly still care? Especially, after all she'd seen down here? No, she didn't.

"Police Central it is," Lenah said and nodded. Another loud clang reverberated behind her. It sounded like cyborg c-nano material banging against the cement floor. She turned slightly, trying to pick up details of the fight. The mages followed her every motion, but they didn't move to attack.

Cassius was on the floor, but the two men were under him. That was a good sign. At least he wasn't losing. Uz and Persia had already tied up the remaining four guards. Lenah turned her full attention back to the mages.

"If you won't unhook them, I'll have to, or my friend, Doctor Lund, will. But I warn you, he's not a real doctor."

"I *am* a real doctor," Doctor Lund called over from where he was still guarding their stuff and clutching his tranquilizer gun with white knuckles. "Just not a medical one, but you show me something related to the warp phenomenon, and I will be able to tell you all about it. In time."

Mage Sureika shook her head at the exchange. "All right." She finally sighed. "I'm willing to risk it for a chance at freedom. It can't get any worse." She turned and walked toward the older mage, then started to press buttons on the machine. The blood inflow stopped, and after pressing a few other buttons, the outflow stopped as well.

Lenah was glad the mage had done this. She didn't know how to operate the machine and would have been forced to rip the tubes out. Even like this, the man winced as Mage Sureika undid the tubes on his neck.

She then moved on to the second mage to repeat the procedure, and, finally, Lenah felt she could turn around and take a good look at what was happening behind her.

It seemed the fight was ending. Cassius had one of the enhanced men down. He was lying unconscious a few meters away, and Uz and Persia were working on tying him up. Lenah edged closer to see if she could help with the second one when Cassius jumped up, then landed again so hard the floor vibrated. But he managed to surprise his adversary from behind. The man, who already seemed to be limping, was unable to turn around in time. Cassius lifted him and crashed him against the wall where he stopped moving.

"That was harder than it should have been. I've never seen suits this good," Cassius said panting.

"Cheung Corp likes to surprise," Lenah muttered.

"What?" Persia asked.

"That's their slogan. Cheung Corp likes to surprise. Probably anyone living on Astur knows it."

"Huh. Go figure."

Lenah turned away, remembering the mages. All four were standing now, but none giving any indication of hostility.

"We need to get you out of here, and we need your help in getting all the other mages too. Do you think you can do that?"

Both the older mage and Mage Sureika nodded.

Lenah pressed the communication button on her wristpiece. A moment later, Lorka's panting voice acknowledged. "Yes?"

"Lorka, have you found a way out? We have the mages."

"We did, it's really long stairs, but the exit ends pretty close to the house. Erm, on a grass field with funny hills and holes. It's not guarded."

"The golf course." Lenah nodded. "That's not too far from the *Rambler*. Where are you now?"

"Almost back down again."

"Okay, we'll send everyone to meet you in the atrium." She cut the connection and turned to the mages.

"We have friends coming, and they will help you gather everyone." She regarded the tied-up guards.

"I hate to ask, but do you think you can bring them out? Not to our shuttle though, just leave them somewhere on the grounds."

"You're not coming?" Mage Sureika asked.

"Not yet, we need to do something else first. In the reservoir."

Mage Sureika looked skeptical, but then she waved for the others to follow her outside.

"One more thing." Lenah stopped her before she could leave the room. "Do you know what we can expect to find in Tract B?"

They shook their heads. "No, we've never seen it. Not even they are allowed in there." Mage Sureika pointed to the doctor who was clutching onto a mage.

30 INTO THE RESERVOIR

THEY MADE IT TO Tract B with no further interruptions. Once behind the door, it looked quite different from the mage's area. The temperature was noticeably cooler, the layout more raw. The small room held no potted plants; instead, the walls were filled with exposed circuitry. The mechanical sounds of hissing and clicking made it impossible to hear anything else.

It was like being inside the gut of a giant creature. Lenah shuddered. Doctor Lund turned a few times on the spot, taking in the place wide-eyed. He was about to say something when Cassius gripped him by the arm in warning. Then Cassius continued toward the only other door that lead out of the room.

There, he stopped to listen, but shook her head. "Too loud," he whispered, before pointing up to the whirring and hissing cables. He pressed the door handle. It didn't give.

Lenah saw a panel next to it and swiped the access card from her father's safe over it. A green light blinked, and the door swung open.

Cassius went first. Immediately, he whirled to the side, and Lenah heard a thump. She rushed in after him, pulling out her tranquilizer gun. A second thump sounded, and she saw two guards had crashed against the opposite side of the wall. They were wearing the iridescent fighting suits and were already scrambling up to join the fight again.

Quickly, Lenah let her gaze sweep around the room. A tall ceiling full of moving circuitry and a chunky body scanner dominated the inside of the space. As her eyes swept over to the two doors at the far end of the room, three more guards burst through one of them.

The mechanical whirring grew louder, but Lenah didn't have time to find the source. She discarded her tranq gun and pulled out her knife. She jerked it up as one of the suited guards reached her and tried to concentrate on his mind while evading his blows. He wasn't wasting time on knives and knocked her hand aside with brutal strength, then lifted his own laser gun with the other. Lenah sent the sensation of burning pain into his mind. He stumbled backward, starting to pat out imagined fires on his body. Before Lenah could breathe in relief or get an overview of the fight, she was suddenly hoisted off the ground.

Something big had grabbed her by the waist, and she was lifted several meters. She looked around frantically to see Persia in the same position as her. A large metal arm, like a tentacle, had grabbed her. It seemed part of the very machine making the whirring sounds in the room.

Lenah looked down, watching as her friends vanished from view when she and Persia were lifted over the wall and into an unlit area beyond. She writhed in the grasp of the machine hand but quickly realized that she might as well not waste her energy.

"What's happening?" Lenah called to Persia, who was wielding her hammer, trying to twist and hit the mechanical tentacle. It was an awkward angle, and she couldn't reach.

She looked at Lenah and yelled, "Where is it taking us?"

Meanwhile, the sounds of the fight faded away.

"Give me that," Lenah shouted, stretching out her arm for Persia's hammer. Unlike Persia, who had been grabbed from behind, Lenah was held from the side and would have a better angle to the mechanism holding them.

Persia tossed the hammer, and Lenah grabbed it, surprised by its weight. She swung her arm like she'd seen Persia do, then brought it around to hit the tentacle that held Persia in the back. It didn't let go, but a couple of the claws-like appendages grasping Persia bent. Lenah swung again, this time with more strength. More claws bent. Finally, the arm gave way and let go of Persia who fell out of its grip with a yell.

Lenah, who was being moved further into the darkness, started hitting the claw holding her. It let go on the third hit, and she plummeted downward. Lenah steeled herself for the impact but was still surprised how hard she hit the floor. The bones in her body protested. She held her eyes shut and didn't realize immediately that the lights in the room had turned on. The sound of running footsteps came closer, and Lenah snapped her eyes open to see two guards, both in Cheung fighting suits, running toward her and Persia, who stood a couple of meters away. The room they were in had several prison cells with metal bars against one wall.

Lenah stumbled up, and, at the last moment, moved away of the guard swarming her, then jumped back, this time more nimbly avoiding his hit. A suited fist hissed by Lenah's ear as she ducked away and tried to gather up enough concentration to feel his mind. But every time she tried, her attacker charged again, and all she could do was scramble out of his reach. Lenah heard air swoosh by her ear once again and tried to duck, but his leg connected hard into her gut, and she bent over, gasping. He grabbed her wrist and twisted with merciless strength. Lenah dropped the hammer, unable to breathe through the pain in her belly as he followed up with another kick that sent her to the floor.

Out of the corner of her eye, Lenah saw that Persia was also on the floor, her knife lying uselessly a few steps away.

"That's enough," a commanding voice from the speaker of her attacker's suit said. "Get them into the cells."

Lenah turned her head as a mechanical noise sounded from above and saw the robotic arm swoop in again. Two of its claws were broken, but in a third one, she saw the writhing figure of Doctor Lund. He was hitting the metal with his tranquilizer gun but to no effect. In moments, he crossed the room and was dumped into one of the cells at the wall. Lenah's attacker grabbed her by the legs and started to pull her over in the same direction. It was now or never.

Trying to concentrate despite her pain, Lenah channeled the painful sensation from her belly and sent it out into the room. The guard pulling her swayed with an outstretched arm as if he were trying to find support against a wall that wasn't there.

Fueled by her desperation, Lenah pushed harder and heard Persia gasp. Lenah was dimly aware that she was influencing all three of the people in the room, including Persia, but didn't have the strength to separate out the two guards. Her captor let go of her leg, but his fist came toward Lenah. His movements were slow though, and she didn't have a hard time evading his blow by rolling to the side.

"How did you do this?" he hissed, going down on both knees. "You didn't even touch me."

Lenah stepped away from him and took a few seconds to separate the three minds she was influencing.

Careful to hold on to the others, she let go of Persia's mind. Her friend stopped clutching her legs and instead lay silent on the floor, breathing heavily. Lenah concentrated on the men. A small slip in her focus and the fight could resume in the blink of a moment. She crouched next to Persia's attacker and checked out his helmet, glad to find a button by the side of his ear. As she pressed it, his suit's headpiece clicked open to reveal a young man staring daggers back at her with pain-clouded eyes. He tried to move again, but Lenah used her own pain to intensify the effect, and he closed his eyes, whimpering. She pulled off his helmet and put it on.

Once Lenah pressed the button, the helmet's UI appeared before her eyes. The sensation was dizzying. Every time she focused on an item, the helmet detected it and zoomed in. Lenah, trying to see how to get the suit off the man, didn't care for any of the menus. She was also still distracted by focusing pain toward the two guards.

"Lenah, what are you doing?" Persia's voice sounded weak.

"I'm glad you're up!"

"I'm alive. Can I have my hammer back?"

The moment Lenah thought of the word hammer, a red outline appeared in her vision through the visor, showing her exactly where it was. Lenah walked it over toward Persia who was sitting on the floor a few meters away, carefully guarding Lenah's attacker.

"What are you doing?" Persia repeated her earlier question.

"Shh." Lenah sat back.

"Why are they doing that?" Persia whispered, pointing at one writhing man on the floor.

"They think they're in great pain."

"They think?" Persia started. "Ah, now I understand… I thought I had gone mad or was dying. You know how they say that your pain gets less the closer you come to death?"

"Shh," Lenah repeated. "I don't want to do this longer than necessary."

Persia stayed silent, but through her visor, Lenah saw the look on her face. Persia wouldn't mind letting these men think they were in pain for a little longer.

Finally, Lenah found an interface at the lower corner of her vision. Several options popped into her view, and finally one of them read 'Off.' She stared hard at it, and within seconds, her visor popped off, and all interfaces disappeared.

The rest of the suit that the young guard behind her was wearing, simply popped off him. Lenah scooted back, shoving it away from him.

"Those things are well designed," Persia said. "I've never seen a smart suit do that. I hear they are a bitch to get out of when you have to go to the bathroom."

"The bathroom?" Lenah asked in confusion. "Do you have a concussion?" She turned back to Persia to see her shaking her head.

"Didn't get hit in the head as far as I know. Should we undress this other one?"

"I'll do it. Can you tie this one up? And go check on Doctor Lund?" Lenah waved her hand toward the cells, and Persia's eyes went wide as she saw who was occupying one.

Lenah turned to the next guard to repeat the process of putting on his helmet and turning the suit off. Before long, both the guards' hands and feet were tied up with shreds of their own T-shirts that Persia had cut using their knives.

"Did you find a key chip on any of the guards?" Persia asked as Lenah joined her in front of Doctor Lund's cell.

Lenah shook her head. They had only worn white T-shirts and boxers underneath. Definitely nothing to hide access chips to the cell.

She eyed the metal bars, then the suits behind her. "I have an idea."

Persia followed her gaze. "If I'm right about what I think you're thinking, then I'm in." She grinned, then turned with a wince.

Lenah went to help her. "Are you hurt?"

"I'm fine," Persia muttered. "But I definitely wouldn't mind the help of one of these suits."

"Just be quick please," Doctor Lund called as they left him.

Lenah bent to pick up the helmets and handed one to Persia, showing her the switch.

"Whoa, that's a lot of interfaces. How did these guys even see us?" Persia blurted as she put on her helmet.

"It's a little like looking at flight controls in a cockpit," Lenah told her. "You learn which one to look at in a given moment and which one to ignore." She put on her own helmet, then went to the suit. "I hope these won't be too big."

Neither she nor Persia were very tall, and the guards were definitely taller. Lenah had to take off her shoes to get the suit on, but it fit surprisingly well. It was too big, yes, but it was almost as if the material was trying to cling to her wherever it could.

As she picked up her boots again, she was surprised to find them weighing almost nothing. Actually, she couldn't really feel it.

The suit's UI blinked in front of Lenah's eyes, asking what mode she wanted to use it in. The options were light, medium, fighting, and heavy load.

"I turned on fighting mode," she told Persia, her voice sounding muffled. Did this thing have speakers?

Scanning the interfaces, she found an audio symbol. There it was: internal and external speakers. She turned both on by letting her vision linger for a second.

"I'm in fighting mode," she repeated her comment to Persia.

"What?" Persia seemed to yell, but Lenah could barely hear her.

"Look at the audio symbol in the upper right. Turn on your speakers. And your fighting mode is in the menu that pops up."

While Persia stood still to follow her instructions, Lenah turned to Doctor Lund's cell. Time to try out her new cyborg strength.

31 BECOMING CYBORGS

LENAH FISTED HER SUITED hand and drove it toward the wall, putting all her strength into the movement. Metal cracked with a satisfying sound, and her fist left a several-centimeters-deep indent in the sheeting. She tried again and again, and every time the wall gave in further, until the panel was so warped she could easily pull it off.

"First my cell and now a wall. You're a cyborg, Lenah," Doctor Lund said.

Lenah grinned under her visor. It did feel amazing. How could Cassius not feel elated all the time? Persia ducked through the hole Lenah had made, and Lenah followed with Doctor Lund. It was dark, but as soon as she thought about it, the room became visible in front of her eyes, bathed in a light that was too bright to be natural. Night vision.

"Wow, we can even see in the dark." Persia's voice carried through her speakers. "These suits are neat."

Lenah didn't answer. She heard sounds of a fight in the next room and went to check the door, but it was locked, and there was no access panel.

She lifted her fist again when Persia interrupted her. "My turn," she said, swinging her hammer, and Lenah smiled despite herself as she stepped back to give Persia room.

Lenah got out her knife and stood at the ready as Persia made quick business of the door. With a few well-aimed blows, the mechanism came loose. Light shone in the room beyond, where the fight became visible. Uz and Cassius stood back to back, surrounded by four adversaries who were still standing. All of them were clad in fighting suits. Cassius was bleeding from a gash at his temple. He was trying to confront three and leave Uz with only one. The four moved at the same time, and Cassius intercepted by swinging his metal arm. What usually had a great effect, barely stopped these guys. Without further thought, Lenah burst through the door, followed by Persia.

Lenah picked the one attacking Uz, and unlike what she'd learned in Cassius's training, she didn't do her usual dance around him. This time, she wasn't the weaker target, and she had surprise on her side.

Lenah put all her anger about her father, her sense of urgency, and her indignation about the mages into the blow. Her opponent pulled up his arm in defense to meet her fist, but Lenah figured he would and adjusted her aim in the last moment. He blocked, pulling up his arm at an impossible speed. Lenah wasn't the only one with better-than-human reactions now.

She gritted her teeth and took a fighting stance after all, then started to dance around him. He attacked next, trying to land a blow to her gut. She evaded, jumped away, and suddenly found herself several meters from the fight. This new strength was taking some time to get used to.

The man followed her with a few controlled steps, launching at her again. Lenah bent and kicked. It hit him hard in the side and he stumbled but didn't go down. She followed up again, but this time he evaded her kick, then turned away and tried to get closer to her. She let him, figuring she could withstand one blow and planning to use the chance for a counter-hit herself.

His fist smashed into Lenah's helmet, and the displays in front of her visor blinked and wavered. Everything was turning on and off at the same time. She stumbled, becoming disoriented, and lost sight of her adversary. A fist in the gut finally told her that he was right in front of her. Pain exploded in her already sore middle, and she gasped, trying to stay upright.

She thought quickly to use her talents on him, but he was coming for her, and she put all her effort into breathing and jumping out of the way. Lenah stumbled and landed on her butt, unable to keep her balance when the suit exaggerated her movement.

The man followed up with a jump himself, only, his was more controlled. His weight pressed exactly where her belly already ached. She wiggled under him, but he wouldn't budge. Instead, he followed up with another blow to her face. Lenah lifted her hand in protection, but he just used his other fist to land his blow. Blinking lights erupted all over her vision again. He definitely knew the weak spots of this armor.

Changing tactics, Lenah grabbed him by his torso and pulled. She used her leg and trapped his thigh next to her. She had practiced this with Cassius's weight and was surprised how easy it was to pull this man down with the suit on. He seemed surprised too, as she was able to pin his arms under her, then roll over. Her stomach protested at the motion, but she pushed through.

When she was sitting on top of him, she targeted his helmeted face and landed several fast blows. The speed at which she moved was incredible.

He tried to protect himself from her incoming fist, but she changed direction, and when he didn't follow her movement, she knew that all the blinking displays blinded him. Lenah fumbled for the button on his helmet and pressed. When she delivered a final blow into his face, he stopped moving.

Around her, the sounds of fighting had ebbed. Persia stood in the room, hammer lifted, and two adversaries in front of her on the ground. Cassius had taken care of the last one and was breathing heavily and wiping the blood off his bruised face.

"Are you alright?" Lenah asked him and closed the distance between them.

"Fine," he said in a clipped voice, then turned away.

Lenah regarded him, taking in his slumped shoulders and wheezing breath. She didn't think she'd ever seen him this exhausted, not even after confronting Kahoot's cyborg in the Syrr temple.

She looked around. Six suited men were in various places unconscious on the floor. It was safe to assume that Cassius had managed to knock out three of them.

Uz and Doctor Lund caught her attention, approaching the door behind the body scanner. It was made of thick material and reminded her of a spaceship hatch.

Persia followed her eyes. "That door looks like the real deal. I bet we finally found it."

Lenah nodded and stepped closer. As Doctor Lund touched the door, it gave a beep of denial, and a panel lit up in its center. Lenah fumbled into her suit to get out the chip card she'd taken from her father. She winked it over the panel and was rewarded by the mechanical sounds of an opening hatch. The door swung upward.

What lay beyond reminded Lenah even more of a spaceship. It was a small chamber, empty but for blinking panels on the wall and an identical hatch door at its opposite side.

"Please step into the decontamination chamber," a friendly AI voice said.

"What will you do to us? Where does this lead?" Doctor Lund addressed the AI. He sounded nervous, and Lenah couldn't blame him. After having to fight all these guards, she was nervous about what else the place had in store for them.

"Please step into the decontamination chamber," the AI repeated.

"Is the farm on the other side of the hatch?" Lenah asked.

"Command not recognized. Please step into the decontamination chamber," it repeated stoically.

Great, a non-intelligent AI.

"For stars sake, I'll do it," Lenah said and walked into the room. Everyone else followed suit.

"We're not letting you do this alone," Uz said.

"You're the only one with an access card." Persia shrugged. Cassius just glowered wordlessly.

The hatch closed, locking them in the small chamber.

"Decontamination in three…two…one," the AI announced. Lenah looked around, unsure what was about to happen, when the room was suddenly bathed in a sickly green light. For a moment, her stomach and every other organ and blood vessel in her body felt as if it were being turned upside down. She was going to throw up. The sensation vanished as quickly as it had come, and the light restored to its normal white color. She swallowed hard.

"Atmospheric adjustment in three…two…one," the AI said, unaware of the discomfort of its decontaminated subjects.

"What's atmospheric—?" Persia asked, but her voice cut off as the room and their bodies suddenly seemed to lose weight. Instinctively, Lenah knew that they were now in a zone of reduced gravity.

"Thank you," the AI announced in its robotic, cheerful tone as the hatch in front of them pulled open, engulfing them in the dark-purple light of the room beyond.

Behind Lenah, Cassius stepped forward to overtake her in the front row. He had his weapons lifted and head turned to listen into the room. Lenah pulled out her knife as she walked out of the decontamination chamber behind him.

The room was empty, except for a large tree that dominated a wide and tall space. Lenah blinked several times to confirm what she saw. It was a tree.

Next to her, Uz took in a sharp breath. Lenah looked over and saw the Cassidian staring open-mouthed and with wide eyes toward the tree.

Doctor Lund joined her. "Uz, what is it?"

Uz didn't react, just kept staring. Her hand went up to the scars on her forehead, and she seemed almost surprised not to find her gyrums there. Lenah looked back at the tree, taking in its sheer size and detail for the first time. It was bathed in purple light, but Lenah could see that the tree, both its bark and leaves, were of an even deeper purple. At the same time, they shimmered in a pearly hue. Was that one of those sacred Cascra trees? Lenah looked back and forth between Uz and the tree and considered her suspicion confirmed. She inspected the tree again, marveling at its magnificence.

The branches started only halfway up the trunk, a good seven or so meters above the ground. They were wide and quickly became covered in a mass of large, blade-shaped leaves, each growing in a circle around the thinner branches.

A red fruit was growing at the very tip of some. It was beautiful and eerie, but a tree after all. Just—what was it doing here?

Behind the tree stood a small production line. A conveyor system was slowly moving something—she couldn't see what from this distance but imagined warp drives—taking it through various stations behind panels. At the far-right side, silvery boxes were neatly stacked up. Lenah had seen those before. Each would hold several hundred of the small hand-sized disks that were the warp drives.

"Rumors have it that Cassidia is covered in vast forests of purple trees. Trees no creature but those native to the planet are allowed. They are set far away from the public meeting places where Cassidians permit the very rare visits of off-worlders," Cassius said slowly. He wasn't looking at the tree but instead studying Uz's face. Lenah followed his gaze. Uz still looked stunned as she gazed upon the tree, incredulity written all over her face. She didn't deny Cassius's words.

"Is this a tree from Cassidia, Uz?" Cassius asked her, his deep and raspy voice sounding softer than Lenah had ever heard him. Uz licked her lips, then slowly nodded.

"This is…" her voice broke up, "…heresy."

"I take it it's not just a decorative tree, given that someone went to great lengths to put it here?" Persia asked from behind.

Lenah shot her a silencing look. Whatever was going on with Uz, she was sure sarcasm wouldn't be appreciated right now.

32   RARE TREES

"IT'S NOT JUST A TREE," Uz said almost mechanically as if Persia's irony hadn't reached her. She slowly walked forward, taking careful steps toward the trunk. Lenah and Cassius followed, worried that security measures were in place.

Doctor Lund took the rear, murmuring to himself. "This place is big," he said twice. "And we only have the few backpacks of explosives."

Uz turned so suddenly, Cassius almost walked into her. He stopped and lifted his weapon, looking around. Lenah searched too but couldn't find anything that had changed in the last few seconds.

"There's no way you're blowing up that tree," Uz growled at Doctor Lund, pointing a long finger at him. "No way. They're the most important living entity in the universe and they belong to the home world only."

Lenah found Cassius's eyes as he arched a questioning eyebrow. Remembering Uz's reaction when Lenah had asked about the Cascra logs on Neeth Station, Lenah thought she understood what was going on. "I think the Cascra trees are more than just a big forest on Cassidia. They are extremely important in Cassidian culture and have something to do with the vertex." She explained.

"They're untouchable," Uz whispered. Then she shook her head, but at least she was no longer staring daggers toward Doctor Lund.

"Do you know what an entire tree is doing here?" Lenah asked her, hoping that turning the conversation away from Cassidia itself would make Uz speak.

Uz shook her head, then looked up again and nodded. But she didn't speak.

"Uz, we're your friends. We won't share with anyone what you tell us."

"But you're here to destroy it," Uz said, still looking up into the treetop. Lenah followed her gaze and realized that the red fruits on top looked like they were pulsing with colorful energy. Was that really a fruit? Or was that the magic Uz had been talking about?

"Are you sure we have to destroy the tree?" Lenah asked softly.

"How could this person do this? Bring a Cascra tree off-world. And for what? For implementing this stupid technology. *Technology*, of all things." Uz shivered.

Lenah had never seen Uz—the most tech-friendly person she knew—have such a mainstream Cassidian opinion. Her gyrums had even been cut off because of her love of technology. It all added to Lenah's confusion.

"Implementing the mage farm?" Lenah said, instead of asking any of the other pressing questions she felt bubbling up inside of her. At least, it sounded like a clue to what was going on here.

Uz looked at Lenah. Their gazes met for several long moments before Uz broke the contact. Her shoulders slumped, and she stared lovingly at the tree trunk. "You can't tell anyone ever what I'm about to tell you. Not to non-Cassidian, and, especially, not to another Cassidian. It's one of the most closely guarded secrets of the galaxy."

Everyone nodded, but Uz didn't even look at them. Nonetheless, she continued. "The Cascra tree, its fruits specifically, serves as an amplifier—a catalyst—to the vertex. It lets us use more warp magic than we actually possess. In a way, it stabilizes the magic, makes it tangible to our vertex sense. The fruit only works as long as it is connected to its mother tree. Once plucked, it will lose power and just be a random crystal with no special use. They are sacred. And what's worse, this tree was taken from Cassidia. For sure without the necessary ritual performed by the High Priest."

"Are you saying that this tree was stolen from Cassidia?" Lenah asked.

"It has to be. There is no other possible explanation." Uz nodded.

"But for what purpose? Stabilizing what?"

"I believe it must be serving a crucial purpose in extracting the warp essence from the mages and storing it on the drives. Destroy the tree and you destroy the farm." Uz sounded really miserable as she said that.

Lenah nodded. She still didn't understand most of what was going on here, but that general notion made sense.

"And why the purple light?" Persia asked.

Uz's shoulders drooped. "It feels like home here. The light, the slightly lower gravity…"

"They're mimicking the tree's natural conditions," Cassius concluded.

"I hate to say anything, but we have less than an hour," Doctor Lund said, putting down his backpack and starting to unpack its content.

"Don't you understand what I just said?" Uz shouted. "We can't damage that tree."

Lenah thought about that, but if this was the secret to how the magic got stored on the warp drives, then there was no other way. "Uz, the tree is already lost to your people. If this is such a closely guarded secret, that's another reason to destroy it."

"No."

"Uz, think about it."

"No."

"We don't have time for such childish arguments," Doctor Lund said matter-of-factly, looking up from the explosives on the floor.

Uz turned. "You think this is childish? What would you do if someone wanted to blow up every single theory USO had ever proven to be scientific?" She breathed hard. "Would you call that childish too?"

"You can't compare that. USO does science. We prove that myth and magic don't exist. You, on the other hand, are getting all worked up about something mythical like a holy tree. I understand that it has a significant cultural meaning, but saving this planet is more important than this tree. It's simple Fungs's Allotment of Rank theory. So, your behavior," Doctor Lund pointed a finger at her, "is childish."

Uz fumed. In fact, she looked like she was going to attack Doctor Lund. If she'd been any other race than a peace-loving Cassidian, she probably would have.

"Uz," Lenah said and tried again, "please try to see our point of view. No one is saying that this isn't a terrible thing to your people. Even if it wasn't an important tree for Cassidians, destroying something so beautiful is awful. But think about the price. Please, think about the price. Humanity might be wiped out if we don't do this."

Uz looked at her, her eyes sad and filling with tears. But she didn't argue, so Lenah continued.

"Do you remember the history of how Cassidians found the human generation ship, and you took us in? Showed us New Earth, didn't even abandon us when we destroyed our new home planet as well? One tree, after making all that effort, is maybe a price worth paying," Lenah said, thinking of history classes where they had learned how the human generation ship had been found, floating with failing solar engines, by the Cassidians. They'd taken in humans, shown them to New Earth, and some had even fallen in love with each other. That had changed humanity forever. They had acquired warp magic. Though Lenah couldn't think of anything that humans had ever truly given back to the Cassidians. They'd quickly started to spread to other worlds, building their military and fighting over territory. It had resulted in the destruction of New Earth due to the same nuclear weapons that had already destroyed Old Earth.

"One tree and a secret kept," Uz whispered. Then she turned around and walked toward the tree where she slumped down with her back against the trunk. She put her cheek there as if trying to console it and didn't speak again. Lenah nodded to Doctor Lund. They would continue.

"Where should we place these explosives?" Cassius asked the doctor in a hushed voice. Lenah appreciated that he didn't want Uz to hear more than necessary.

"I don't know for sure yet. It's a really big area to cover." Doctor Lund walked closer to the tree, then the production line in the back of the room. All the while, he kept muttering and taking notes on one of his devices.

Lenah helped Persia unpack their cargo, while Cassius assumed a guarding position halfway to the hatch door. He kept squinting back at Uz, however, and looked as miserable as Lenah felt for the Cassidian. Funny how she'd once thought his face expressionless. You only had to look closer and see the emotions in his eyes.

After a while, Doctor Lund joined them. "I think I have it figured out. We can place much of the explosives under the roots and spread out the remains along the production line and the storage over there. I'm confident that even a deeply rooted tree won't be able to withstand that much. I asked her if she knew how deep the roots are, but she won't talk to me." He shook his head.

"Alright, just tell us where to place all these things, and we'll follow your instructions," Lenah said, picking up some of the spheres.

"Right. Let's first bring a good twenty to the tree. Then we place the remaining around the back area."

Each of them began cradling the round spheres in their arms and making their way to the tree trunk. When Uz saw them approach, she slunk back and sat by a low-hanging branch, her stiff back turned toward them. Doctor Lund stayed behind, muttering calculations to himself with the help of his notes, while Lenah and Persia made another trip.

"They can't blow up if I drop one, can they?" Persia asked, balancing a mountain of spheres in her arms. Lenah grunted. She had no idea but could only concentrate on her own mountain. "Whoever designed these to be round was a stupid person."

"They're Craff made," Doctor Lund said, looking up. "I believe for them it's a handy size to fit into one of their claws. And they won't explode just like that. The inside is filled with exmangonium. A rare mineral found deep down in the crust of their home world. Once we turn the switch and set the timer, it'll slowly cool down the liquid exmangonium inside."

"Cooling, huh. Typical Craff," Persia muttered, probably thinking of the alien's like for extreme heat.

"It's pretty safe if you live surrounded by lava," Lenah said.

"Guess so."

Doctor Lund accepted the additional spheres, then waved for Lenah to stay.

"Can you help me stick them to the trunk over there?"

He showed her how she could activate the little stick legs that came with the devices, then got out a small laser to mark the spots. They worked in silence until the trunk and its surrounding roots were evenly covered with the bulbs.

"You think thirty minutes is enough?" Lenah asked him, adrenaline spiking in her again as she programmed in the timer. They still had to place the remaining explosives and leave.

"It'll have to be. That's all the time we have left."

Lenah nodded and started working more quickly. As they turned to leave, Cassius stopped. "Where's Uz?"

"She…Stars, I don't know. She was just here." Lenah turned around to go looking for Uz, but she appeared a few moments later, her own empty backpack strapped over her shoulders. She was crying, looking the picture of misery.

Lenah patted her on the forearm. "Let's go, Uz. We need to get away from here."

The Cassidian nodded, not meeting her eyes. Together, they stepped through the hatch door and back into the decontamination chamber.

33 BOOM!

"FASTER, MOVE FASTER," Cassius urged, taking the lead as they jogged across Callo mansion's impeccable lawn. Lenah followed him, looking back at the house. How far away was the lab from the estate? Would the house get damaged in the explosion? She didn't know how she felt about that. At this point, coming back to live here seemed out of the question. The *Rambler* felt more like home than her old rooms. Despite the perks of having delicious food, as many hot water showers as she wanted, and the walk-in closet.

The underground location of the lab made it hard to know exactly how far away it was, but if it had been built close to the lake as the original plans had indicated, that meant it was at least a klick away. Just to be sure, Lenah took one last look at the mansion behind her.

Their escape back through the house had been easier than anticipated. Everyone was gathered outside in the front yard, staring up at the crafts visible in the air: the Cheung army. Lenah's group hadn't run into anyone while slipping through the back of the house. She looked up where dozens of small ships were flying above them. Had a battle started? Were the Cava Dara here already, high above them?

"Lenah," Cassius urged again, and she turned, hurrying.

"I'm here," she said, catching up. They hiked in silence next to each other.

"Do you think Lorka and Zyr made it with the mages?" Persia panted.

"We'll see soon enough. I can't hear them yet," Cassius said. He was the only one not out of breath.

"One minute," Doctor Lund puffed and stopped dead in his tracks, looking down at his wristpiece. "By the stars, only one minute."

"Keep walking," Cassius told him, and they all continued in silence. Maybe everyone was trying to count down the sixty seconds, as was Lenah.

"Ten seconds," Doctor Lund announced. Uz gave a short whine, then started to pick up speed, getting ahead of them all.

"Five. Four. Three. Two, and..." Doctor Lund's last words were cut off by a loud boom, followed by a low rumble. The earth shook under them, and they were showered in dried leaves from the trees above. The forest rustled and cracked, then everything fell silent. Lenah turned to see what had happened back at the house, but they were too far away by now. All she could see was the forest. Faint human voices drifted over from the direction, and she hoped no one was hurt. That it was only from confusion and worry about what had exploded. Her father would know exactly what had happened, of course. Had he been found by now? Would she ever see him again? Or talk to him again?

Cassius touched her lightly on the shoulder, and they continued walking. Lenah kept looking up at the sky. Had the Cava Dara turned around to sleep for another six thousand years?

Finally, they reached the ship. Zyr was floating in front of the dusty hatch, looking as grumpy as a stone-made drone could. Which meant quite grumpy.

"What's wrong, Zyr? Did something go awry with the mages?" Lenah asked as she approached.

"Yes," he said, snuffling and not reprimanding her on the use of his nickname.

"What happened?" Images of a dozen mages blowing up with the farm appeared in her mind.

"They are there. In there. *All of them*," Zyrakath pressed out and fluttered higher.

She let out a long breath. "Thank the stars. But…isn't that good news?"

"No."

"No?"

"Too many people. Talking, crowding. I haven't been with so many people in millennia."

"Oh. Well, it won't be for long," Lenah said, trying to sound understanding. Even she felt like being alone after today's events.

"It's almost time for you to fulfill your promise to take me back home. I'm being very patient with your underdeveloped plans of mayhem and destruction. You should have really consulted your Elders before coming here. Now, I'm getting stuffed with so many people in your small space box."

"You're welcome to come hang out with me in the engine room," Uz offered, waving her hand over the hatch's sensor panel and climbing up before the hatch had fully opened.

"They might be in there, too," Zyr said but followed her inside.

"How many mages were there?" Persia asked Lenah, stepping next to her into the ship.

Lenah could immediately tell that it was far more than she'd thought. At least a dozen sickly looking people were huddled all over the cargo hold, but she could hear soft conversations from further up the corridor as well. And laughing.

Lenah nodded to the mages who looked up at them as they entered the ship. One person, the doctor she had influenced into showing them around, stood up and walked toward her. She looked guarded, but urgency was written all over her face. "What was that blast? Did the farm really blow up?"

"Yes. It's gone," Lenah said loudly, so that everyone would hear. A general sigh went through the room, and several mages smiled. That made Lenah feel better.

The doctor put a hand to her heart. "I can't say I feel sorry about that." Then she nodded to Lenah, and a silent understanding of peace passed between them.

Lenah continued up the corridor and found Lorka in the common room with another group of mages.

"Lenah," he called when she passed by, and he stepped out into the corridor.

"What is it?"

"I...well, um. I don't know how to say this. You are a great team, and..." he broke off, wringing his hands.

"Be quick, Lorka." Lenah felt anxious to depart.

"Okay," Lorka said. "I really like it here with you guys, but these are my real people." His voice drifted off, and he looked away.

"And you want to stay with them?"

His head snapped back, then forward. "Yes."

"That's understandable. You helped us get off UPL station, and I'll always be grateful. But, of course, you won't give up your whole life to come stay with us. You're always welcome to come visit, and when you do, I'll finally show you how to fly this ship." She forced a wink to the young mage.

His eyes lit up. "And you should visit me. Us. My father." He corrected himself. "You should come talk to him about the possibility of him training you."

It was Lenah's turn to look away, but Lorka continued, "At least come and see if there's material—books or videos about," he trailed off, "your condition," he finished, glaring at the mages sitting a few steps away.

Lenah nodded. It was tempting, of course. And she might have the time. If the Cava Dara left, what else would she do?

Was it even a valid plan to fly around the galaxy and enjoy her freedom?

"I'll think about it," she finally said, and it seemed to satisfy Lorka.

"And I could present you to all my friends! If they take me back in, that is…I mean, I didn't complete my internship, but I should get some leeway for bringing back all of these guys." Then he bent down and engulfed her in a short hug, the kind only tall and lanky people could give. Before she could hug him back, he'd already stepped back into the common room with sweeping robes that showed off his yellow socks.

Smiling despite herself, Lenah continued into the blissfully empty cockpit.

34 BACK IN ORBIT

"WE'LL BE HITTING the atmosphere in the next few seconds," Lenah announced to Cassius and Zyr, who were sitting and hovering, respectively, with her in the cockpit. She'd wanted to be alone up here, but Cassius has insisted in case she needed someone to man the only two aft lasers the *Star Rambler* had. She'd grudgingly nodded, but the Cassius she wanted to be with was the version from before the events of today. The one before she'd invaded his privacy and before he'd repeatedly shamed her for her social status—former social status.

After dropping off the mages and Lorka at the Central Police Station, it had taken them a long time to regain height. The sky above Asturis I was swarming with Cheung army fighters, and Lenah had flown a good distance away to come up over the forest.

She fidgeted with the *Rambler*'s controls as they approached the atmosphere. Once through, they'd at least be able to see things for themselves. She had to admit that she didn't want to see, didn't want to confront the terrible things she feared laid out there. If the Cava Dara were backing off, then why were there still so many fighters patrolling the capital? It all led to the same conclusion. The Cava Dara were still attacking, and their efforts had been in vain.

The ship shook, momentarily blinding them in orange light of a breached atmosphere, and they were in open space.

Lenah peered into the surrounding blackness. There was nothing there, probably because they had come out over the endless forests that dominated the region east of Asturis I. But a few hundred klicks toward the west, there was— "Blazing stars."

A battle was raging ahead of them. Lenah's heart raced as she tried to decipher exactly what was going on.

She saw big ships fire a barrage of lasers toward small floating objects, many of which were vaguely humanoid in shape. There were so many. An endless swarm. Lasers pierced holes into their lines, but every time, an equal number of Muha Dara would close the gap. The *Star Rambler* hovered too far away for Lenah to see details, but she shuddered at the thought of former Syrr floating in space.

At some point, the lasers had to kill enough to cut holes into their masses, right? That was, as long as the Cava Dara didn't reach the humans inside the ships to restock their ranks.

A sharp beep interrupted their shocked silence. A message.

"Someone's trying to comm us." Cassius stated the obvious, and Lenah absently nodded as she accepted the connection.

"Civilian ship, back off," a clipped male voice said. "There's a battle going on, and we won't be held responsible if a stray laser beam finds you. I insist. Back off, go back planet-side. This is no place for onlookers."

The message ended, but no one moved. Instead, they kept staring at the battle ahead.

"The Cava Dara are still coming," Lenah muttered, feeling defeat crawl its tendrils through her whole body.

"Maybe they haven't yet realized that the mage farm was destroyed?" Persia said softly from the hatch. Lenah hadn't even realized she was there.

"But aren't they magical beings that should—somehow, I don't know—feel this? Something like that happened when they awoke, no?"

No one answered, but she hadn't expected them to. Had it been stupid to assume that fixing the trigger would stop the attack? Either that wasn't the case, maybe once triggered, the Cava Dara came for their victims no matter what, or the mage farm wasn't the only trigger. Except, that didn't make any sense.

"Zyr, once the trigger is removed, shouldn't the attacks stop?"

"I understand that *Zyr* is a form to address me with respect, but I would much prefer that you call me Elder Zyr," the little drone said behind her, managing to sound indignant and stately despite his high-pitched voice.

"Okay, *Elder* Zyr. Do you know how the Cava Dara work?"

Silence.

"Stars, seriously? Elder Zyr, would you please answer my question?" she repeated a third time, trying to cut the sarcasm out of her voice. She found his reaction childish. A six-thousand-year-old drone that behaved immature but might be the key to valuable information. Just what she needed right now.

A hand, Cassius's, came to lay softly on her forearm. Lenah moved her arm to adjust a switch on her console. She didn't need this right now. And, especially, not from the guy who had created a canyon between them earlier.

"Even in situations of stress, you should never forget who is in charge," the drone finally said.

"Situation of stress?" Lenah echoed. "Are you serious? My race is being attacked. Only one corporate army is currently fighting here and the big solution we had, seems to have had no effect whatsoever. Maybe, we should have never left UPL station, but instead, started a political campaign for greater army resources, not stolen explosives on a freaking illegal space station and blown up trillions upon trillions of magic in CGC, as well as Uz's holy tree!" Tears were starting to well up in her eyes as she spoke, and she couldn't hold them back.

Zyr nodded. "I do not know why the Cava Dara are still attacking. I believed, like you, that the attacks would stop once the trigger was removed. That is either not the case, or there is another trigger."

"Another trigger?" Persia whispered. "Like a second mage farm?"

"Yes," Zyrakath answered. "Or something else entirely."

"I don't think there's another mage farm." Lenah shook her head. "So, what could that other thing be? This is a disaster and—*stars.*" Her voice hurt. "Are those Cheung ships firing at each other?" She stared up ahead, then back onto her screen. Fireworks of laser beams shooting in all directions had replaced the well-aimed shots at the incoming Muha Dara. What had seemed like a difficult battle with two clear fronts, now looked like pure chaos.

"Stars, you're right," Cassius exclaimed, also staring out of the window. "What are they doing?"

"They have been turned," Zyrakath said gloomily.

"But are they conscious enough to shoot? Aren't they supposed to start floating through space and attack the other ships that way?" Persia asked, leaning over Lenah's shoulder. "I mean, the turn is instant, no?"

"It is," Zyrakath attested. "I do not know why they are doing this. With my people, it was different. The turned attacked the remaining Syrr flesh-to-flesh as we didn't have flying boxes available to us.

"I'll get us closer," Lenah said and moved the *Rambler* forward without asking for their consent. No one mouthed any objections.

She flew slowly, scanning the surrounding space. Up ahead, small moving figures took shape. Some were tiny specks of upright floating humanoids. Syrr. Others were larger, darker, a sharp stinger hovering over their bodies. Those were Bartoc. Lenah's head itched as she remembered how the only Bartoc she'd ever encountered had pulled her toward that stinger by the hair. If Cassius hadn't rescued them right then and there…imagine what these versions of Bartoc could do with just a bare touch.

A gasp followed by a slight crash made her turn. Zyrakath had apparently stumbled back in the air and hit the wall. His mouth was open wide, and his stony eyeballs appeared to balk at what he was witnessing. "By the souls of the Elders, those are my people."

"They no longer are," Cassius said softly. "They haven't been for six thousand years."

Zyrakath shook his head. "If I wouldn't have left. If I had stayed to keep watch over them."

Lenah shivered, remembering the creepy stone army they had encountered on Masis III. Zyr had been there with them for six thousand long years.

"What are they doing to the hatches?" Persia asked.

Lenah pulled her attention back to the view in front of them.

"They are pulling them open, and, oh no—" Persia trailed off.

Lenah didn't say anything. She could only watch in horror. How could a tiny Syrr body, Muha Dara or not, be strong enough to pull open the hatch of a spaceship with their bare hands?

"By the stars, they're going in," Cassius whispered.

Moments later, shapes filed out of the ship closest to them, humanoid, but bigger than the Syrr. Floating, somehow no longer in need of oxygen. Humans.

"Lenah, get us away," Cassius said, urgency in his voice. "We can't do anything here. At any moment, one of those things will get close enough. Move us, Lenah. Or I will." He seemed serious about it. Even calling her by her name again.

Slowly, feeling shock take hold of her body, Lenah moved her hands to the controls. Her father had done this. He had caused this horror and she had failed to avoid it.

"Look, one of the Cava Dara. There." Persia pointed sideways. A tall figure, bigger even than the humans, appeared a few klicks away from the *Rambler*. Its black silhouette shone brightly against the backdrop of the planet below and displayed every crease and curve in the unmoving wings and regal face. Its purple eyes seemed to bore into Lenah, even across the distance, as if it could see her, sitting here, protected in the cockpit. Lenah shook herself and looked away, and the creature did the same almost as if they really had shared contact. It then moved its wings, stretching them high over its head in an almost lazy motion. A moment later, it vanished from their field of vision.

"What can we do now?" Lenah asked in a soft voice. "How can we help?"

Cassius shook his head.

"Stop them from destroying your home, of course," Zyr said.

Lenah turned to look at the drone. "And how would you suggest we do that?"

He hovered close to her face. "Use your magic. What else? You and the other one. The one you fought with at my temple."

Lenah gaped. "Corinna?"

"Why by the stars would we fight with Corinna?" Persia said, shaking her head. "She tried to kill us."

Ignoring Persia's comment, Lenah asked, "What do you mean, Zyr? Use my magic?"

Zyr gave her an exasperated look, and she figured he was debating whether to complain for not being addressed properly or explain. But then he spoke. "I had access to the temple's great library for six thousand years, and I read each of the 2.14 million books several times." For someone unaccustomed to human numbers, he certainly was using a lot of them. "I no longer need to sleep since I transferred into this artificial body."

Lenah tapped her fingers on her armrest but didn't interrupt him. At least, he was talking to her. Even if his story sounded self-important, it would hopefully lead somewhere relevant.

"There were hundreds of Cassidian books in the library. Some of which told the history of the Old Cassidians. And their extinction." He shook his small head. "If we'd have known that the Cava Dara would come for other races as well, maybe we could have avoided our fate." He took a deep, theatrical breath. "In one of those books, it was written that the Muha Dara could be influenced by Cassidian mind controllers as long as there is not a Cava Dara nearby."

"But I'm not one of those Cassidian mind controllers." Lenah shook her head.

"You are a human, but a mind controller none-the-less," the drone answered.

No one spoke as Lenah processed that. Could her magic originate from the Cassidians? It would make sense, considering that was how humans had acquired warp magic. But the Cassidians Zyr was talking about had gone extinct eighteen thousand years ago. Then again, did it matter right now?

"You're saying I can stop these," she said. "As long as I'm far enough away from the Cava Dara?" Lenah could not hide the skepticism in her voice.

"They are most likely susceptible to your powers," the little drone answered. "As well as the other woman's."

"Corinna?"

He nodded. "The mind controllers even united their magical powers together and were able to multiply their effect. Nonetheless, in the end, they lost."

"You might be a genius, Zyr," Lenah said and was rewarded with a smile and appreciative nod from him. She almost wanted to hug the drone, but the mere thought of him giving her another lecture on elder respect stopped her.

"We should test this theory of yours," she announced and guided the *Star Rambler* back toward the Cheung army ships.

"I think getting closer won't be needed," Persia said, staring at the sensor panel. Lenah followed her gaze. Four ships were coming their way, and they were shooting at each other.

"Stars, where did they come from so quickly?"

"Concentrate," Zyrakath's calm voice said from behind her. Lenah listened to him.

At first, all she could see were the minds of her friends, but then she discovered something else, like a mist that was surrounding the approaching figures. Was that their version of a mind? So weak, it looked like transparent fog instead of the well-defined cloud she was used to?

"Lenah!" Persia yelled into her ear, and Cassius's shoulder rammed into hers. Lenah jerked her concentration back into the cockpit. The proximity sensors were beeping loudly. Cassius's hand was on the flight stick, the *Rambler* angling sharply downward. They were moving away from a ship that had closed in above them, but there was another ship halfway under them, and they were going right toward it. How had they closed in this quickly?

She pushed Cassius's hand away from the flight stick and pulled the *Rambler* sideways, rapidly accelerating. The ship creaked in protest at the sharp turn, but she knew it would follow her controls. Her *Rambler* was old, but agile. They soared through a gap between two of the incoming ships.

Belatedly, Lenah realized the planet's atmosphere started right there, and the ship shook hard as they plummeted through.

35 MAKING A CALL

"I'M REALLY NOT SURE she'll answer at all," Uz commented, and not for the first time. Her eyes were puffy, and she didn't look one bit better than she had back at the tree. But Lenah was glad she'd agreed to come out of the engine room and help her call Corinna. Only, Corinna wasn't picking up.

"Let's send her a comm then. I'm not wasting any more time on this annoying woman," Lenah grumbled. "She's there when you don't need her and not there when you do need her."

"In the message, what do you want to tell her?" Uz asked, looking skeptical. Or depressed. Probably both. Lenah was glad she was thinking of something else rather than the destruction of the tree.

"The truth."

Uz shrugged and swiped the recorder. Then nodded toward Lenah. "Ready."

"Corinna, this is Lenah Callo. Before you hang up on me, I'll get straight to the point. Mind magic can influence the Muha Dara. Our combined strength will be even stronger. More than we can both do separately. I have it from an ancient, but reliable source. I'm going planet-side and will help in the city. Just for today, let's forget what happened between us and work together. For the good of Astur." She nodded for Uz to turn off the recording.

They both stared at the device for a few moments.

"Do you think she'll come?" Uz asked.

Lenah bit her lip. "Not sure. On Masis III, she was very proud of being in control of this matter. Remember how she said that it should be in capable hands, implying her own? And how she chased us halfway across the galaxy to get factual proof of this mystery?"

Uz nodded.

"I believe she'll be intrigued by this new fact and by the control she could gain over the situation. Which she seems to have lost out in space."

Uz pursed her lips. "I guess that makes sense, but she's still our enemy. Apart from the Cava Dara, we're the last people in the galaxy she wants to cooperate with."

"True," Lenah said and nodded. "But we're better than the Cava Dara and that's all that counts right now."

They sat in silence for a little while, then Lenah turned back to her controls. She had a ship to bring down to the surface and a population to help. It didn't matter what Corinna Cheung decided to do. Lenah would give her best anyways.

"Lenah, look at that." Uz pointed at a stream of figures visible in their view window.

"Stars, how can they be so fast?" Lenah said as she watched the mix of Syrr, Bartoc, and humans float toward the capital. "First, they rip open hatches, now, they fly faster than any spaceship."

It was eerie. A body should not be able to withstand this. But whatever had become of these former humans, Syrr, and even Bartoc, they seemed immune to the very forces of nature, like gravity, the vacuum of space, or the friction of atmospheric reentry.

"Uz, can you check what's going on in Asturis I? News sources, video feeds?" Lenah asked with renewed urgency.

Uz nodded and started typing commands into the *Rambler*'s starnet console. A short while later, a public camera view came up, showing the center of the capital's office district. There was no commentary, only a camera feed depicting office workers running out of buildings, their faces contorted into panicked masks. Quick-moving shadows cast darkness over the crowd, even though the sun was out and not a single cloud was visible over the city. Lenah could guess what that meant.

"I think they are ripping off windows," Uz said, pointing to several blurry specks in the background.

"Where are the guards? The police? Why is no one there to defend these people?" Lenah asked, her throat constricting.

Uz shook her head, but before she could answer, the beeping of an incoming message interrupted them.

They stared at each other for a few seconds before Lenah pressed the play button.

"I'm in a transport vehicle outside the city. Hidden Creek's area. If what you're saying is true, I am interested," Corinna said, her voice mixed with the chatter of several people and the hissing of guns in the background.

Lenah took a moment to think before answering. Should she fly the *Rambler* right into the office district or should she join up with Corinna at the Hidden Creek's Park? The park entrance was about a klick from the offices and would hopefully give Lenah a chance to land the *Rambler* before gambling to use her powers on the Muha Dara.

She pointed for Uz to press the record button. "We'll meet up at the Creek's Park entrance. I'll come as quickly as possible."

"Where is that?" Uz asked when she ended the communication.

"It's a *big* park, and the entrance is close to the city. It will be a short walk into the city center and toward that." Lenah motioned to the news feed. "Turn it off, will you? I can't concentrate on flying if we're watching that."

Uz complied. After a short moment of sitting in silence during which Lenah returned to her ship controls, Uz asked, "Is there anything else you want me to do?"

"Not now, no." Lenah shook her head. "But I want you to be ready when we land. All of you."

Uz nodded and got up. "I will be. For now, I'll be in my cabin."

36 CITY IN PANIC

"YOU CALL THIS A PARK? This is a jungle." Persia's voice sounded over the speaker in her suit.

"It's a big park. Asturis I has lots of green areas. That's the one priority the founders had, to retain the wilderness all around, even though the city itself is organically built and not planned," Lenah said absently, repeating what she'd said many times before to guests of the Callo family. "This park was built to balance out the size of the temple."

"No kidding," Persia said looking over at the giant pyramid that was the temple of the Life in Paradise Church, Astur's oldest and most traditional religion. Nowadays, its ancient house of worship was the city's biggest tourist attraction.

"Where's Zyrakath?" Lenah asked, turning away from the city to look for the drone.

"He's pouting over there." Cassius pointed toward the park's tall stone gate. "He told me he's not a fighting drone but a knowledge worker. I told him to suck it up and come with us," Cassius said, his breath puffing out in a white cloud. Somehow, the temperatures of the planet had dramatically dropped since they'd left it a couple of hours ago. Lenah hadn't noticed at first as she'd donned her Cheung fighting suit again and was isolated from the temperature, but the others had immediately started to shiver.

Lenah followed Cassius's pointed finger to the small drone hovering several meters behind them under the gate. She didn't know if it was on purpose, but it looked like he was trying to make himself invisible next to the gray stone of the thick column. Lenah nodded to Cassius. She couldn't blame him for losing his patience with the drone. She'd done so herself.

Carefully, she approached. "Zyrakath, is there anything else you can tell me, anything you might think is helpful with these creatures?" She didn't like one bit that she hadn't been able to influence any while still onboard the *Rambler*. For some reason, her ship felt so much safer than walking out here. Even though she'd seen firsthand how the hatches of the military ships hadn't kept the Muha Dara out.

"I only know from the literature that they can be influenced," the drone answered. "I do not know how." He wrinkled his forehead. "From my own experience with my people, I saw how these creatures cluster together in one area. They invade it like a swarm and touch everyone until only

Muha Dara are left. The grown swarm moves on to the next area. They also leave behind this lingering frost. On my home world, it only went away a few cycles after the masters left and the Muha Dara were asleep."

"Muha Dara is old Cassidian for Mindless Frost," Uz reminded, and the drone dipped his head in the affirmative. "Cava Dara means Winged Frost," Uz said, looking up at the sky where hundreds of floating figures were visible.

Lenah nodded her thanks to Zyrakath.

"We know that the city square is the area they're targeting. Unfortunately, it makes sense. I wonder how they knew. But if you want to create as many Muha Dara as fast as possible, you'd go right there. There are so many offices in the area."

"Offices?" Zyrakath asked. "My internal language programming wasn't able to translate that word."

"It's a building where common people go to work for the families. Knowledge workers, people working mostly in tech or finances," Lenah answered. Zyr's eyebrows pulled together on his wrinkled face.

"Doesn't matter," Lenah said, shaking her head. "It's the middle of the work week, and this is where most people are clustered together on the whole planet. Oh stars, it's even the week of the harvest holiday. People from all over Astur come to sell their produce on the plaza and have spiced kaleh."

"I always wanted to come and have a real Asturian kaleh," Persia wistfully said. "Seems I picked the worst year to finally show up."

Zyrakath ignored Persia and turned to Lenah instead. "Are we waiting for your adversary?"

"Yes, I'll comm her again."

"Lenah," Cassius called her back over, then pointed upward. A small group of Muha Dara, all of them Syrr, had turned away from the city square and were rapidly approaching.

This was it. Lenah gathered her concentration, holding up a hand to halt the others. She wanted to see what she could accomplish first. "Just give me a minute."

Again she could find the weak fog of the approaching minds. During their journey down to the planet, she had pondered what she wanted to show these creatures. Now, she sent them the image of stopping their approach and attacking each other. She used the images she had seen up in space of them opening up hatches to project the visual of them ripping at each other's shiny gray limbs instead.

They reacted. Within seconds, they turned on each other, ripping apart arms and legs, even heads, which came off neatly, not fleshy at all, more like stone statues. Lenah shivered and struggled to hold her influence. Gray torsos, like deformed snowballs, crashed to the ground. When only two of them were left, a streak of laser blasted out. When Lenah checked, she saw Cassius lowering a pistol.

Lenah took a deep breath, trying to shake the shivers. Something amazing had happened. There was hope.

A grin spread on her face as she looked at Cassius and the others, who were breathing a sigh of relief. Getting rid of almost two-dozen enemies had been easy. He flashed his own grim smile before walking over and looking down at her. All remains of his smile had vanished. Her belly churned. What was he going to do?

"I want you to be careful out there," he said, his voice solemn. "I know you think you've got this. And I know you feel at least partially responsible for what's happening. But you need to be careful."

The truth of his words sobered Lenah. Especially coming from him after he'd been so cold to her since the elevator scene. A coldness that she had deserved.

A little bit of fear, probably healthy fear, bubbled up in her belly. She had defeated twenty now, but there were so many more. Hundreds, if not thousands. She was going to have to confront humans as well. Evil turned-to-stone humans. It was dangerous, and she still had so much to do. She reached out with her gloved hand to touch his.

"I'll be careful. Will you too? Will you keep the others safe?"

His eyes darted over toward the group, and he didn't say anything at first. Finally, he nodded and wrapped his second hand around hers. This small moment of intimacy felt so good, and Lenah wanted to hug him, but a hovering vehicle appeared in the distance from the direction of the park. It was a sturdy, black box, unmarked, but Lenah knew who was in there when she saw the tendrils of mind magic seeping out of it.

Like a swarm of angry makkah crickets, a handful of Syrr and one Bartoc swept at the vehicle and started to target the doors. It shook and almost toppled over in the air.

Lenah gathered her concentration and sent the idea of attacking each other toward the Muha Dara again. But this time, nothing happened.

"Why is this not working?" she hissed toward Zyrakath. "I can see their minds. But I cannot influence them. It was easy with the other ones."

Zyrakath looked around before answering. "I do not see any Cava Dara close-by. Are you doing anything differently this time?"

"No, I have their minds, and I'm telling them to attack each other. Just as I did with the other ones…" she trailed off, trying again. Nothing. Instead, the driver's door snapped off its hinges with a sound of crunching metal. She watched the man's panicked face as he was pulled out of the flying vehicle and started to fall. A moment later, the brown tone of his skin turned gray, and he simply stopped in the air, hovering.

Frantically, Lenah thought again, trying to re-step exactly what she'd done before. She was sending the same suggestion—attack the others—but was she short-cutting it? Hadn't she imagined it more vividly before? She made the effort, sending an image of the same group of Muha Dara getting away from the hovering vehicle and ripping off each other's limbs. They complied. A few seconds later, Cassius fired at the last few. Lenah allowed herself a moment of hope. Corinna had really come.

Her group watched in silence as one of the passengers scrambled into the driver's seat and the vehicle set down. The back door opened and Corinna stepped out first, her blonde hair tied into a tight top bun, lips painted a red so dark it was almost black. Guards filed out behind her; guns raised. Lenah wasn't too surprised to find them pointing the guns at her instead of the sky. She hoped this was only a precaution and Corinna had been honest in her agreement to cooperate.

"Nice suit," Corinna said, eying Lenah and Persia with a smirk.

Right, Lenah had forgotten they were wearing stolen Cheung Corp suits. An obvious proof of where they had recently been. She also assumed that Corinna already knew.

"They *are* nice. Don't worry, you'll get it back once this is over," Lenah answered, trying to regain her footing, unsure what else to say. It seemed she never got the time to express what she now thought of the woman she admired for so long.

Corinna clenched her fists, a fire burning in her eyes, and Lenah was pretty sure it wasn't about the suit.

"Thank you for coming." Lenah changed the subject.

Corinna regarded her, then the broken pieces of stone scattered around.

"As I just saw, you seem to have spoken the truth."

37   MUHA DARA

THEY ENTERED CHAOS. Screams sounded everywhere. People were running. An elderly man in a blue business suit stumbled, but the ones behind him didn't falter in their steps. Lenah ran forward to help him up, but she was pushed over by the heaving masses going the other way, and his body vanished from her sight before she'd even closed half the distance.

Up above, it was no better. Shadows covered the perfectly blue, late-afternoon sky. Flying figures came swarming down, a constant downpour, all directed toward the office district, but the running people hardly looked up. Everyone was trying to get away as fast as possible.

Asturis I's business district was the city's prime real estate. High rises, several hundred stories tall, housed the offices of every corporation and company that had any importance on Astur. Tens of thousands of commoners worked for the families right here, within one square kilometer. The glass towers were immaculately clean, their fronts shimmering and reflecting off each other. The plaza in the center of the ring of ten high rises had been planted with exotic trees and flowers. Now, the flowers were trampled as hundreds of people tried to escape at the same time.

Something crashed onto the concrete floor nearby with a deafening shatter. A window. Ripped off to give the Muha Dara access into the building. Lenah turned in a circle, unsure where to start. There was so much work to do, so many Muha Dara.

She ducked behind an overturned hovering car. "How are we supposed to get closer? We can't run against that. Not without hurting anyone," she said, thinking of how she, Persia, and Cassius could probably hold against the crowd with the fighting suits and his cyborg strength.

"Easy," Corinna said. "We make them give us room." She sounded like she was talking to a child.

"How?" Lenah asked, trying not to let the arrogant tone get to her. She'd chosen to work with this woman. Now she had to actually work with her. *Clearly.*

Corinna didn't say anything else. Instead, she got up. A moment later, the masses parted in front of them, leaving a narrow corridor. Corinna walked toward it, waving them on. Reaching out with her senses, Lenah followed. She could see a wall of force emanating from Corinna, like a shield. A suggestion to not step there?

She'd love to know, but asking Corinna was out of the question. Maybe she should go to the Guild after this, as Lorka had suggested. One thing at a time.

Walking behind Corinna, Lenah looked up to the closest group of Muha Dara. They were flying toward a low window in the tower next to them. She concentrated, imagining how they'd turn on each other with an emotion of hatred that she didn't have a hard time conjuring up. They stopped and started attacking each other in a heap of flying arms, legs, and torsos.

As Lenah watched a Syrr rip off the arm of another, her own arm was suddenly pulled hard, and she was jerked sideways. With a burst of adrenaline, she realized that she'd stepped sideways and it had been Cassius pulling her back and not a Syrr ripping at her. She nodded her thanks and looked back up, conjuring the same images again.

A high-pitched scream right behind her head brought Lenah's attention back a few moments later. She turned to find its source and realized that Zyrakath was hovering low behind her as if using her back for cover.

"Lenah," Cassius yelled, pushing her over. *What? She hadn't stepped out again.* Looking around, Lenah noticed a bright streak—a laser—being fired at her chest. The suit was apparently fully absorbing it because she didn't feel a thing. Behind her, Zyrakath gave a shrill yelp, and she turned, trying to protect him with her body, but it was too late. He stared at her in horror, eyes wide while clutching his blackened leg.

Lenah turned again, trying to find the source of the fire. Why were they even being fired upon?

Before she could answer that question, a weight crashed into Lenah. She went down, taking Zyrakath with her as she tumbled. Barely able to avoid him getting crushed under her, Lenah managed to get up again.

Turning, Lenah realized it had been Corinna falling into her. She'd been flung backward, at least six people overrunning her as they made their panicked escape from the buildings. She'd dropped next to Lenah, who rolled over, putting her suit protectively in front of Corinna. Their gazes met for a moment before Corinna's gaze became absent of emotion. A moment later, the trampling stopped. People were leaving a corridor for them again.

"Thank you," Corinna panted as Lenah helped her up. "Lost concentration when someone started shooting at us."

Lenah nodded. She could relate to that. She turned to scan their surroundings. Who had been shooting? Had it only been a stray laser?

"Over there," Persia shouted and pointed, having taken Lenah's position in front of Zyrakath. Lenah followed her outstretched arm. A man dressed in a guard uniform was squinting and aiming a weapon straight at them. He was part of a whole group of guards, who were all firing lasers up at the Muha Dara. What was this one doing, shooting right into a mob of running people? Then she understood. "Hide, Zyr," Lenah said to the drone. "This guy thinks you're a Muha Dara."

"What?" Zyrakath wheezed, his voice a squeaking tremble. He was clutching on to something that he held cradled in his arms. His leg had fallen off.

"Zyr, oh no. Is that going to—err—interfere with your functioning?" Lenah asked him, unsure how to phrase such a question to the drone.

"I'm still in full hold of my mental capabilities," the drone said, hovering more upright. If he was trying to look like a dignified Elder, he wasn't successful. The charred leg in his arms saw to that.

"Let's get shelter over there," Cassius said and pointed to a pagoda rooftop that stretched over a market stand. A fallen sign read out the price list of the available drinks: mostly wine, kaleh, and beer, each offered in several tastes. "And you, stay low," he added, pointing at Zyrakath.

"Shelter?" Corinna asked. "You call it shelter to go up and expose yourself to those things?"

"Do you want to use all your concentration on *those things* or keep making this corridor?" Cassius asked, looking annoyed.

He didn't even wait for an answer, but instead jumped on the roof as if it were no more than a stair. He held his hand down, offering it to Corinna. She snorted, but took it. Next to Lenah, Persia jumped straight up, landing easily on the roof next to Cassius.

Lenah bent her knees, then jumped with all her strength. Suddenly, she was soaring high above Cassius's head. She landed softly next to Corinna, who arched her brow.

Ignoring that, Lenah addressed Corinna. "We need to picture them attacking each other. They don't react to language or any fuzzy ideas. The images you send have to be as vivid as you can make them."

Corinna nodded, looking up to a nearby swarm of Muha Dara. Moments later, they started attacking each other. *Of course, she'd get it on her first try*. Lenah snorted and got to work as well. After a few minutes, she found a steady rhythm. So had Corinna, it seemed, judging by the constant rain of stone chunks she was causing to come down.

"Would you mind if we went to help out down there?" Cassius's voice interrupted Lenah's concentration.

Lenah looked away from the sky to see him pointing at the masses of people still fleeing below them.

She nodded. He was right. They could be more useful down there. A moment later, he jumped from the pagoda roof, followed by Persia. They helped Uz and Doctor Lund down; Lenah was left with Zyr, Corinna, and her guards.

She concentrated back on her own task.

"Try to unite your powers." Zyrakath interrupted her. He was hovering above the pagoda roof, still cradling his leg like a baby.

"And how are we supposed to do that?" Corinna frowned down toward the drone.

"My books didn't specify how," Zyrakath answered, looking unfazed by Corinna's skepticism.

"Books?" Corinna echoed. "That's your reliable source? An ancient machine that read some books?"

"Yes," Lenah said flatly. "If you haven't noticed, Zyr is no ordinary drone."

"Elder Zyrakath," he corrected, but Lenah ignored him. If Corinna were already not taking him seriously, his talks about his elder wisdom surely wouldn't help.

She continued, "He's no mere machine but the soul of a real Syrr. A full-blown person in all but body."

Corinna blinked, then thoughtfully looked down at the drone. Lenah hoped she wasn't plotting Cheung Corp's next great invention and make Lenah regret sharing this information.

"The Syrr library held incredible knowledge. I believe him. We need to figure out how it works," Lenah said. "Let's try to unite our efforts. You lead." She figured Corinna would enjoy that. "And I pour where you pour."

Corinna looked down at the drone with pressed lips. "Can't hurt, I guess," was all she finally said before turning back to the sky.

Lenah saw that she had started to target a group of mostly human Muha Dara who had come out of the open window of a building. She concentrated on the stream of Corinna's mind magic.

Lenah's magic flowed up toward the group where she imagined them attacking each other. While most did, some hung in the air, not doing anything. When Lenah concentrated specifically on them, they finally turned on each other. Was this how it was supposed to work? Was she making it worse instead of better? Not willing to give up yet, Lenah kept pouring.

It happened a few more times, but they were quickly able to move on to the next group. Maybe Lenah had overestimated her area of impact before this. She followed Corinna's lead to target a huge swarm that had arrived on the scene. When a Muha Dara looked as if it wasn't following their instructions well, Lenah corrected with a targeted push.

After a while—Lenah didn't know if it had been ten minutes or an hour—her limbs started to feel as heavy as lead. She took a deep breath and looked around the area. Twilight had fallen over Asturis I and was hiding many of the details of the fight, but she could still make out how everything was littered with gray stone, covering most of the ground.

She saw a man run toward the temple area, a thickly walled building with only the occasional slit for windows, where he joined a whole line of people making their way there. Close to the temple entrance, Lenah recognized the suited figure of Persia, waving people inside. Uz and Cassius stood next to her, guns lifted and shooting any Muha Dara who were threatening to get close.

"Keep in line, there's room for everyone. You over there, come here." Lenah could hear Persia's distant voice, enhanced by her suit's speakers. She sounded perfectly calm, and it gave Lenah hope that they had a chance.

"You're not uniting your powers. Why?" Zyrakath asked from beside her. He had hovered close, and his stone features were looking concerned.

"What do you mean, Zyr? We're both pouring in the same direction."

"You're focusing separate efforts in the same place, but in order to make a more powerful idea, you need to unite your powers."

"Is that why I suddenly feel I'm doing worse since she started to do that?" Corinna asked, pointing a finger at Lenah.

"Me?" Lenah huffed, but stopped herself. If Corinna didn't realize that now was not the moment to fight between them, then at least Lenah would.

"What are we supposed to do differently?" she asked Zyrakath.

He frowned and shifted the leg in his grip. "I'm not really sure. The books weren't very specific about this, but I believe that one mage yielded to the other and let them use their power."

"Yield? To her?" Lenah whispered. She caught Corinna's gaze, who snorted. *Yep, that wasn't going to happen.*

"Yes, one of you needs to give the other control over them."

"I'm not letting *her* control my mind," Lenah said. "No offense."

Surprisingly, Corinna's mouth spread into a wide smile. "None taken. That's the most reasonable thing I've heard you say."

Screams and fighting noises pulled their attention toward the temple. All of a sudden, the entrance was clouded by a heaving mass of hundreds of Muha Dara, all trying to keep the stream of fleeing people from reaching the building. It was a dreadfully rational choice.

Persia's voice stopped giving instructions. She, Cassius, and Uz were standing side by side, steeling themselves against the incoming masses and bombarding them with a constant shower of laser blasts from their guns. But it wasn't enough. They were going to get swarmed.

Lenah gathered her concentration, reaching out to the Muha Dara. She could no longer see Cassius and Persia. Were they even still firing? She wasn't so sure.

Lenah tried to cover the whole area of attack with her influence, but hundreds at once, determined to go at the same spot—the entrance to the temple—was impossible. Lenah's focus kept slipping away, becoming too weak to overwrite whatever internal command the Muha Dara were following.

She saw that Corinna was having similar struggles, targeting the same area.

Suddenly, Lenah saw something fly high. A human figure clad in a sleek suit.

Persia. She had jumped up and was almost caught by Muha Dara who threatened to touch her. Lenah concentrated her effort there. Anything to get them away from her friend. The mob around Persia tore at each other. But where was Persia?

"There are too many," Lenah croaked out, feeling helpless.

"Join forces," Zyrakath's voice sounded from right next to her.

Lenah concentrated back on the fight.

"There's a big group coming for us," one of Corinna's guards said, the constant firing of his lasers illuminating the sudden darkness.

"They're here, they're coming!" he yelled a few moments later, his voice sounding even more urgent.

Weight crashed down onto Lenah. She hit the roof under them hard.

"Join forces," Zyrakath urged again.

This time, Lenah succumbed. She thrust her mental self over to Corinna, some part within her knowing how it could be done. She poured power toward the woman, but without an idea in mind. Just the power.

The weight moved on top of her. A guard. He'd thrown himself on her when the Muha Dara had come too close and provided her with a human shield. He moved again, and Lenah fully jerked to attention when she saw his skin turn gray only a few centimeters in front of her face. Suddenly, his eyes shone purple. She wiggled under his weight, trying to reach her gun. He came closer, touching her suit with his gray hands. *Stars, he wanted to expose her skin.*

Suddenly, his head exploded into a cluster of flying stones. Other parts of his body followed, and Lenah could finally move away from him. She looked up.

Zyrakath had let go of his leg and was holding a gun, the guard's own gun, that was almost as tall as him. *Thank the stars.*

Resolve forced Lenah on. She started pouring into Corinna again, and their eyes met. Corinna's widened in surprise, and then the haze of her influence grew. She closed her eyes, sending a huge wall, several hundred meters, upward.

Stone—limbs, heads, and torsos—started to rain down on them. One hit Lenah's visor, and the displays blinked wildly in front of her eyes. She shut them and kept pouring into Corinna.

In that moment, she was aware that Corinna could make her do and believe whatever she wanted to, and she could even use Lenah's own magic to do so.

Yet Corinna was only strengthening her suggestions toward the Muha Dara. Images of killing each other, no, the *desire* to kill, the emotion of hatred, all ran wildly through Lenah's mind, and she struggled to keep still. She wanted to join the fight, rip someone's limbs off. *I'm only the funnel*, she told herself over and over, with the small part of her mind that was still Lenah.

I'm not one of them.
I'm NOT one of them.
I'm Lenah.
I'm...

38 CAVA DARA

SUDDENLY, THE URGE to attack ceased. Simply ceased. Lenah, who had been fighting over it with all her willpower, buckled when her limbs were suddenly no longer able to move. Then, a presence stormed her mind. Just ran her over, flattening out the part of Lenah that she'd been holding onto.

She was horrified, she was angry. About everything spinning out of control, dread of what was happening, guilt about being a driving force in it. How could she have been so wrong? How could she have lost everything in just one day? The mage farm gone, lives lost, and the anger at the one person who'd caused so much of it, this daughter of a business partner, who could have been an ally, but who instead turned out to be a deceitful child. She wanted to make her hurt, to pay for it, so that she wouldn't have to shoulder so much anymore.

"Both of you, stop it." A voice demanded, way too close to her ear. "Lenah stop, other mind controller, stop." The voice insisted.

She didn't want to. This anger felt good. This power over someone else felt so good.

But, you're Lenah... A tiny voice in her head wailed. It was so low; she chose to ignore it. She was Corinna Cheung, and she had proven multiple times that she deserved to be in charge. It always turned out better when she was. But today, she'd lost control. Today, so much had been lost.

"Lenah! Push back!" The annoying voice yelled again; this time accompanied by a shake to her shoulder. She felt her head roll as if it was lying on the ground when she knew that she was standing, looking down on the spread-out and twitching figure of her forced ally.

Something was not right about that... The fraction of Lenah in her mind nodded frantically. Started begging her for more control. *Let's take our power back*, it whispered.

With a jerk, she became aware of a steady stream of energy leaving her. Why was she doing this?

The Lenah corner yelled at her: *That's it, that's what we need to stop!*

Yes, she should. It was hard work, and she was starting to feel really, really tired. She concentrated on stopping the outpour, and, suddenly, the anger stopped.

A yell sounded next to her as Lenah opened her eyes. She saw that Corinna had gone to the ground and was clutching her head, tears streaming out of her eyes. Lenah lowered her head again. She was so tired.

"Miss Cheung!" A loud male voice made her wince.

Lenah had a killer headache herself. With an effort, Lenah opened her eyes and looked at Corinna.

One of her guards—the only remaining one—was bending over Corinna. She swatted his hand away and tried to get up.

"Thank the stars, you're well. And you defeated them all," he exclaimed at her show of energy.

Corinna looked up at the sky, and Lenah followed her gaze. The sky was clear, not a single cloud of Muha Dara obscured the colorful sunset.

"Are they all gone?" Lenah croaked. Surprised by how dry her throat was.

"Yes, we defeated them all," Corinna said, looking at her. They stared at each other for a few seconds, and Lenah remembered the anger this woman had just felt toward her, then the overpowering guilt. Corinna gave an almost invisible nod of her head. "We really defeated them all." She repeated.

"It was incredible, all of a sudden all of them started to attack each other. The whole area at once," the guard said, putting away his weapon.

Lenah turned to see Zyrakath hovering low on the roof.

"How did we do, Zyr?" she asked.

He flew closer. "It did not look like what the books described. You seemed to lose control, but you still did it."

"Lose control? That's putting it nicely," Lenah winced, turning her head. Corinna was still clutching her temples.

"Are you all right?" Lenah asked. Had the experience been even worse for Corinna? Lenah couldn't image what was worse than losing complete control over herself and being swarmed by someone else's emotions like that, but Corinna had influenced thousands of Muha Dara at once. "Corinna, are you all right?" she asked again.

Corinna groaned something that remotely sounded like a yes, she was okay.

Slowly, Lenah sat up, fighting a wave of nausea. The area around them was barely recognizable. Instead of the beautifully planted plaza with food and drink booths, it was a war zone littered with light-gray rubble. Some pieces had shattered by falling from up high and looked like mere rocks. Others still had the shape of a face or a limb. Windows were missing from all the office towers. The only building that had seemingly withstood the past few hours without so much as a scratch was the temple of Life in Paradise.

Persia! Stars, where was Persia? Lenah frantically tried to see better through the rubble at the foot of the temple, her suit helping her as it turned to night vision and zoomed in by itself. Her friends weren't there. Were they buried under the destruction?

But then she saw the gate to the temple open. Cassius's familiar figure peeked out. After scanning the sky, he stepped into the evening light.

Persia was right behind him. Lenah breathed out a big sigh of relief, grinning widely and waving as she saw them look toward the pagoda roof. Thank the stars, they were both okay.

But Cassius didn't wave back. With a sudden movement, he jerked up his laser and started shooting. Lenah followed the trail of his weapon, and her heart skipped a beat.

"Corinna!" she yelled, shaking the woman who was still lying on the ground. Corinna's eyes snapped open.

"Give me your magic," Lenah urged, watching the two winged figures descend. She heard Corinna gasp, then felt the inpour of magic. Lenah sent everything they both had toward the Cava Dara. *Attack each other. Go away.*

But they kept coming.

Suddenly, it was so cold, Lenah could feel it even through her suit. Laser beams, several at once, were hitting the Cava Dara and were leaving scorch marks on their white bodies and wings, but it didn't stop their descent.

The creatures were less than ten meters away from Lenah now, and for the first time, she could see them with all their terrible detail. They were naked, their skin not resembling any material Lenah had seen before. It didn't look like skin; instead, it shimmered as if made of something between polished stone and c-nano, but with an iridescent silver tone. And those purple eyes—sentient, and so cold. Otherworldly.

Lenah felt sweat run down her forehead, then stop as it turned to ice.

The creatures descended in a slow glide, wings unmoving, as if gravity didn't apply. Maybe it didn't for them. Then their eyes met, and Lenah's heart became stone cold. Her magic faltered and faded. All she could do was stare back.

Seconds, or maybe minutes, ticked by. She didn't know. Until a terrible shriek—like a piercing blade of ice—rocked her out of her lockdown. Lenah broke eye contact and saw the second Cava Dara teetering under the constant barrage of laser fire it was receiving from the temple entrance and from Corinna's guard. Its wings moved, giving two mighty beats, but instead of going up, it tumbled down. Another shriek sounded, and Lenah was pushed backward by what felt like a wave of icy air. With a crash, the body of the Cava Dara hit the ground where it splintered into thousands of pieces.

Lenah looked back at the first Cava Dara, the one who'd stared at her. It was now the sole recipient of Cassius's and Persia's laser fire. The moment she looked, the creature found her eyes again. Emotion, hatred, an image of herself dying blasted through Lenah's mind, and she felt herself fall backward, unable to catch herself. Lenah clutched her heart, suddenly sure that it would stop at the next beat. But she couldn't feel anything through the suit. Panic flooded her as a third shriek interrupted the silence. Lenah looked up to see the creature flap its wings once. And then it was gone.

Lenah blinked and looked around. The Cava Dara had moved several hundred meters away and was rapidly gaining height. A few moments later, it had vanished.

Lenah closed her eyes, trembling. She'd never felt this helpless. And this cold.

"Why is it so cold?" she asked through shivering teeth, clutching onto the one thing she could at least explain. She knew cold. The rest of the encounter had been too eerie to address.

39 AFTERMATH

SLOWLY, THE PLAZA WAS coming back to life. A constant stream of survivors walked out of the temple and into the evening twilight. Lenah watched as almost everyone had the same reaction.

Hugging themselves against the cold, people looked up fearfully, then down in disbelief about the rubble that covered the whole area. At first, no one talked, but after a few minutes, a crescendo of whispers, then shouts of happiness filled the plaza. They hadn't believed it possible, but they'd won the day.

Their relief was contagious, and, slowly, Lenah felt herself getting warmer. And lighter, as she watched the people around and was able to push the encounter with the Cava Dara into the back of her mind. She was also starting to feel the effects of her suit's inner heat regulators. Not feeling like she was about to freeze to death considerably helped to lift her spirits.

Corinna wasn't fairing so well. After Cassius had helped her off the roof, she'd collapsed onto the ground, shivering and barely able to speak. Now, her guard was holding her upright as they made their slow way back to the ship. Maneuvering over the rubble was tricky, and they had to pick each step with care.

Lenah felt exhausted, too. If it weren't for her suit giving her extra strength, she might be right there with Corinna who had stumbled again and didn't seem to be able to support herself when the guard tried to pull her up. Without comment, Cassius stored his weapon in his belt, then lifted her in his arms.

They continued with Cassius carrying Corinna in front, the guard, Lenah, Persia, and Doctor Lund in the rear. Uz trailed several meters behind.

"Do you think this was it?" Persia asked softly into the silence.

Lenah swallowed. She didn't want to think about this.

"There were hundreds of Cava Dara in the Syrr princess's video," Doctor Lund spoke out loud what Lenah was thinking. "Where's the rest? We only saw two today."

Persia sighed and looked like she'd already come to the same conclusion but had wanted to hear something else. Lenah shared the feeling.

"Maybe something happened during the last six thousand years," Lenah said and shrugged as they reached the *Star Rambler*. The ship stood where they'd left it as if nothing had happened.

"The probabilities of that are close to zero. This mechanism has worked for eighteen-thousand of your standard years," Zyr answered, and Lenah glowered at him. She didn't feel like hearing this right now.

"There's a positive side as well," Doctor Lund said as he walked up the small ramp of the *Rambler*. "We won today. You two," he raised his arm and pointed at Lenah and Corinna, "pushed the Muha Dara back. And you," he pointed at Cassius and Persia, "destroyed a Cava Dara. We have powerful weapons that the Syrr didn't have."

"Right now, I don't feel like a powerful weapon." Lenah winced as she struggled to make the small climb up the ramp into the ship. "I only want to sleep with a heating blanket over my head for the next three days."

"I think it's time for a round of Cassidian marches tea," Uz said from behind. "For everyone." She added after looking at every one of them, except for Doctor Lund whom she seemed to be pointedly ignoring. She overtook them and vanished into the common room.

Lenah grunted her agreement. The tea sounded like the ideal next step. Maybe then, she'd be able to think about what to do next.

"Zyrakath, do you think we can train to become better at this? Not lose control?" Lenah asked the drone.

"I suppose," he said distractedly. He was putting down his leg that he'd carried all the way back to the ship. "I'm not the right person to tell you. You need someone with knowledge about mind mages."

Lenah nodded, then sighed. She knew where she could get that kind of knowledge.

She walked behind Cassius, who was carrying Corinna into the common room where the scent of Cassidian marches tea had already taken over. Lenah pulled off the helmet of her suit and collapsed onto the chair next to Corinna. Cassius sat opposite them.

"What should we do now?" he asked, looking directly at Lenah.

She shrugged. Was it cowardice to want to think about anything but that right now? But soon, they'd need to fly the *Rambler* somewhere, and by then she'd better have come up with a good plan.

"We should prepare for the next attack. Get better at this." She waved a hand in between her and Corinna's head.

"And how would we do that?" Corinna stuttered through clattering teeth. Uz, who had been about to give Lenah the first cup of Cassidian marches tea, adjusted and handed it to Corinna. She accepted with only the slightest grimace, then took a big gulp.

"We go to the Guild," Lenah said as Uz handed her the second cup of tea.

Corinna shook her head. "The Guild where they train warp mages?"

"It turns out they might have some experience with mind mages as well," Lenah said, taking a deep sip of her cup. Warmth exploded in her veins, and she sighed. A plan started to form in her mind. "I think we should give a certain group of mages a ride to their home base."

She saw Cassius's eyes dart toward Corinna in alarm and followed his gaze. Corinna was studying Lenah. "You mean the mages who escaped from the farm," Corinna said flatly.

"I mean the mages that we freed from an abusive job."

Corinna's eyebrow lifted, but instead of objecting, she took another sip from her cup. "And hypothetically speaking, you think the Guild would not only be able to train us, but this group of mages will show us the way to their base?" she asked.

Lenah raised her chin. "They'll need *some* form of transport. I doubt the Guild has a ship just parked around on every planet. The *Rambler* might be their best way to get home fast."

"The Guild. Most secret location in the galaxy." Cassius shook his head, but his eyes crinkled with amusement. "Wow."

Lenah wouldn't argue. No one knew where the facilities were located. But Lorka had offered, hadn't he? And there was also the question why the Cava Dara were still attacking.

"There's only one mage farm, right?" Lenah asked Corinna.

The other woman looked up at her in surprise, then nodded. "Why?" she asked.

"Because the attacks didn't stop when we destroyed the first one."

"Are you implying something is still triggering them?"

Lenah nodded, hoping Corinna would explain. But she just stared ahead grimly, lips quivering from the cold. Thoughtful? Angry?

"No matter what, we'll go to the Guild first," Lenah said more to convince herself than anyone else. She hoped they would be allowed to leave again. Especially, without going through the decades-long training mages usually took. She only had days, maybe weeks, until the next attack.

Once this was over, the last thing Lenah wanted was to be institutionalized again. She was ready to live her own life. See what she really wanted and maybe what was between her and Cassius. His intent gaze met hers as if he knew exactly the direction her thoughts had taken, and despite all her worries, butterflies fluttered in Lenah's stomach. She smiled as she took another sip of her Cassidian marches tea.

EPILOGUE

"YOU REALLY WANT this white?" Cassius asked Lenah for what felt like the hundredth time.

"Yes. Besides, it's not for eternity. I can always color it back."

The truth was, she'd be happy with any hair color that would stop people from seeing the similarities she shared with her father. And if she ended up looking unlike Lenah Callo, she wouldn't mind that either.

"How do you like the new cut?" she asked Cassius, shaking out her chin-length bob.

"I, um, it's nice."

She lifted an eyebrow at him. "That was either the worst lie, and you think I did a terrible job cutting my own hair, or you're very rusty with women."

Instead of answering, Cassius looked back at the label of the hair kit they'd picked up on Neeth Station.

"Really? You're not going to answer?" Lenah inquired in what she hoped was a light tone. She didn't want to make her hairdresser nervous. And she was happy with her hair.

"It's not because I don't like it," Cassius answered. Then he lifted the box. "Why didn't you ask Persia again? She bought this, after all." He looked at it dubiously.

"I told you, I don't trust Persia with hair. She shaves half her scalp with the kitchen knife. I saw her do it the other day."

"Uz?" He started to sound slightly desperate.

"She's still in her cabin, sulking about the tree and won't come out." Lenah sighed. She felt bad for Uz but also couldn't fully understand why she was so protective of one tree. Especially, being an outcast from her own people. As sad as it was to lose a precious object, was it worth being mad at your friends?

Cassius mumbled something she decided to interpret as agreement. Or resignation. He lightly touched the hair on her neck, bringing Lenah fully back to the moment. She pushed the unpleasant thoughts away for later and enjoyed how the touch of his fingers felt on her skin and gave her goose bumps all over.

The truth was that Cassius was her preferred person for helping her dye her hair. Even though her arguments for not choosing any of the female crew were true. Especially, Persia. She'd never let Persia loose on her hair.

Cassius started to brush her short strands back before helping Lenah ease her neck down on the washing basin. As she got comfortable, she fully admitted to herself that this intimacy was why she'd asked him. He might be a cyborg with cyborg strength, but he could be gentle. And he had diligently spent several minutes reading the instructions on the box of hair dye. It had been really adorable. Though she wouldn't tell him *that*.

Lenah closed her eyes as Cassius adjusted the water to a pleasant warmth and started to get her hair wet, then rip open the dye pack and apply the creamy paste to her hair. Was he massaging her scalp as part of the treatment or was that on purpose? Lenah opened her eyes and found him smiling down on her. Awareness shot through her whole body as their gazes locked, and she remembered how nice it had been to kiss him earlier this week. She might feel more distance between them since their fight in the Callo mansion, but her body wouldn't. Her body also didn't want to talk about it, something they had both avoided. But her mind told her that it needed to be done.

"Cassius, I…" Lenah started.

His face grew serious.

"I want to apologize. It was wrong to influence you against your will, and I promise it won't happen again."

He regarded her, then asked. "Why'd you do it then?"

Lenah shrugged, causing warm water to trickle down her neck and into her clothes. She ignored it. "I guess I wanted to see what was up with you. You were so distant. And I—" she took a deep breath. "I was worried that seeing my house might change how you see me. How you all see me." She shook her head, causing more water to enter her shirt. "And then, when it really happened, and you called me a rich girl, I was desperate to know for sure."

His eyes held hers the whole time she was talking, but now he looked away. His hands left her scalp, and Lenah held her breath.

"I hadn't seen it that way," he said, slowly. "I didn't realize you felt that way and I'm sorry for calling you that."

Lenah didn't speak. She didn't want to say anything wrong.

Then he looked at her. "I guess I can see how it happened." Cassius gave a lopsided grin. "And we still need to work together, anyway, so try not to do it again, will you?" His hands found her scalp again, and he continued massaging in the cream.

Lenah grinned back, nodding. "Promise." Then she thought about his words. They were only working together? Wasn't there more? They *had* kissed, after all.

"What's your plan when this is over?" Lenah asked him, changing the topic and making an effort not to be disappointed. She should be happy that he'd forgiven her. And she shouldn't even be this interested in him. After all, only a month ago, he'd kidnapped her and been anything but dating material. No need to get all worked up about him.

"Maybe I get myself a remote cabin in the woods with my grandfather," Cassius answered.

"Really?" Lenah studied his face. "I didn't take you for the hermit type." After all, he'd made them deposit him on Oscuris, a planet full of smugglers and dirty air and with not a single forest growing on it. "Or the family type," she added, thinking back to meeting his father and brother.

Cassius cocked his head. "I've lived in space almost my whole life, moving from one place to another and never staying anywhere on the ground long enough to see the leaves change color in the fall. At least not anywhere that's not Victory II's endless dust. I imagine it's charming."

Lenah chuckled. "You're from Victory II?"

He shrugged. "Yeah, and the only thing we have a lot of there is sand."

"I can only imagine. It's Astur's neighbor, but I've actually never been there. So, a charming cabin and forest, huh?" She closed her eyes again, going back to enjoying his touch. "I guess it's a nice plan, though, for me, it always sounded boring to be stuck on a planet all the time and never seeing the wonders of the galaxy."

"The wonders of the galaxy, right." It was his turn to chuckle. "You seem to think that making a living out there is a scenic tour instead of years spent inside warp bubbles with nothing to do but train in the gym or seeing the same annoying people over and over again."

"Annoying people? Like us here?"

"I was referring to my—family." The last word came out pressed, and judging by the way his father and brother had treated him in their brief encounter on Neeth Station, Lenah couldn't blame him for wanting to get away from them.

"Do you think your father will come after you?"

His lips pressed into a thin line. "At some point, yeah. But he must know that right now I won't have the money to pay him back for my enhancements. And my father is nothing if not profit-oriented."

Lenah nodded. In that way, her father and his weren't so different.

"What about yourself?" Cassius asked. "What's your plan once this is over?"

Lenah appreciated how he phrased it as if that were a sure thing.

"I'd like to see the galaxy. Hopefully, stick to the *Rambler* and take it out for a few spins, maybe start hauling some cargo. I don't want to get stuck again on one planet, doing the same thing over and over." *And be free to have the adventures I want to have,* she thought, but didn't mention it as thoughts of adventures like kissing him popped into her head.

She felt her cheeks heat and closed her eyes, awareness tingling in her belly once more. When had she broken up with Mason again? That was over a year ago now, and she hadn't been on a single date ever since. No wonder she was flinging herself at the first guy she met.

"What are you grinning about?" Cassius asked, his voice taking on a lighter tone. Lenah felt her cheeks flush even more.

"Oh, nothing special. I was ogling over your biceps."

He licked his lips. "You had your eyes closed."

"Well, imagining it."

"Ah," was all he said.

She wanted to hide her face in her hands. When had she gotten so rusty at flirting? Ogling over his biceps? *Really*? Maybe she should reconsider her flirting strategy before thinking about kissing him again.

"You did send me that image of you in the negligee," Cassius said into the increasingly uncomfortable silence, causing Lenah to pop her eyes open. Was he flirting back? His green eyes twinkled at her.

Definitely flirting back.

"I did," she said, remembering that she'd taken it from her room in the mansion. They once again fell into an awkward silence. After a minute, Lenah decided to close her eyes and enjoy his hands in her hair.

Soon, he started to wash out the dye, then wrap her hair in a towel.

"All done."

Reluctantly, Lenah got up, checking out the now white strands sticking out from the towel wrap. They seemed to make her brown eyes pop more. Definitely a change.

They cleaned up the lav unit in an easy silence, and Lenah imagined what they might do next—maybe have dinner together in her cabin—when Persia stuck her head in.

"Ah, there you are. And you had a guy dye your hair?" She put her hand to her heart in a dramatic gesture. "Really, Lenah. I'm hurt. I thought I was your closest friend here."

"You also love knives too much and carry a hammer," Lenah commented. "That made me nervous."

"You thought you would rather get help from a cyborg with an implanted arm and a weapon mounted to it?"

"She has a point," Cassius commented.

"The gun doesn't work," Lenah said, patting his cyborg arm.

"Ah, I see what's going on here." Persia grinned so wide, Lenah could see every single one of her teeth. "In that case, I'm sorry to interrupt, but Corinna wants us all in the common room in five minutes."

"And what gives her the right to call us all to meetings like that?" Lenah grumbled. Corinna Cheung might have helped out with the Muha Dara, but that didn't mean that Lenah was happy to have her on board her ship. Especially, if she started to take control as if she were the captain.

"Don't blame the messenger," Persia said and turned around to go knock on Uz's hatch.

"I can't wait to get rid of her," Lenah mumbled to Cassius before turning and making her way to the common room. He grunted in return as he followed.

They found Corinna sitting at the head of the table, her guard looming behind her back. But at least he'd finally stashed away his weapon into its holster.

Corinna gestured for Lenah to sit as she and Cassius entered. Annoying woman. This better be important. It wasn't good for people to be overly used to being in charge. And this was still Lenah's and Persia's ship.

Doctor Lund, Uz, and Persia filed in, and Lenah glared at Corinna as she welcomed her crew with the same gesture.

"I was able to talk to High Ambassador Pantha," Corinna started, and Lenah's anger evaporated. She shouldn't be mad at Corinna if she were able to provide them with useful information. Information that Lenah wouldn't be able to get by herself.

"He has informed me that more Cava Dara were spotted."

There were several sharp intakes of breath.

"They're far away right now, going toward the Last Inhabited Worlds, close to the Saltoc sector."

"How far away are they?" Cassius asked at the same time as Uz remarked, "Saltoc sector, interesting."

"At their current speed, they're about three and a half weeks out from the closest human settlement," Corinna answered. "A UPL army will meet them there. This time, it will be a large one with forces from many corporations and under a central UPL command." Lenah noticed that Corinna seemed fascinated by the rusty mark over the hatchway as she said that.

Having gotten a glimpse into the woman's mind the day before, Lenah could only imagine how it had to hurt Corinna's pride to be outmaneuvered like this. In the end, Lenah had been right about the nature of the threat, and, finally, UPL was moving.

"How many more are coming?" she asked.

Corinna looked at her. "About twenty times as many as we fought on Astur."

No one said anything.

"We need to become better at influencing them," Lenah finally whispered into the silence.

Corinna nodded. "Your claim that the Guild can help us better be true." Her voice pitched a little as she said it.

Lenah couldn't help but feel a little smug for knowing something Corinna Cheung hadn't figured out yet. "We have a contact inside the Guild. He's trustworthy. And he's offered me to come. I'm sure you would be able to join."

"And what exactly does your contact know?"

Demanding Corinna was back.

"That there's a secret facility on their base where they train—or used to train—mind mages."

"A secret facility inside of a secret facility?" Corinna asked, looking directly at Lenah, who stared back without answering. She had said what she had to say.

Corinna broke eye contact first. "If there's even the smallest chance to get that much better at influencing them, then this crazy trip is worth it. You still plan to bring along all those mages?"

"Yes," Lenah answered. She'd contacted Lorka earlier, and they were scheduled to pick up over a dozen mages the next morning.

Corinna's chin came up, and Lenah wasn't surprised. As one of the main culprits of the terrible treatment the mages had suffered, it would be a tense ride for Corinna to the Guild location. Wherever that was. Lorka hadn't told her anything yet. Only that it was under a week away.

Lenah turned toward her crew. This was the part of the plan that she feared almost more than fighting twenty times the Muha Dara.

"I realize this is not where any of you want to go next. If you want to stay here on Astur or be dropped somewhere along the way, I'm happy to do so," she finished quickly. Truth was, she didn't want any of them to leave. Especially, Cassius and Persia who had become true friends. In the case of Cassius, maybe even something more. Her eyes met his, and his green gaze was thoughtful. Was he thinking about where he wanted to be dropped off?

"I want to stay." Uz interrupted Lenah's thoughts. "If I get to keep my own, private cabin." She shot a look over her shoulder toward the hatch. "And maybe you'll need an engineer at some point. Or want to employ one once this is over and you decide to start hauling cargo?" She gave Lenah a questioning look.

"I'm not sure yet what I'll do once this is over. But getting into the cargo business is top on my list."

Corinna snorted.

"I'd be happy to have you on board as my engineer," Lenah said, ignoring Corinna. She was over what she was supposed to be doing as a family member.

"I'll probably get off on Astur," Doctor Lund said. "I need to contact my order and see if I can get picked up. I'm fed up being stuck on this ship." He looked around the room with disgust.

Lenah couldn't blame him. After all, he'd been on board the *Rambler* for longer than she. And as a hostage. She would still be sad to see him go.

She looked at Cassius to hear what he had to say—he still looked serious—but Persia spoke first.

"I'll stay. No way am I leaving you alone. You'll need someone to protect you when doing your mind stuff." Her hand patted the hammer she was carrying slung over her back. "Besides, I have no job, no boyfriend, and no apartment."

"I can't help with the boyfriend, but you own half the ship, and there's a cabin and a job for you here," Lenah said, feeling lighter, knowing that at least Persia was going to stay.

"That's because you started to ogle the cyborg first, and he's the only eligible candidate on board. If he hadn't kidnapped us, that is," Persia said.

Cassius's face went from mildly annoyed to serious again, and Lenah wanted to slap Persia. She wasn't helping in making Cassius stay. Besides, Lenah wasn't keen on having her relationship with Cassius announced in front of everyone, especially Corinna.

"If the cyborg gets off, maybe we can get another candidate on board," Persia continued, unaware or not caring about Lenah's discomfort.

"I saw a lot of mages in your age range," Cassius commented from the sidelines. At least, he looked like he hadn't taken Persia's comment too badly. Then he continued in a more somber tone. "I have things to do, to make up for a negative balance with the universe, so to speak."

Lenah's heart sank. He looked around the room but finished by fixing his gaze on Lenah. She braced herself. She was being dumb wanting him to stay so badly. Cassius was trying to start an independent life somewhere and being dragged along with her adventure surely wasn't that. His leaving was for the best.

"I might have to go back to Oscuris while you train at the Guild. Then I'll stay until this is over. It's—I have a family thing," he finished, but Lenah had only really paid attention to the middle part of the comment.

He would stay. She couldn't hide her grin. The fight of her life was coming, but she would be in it with her friends. And that was a lot better than what she had hoped for.

THE END

ABOUT THE AUTHOR

CLARA WOODS is the author of the Lunara Station universe. As a writer as well as a reader, she enjoys quirky characters on an epic adventure, humor, and a little bit of romance. Even better, if it has spaceships.

Her other obsessions, apart from books, usually involve coffee, her rescue dog, Sofi, and having way too many calendars and planners lying around.

Clara lives in Costa Rica, where she decided to move six years ago to be with her better half and now enjoys the sunny weather all year around.

Made in the USA
Las Vegas, NV
28 February 2022

44733847R20204